Tarkine Mist

D. Alan Petersen

A catalogue record for this
book is available from the
National Library of Australia

ISBN-13: 978-1-922343-92-5

Linellen Press
265 Boomerang Road
Oldbury, Western Australia
www.linellenpress.com.au

Contents

Chapter One

"It goes up by the stairs and down by the elevator." That old adage about the share market was the only conclusion I'd come up with after three hours warming a seat in the departure lounge at Gate Seven of Honolulu Airport. A piece of investor folklore was also a summation of my adult life, the slow building of a dream to find happiness in financial independence and the social status that serious money brings.

No sooner had that goal been achieved than, in the blink of an eye, it was gone – the happiness, not the money or the status.

That eye blink happened in 2032, just after my thirty-second birthday, when a burst appendix had me almost dead. I was rushed into surgery, to die on the table, but then revived. All that was merely pressing the button to summon the elevator.

The stepping in and finding no floor occurred in the recovery section of Intensive Care when my wife, my dearest Lucinda, was allowed in for the first time.

I was still groggy when the nurse ushered her into the room; she remained a blue shadow by the door whilst Lucinda tiptoed quietly over and peered down at me. It took a while to get her into focus, then there she was, her angelic smiling face floating above me framed by a blur of white walls and strange equipment. Though designed to reassure, her smile chilled, then choked because it was too thin to hide the sentiments behind it. She was just going through the motions – less the concerned wife and more the disinterested scientist studying a newly acquired insect specimen in a museum cabinet.

It was then I knew our pretence at marriage was finally over. The concept of the happy life I'd been sold was a dud.

Since then, I've put all my efforts into firstly, regaining my health, at a fancy health retreat in Arizona, then delaying the next step here in Hawaii with eight weeks of surfing and kayaking.

Eighteen months on from the operation my health was back. In fact, I was in better shape, externally and internally, than I'd ever been. My procrastination now was brought on by the need to reprogram my worldview, specifically, to understand what I needed to do in my 'second life' to make it better than the first. To find the happiness money alone didn't supply.

Even though I had a ticket and a destination – Bangkok and then a Buddhist monastery – I lacked the certainty of purpose they implied. Instead, I wavered between going and cancelling. Head back to Melbourne? To what? Resurrect some semblance of my former life? That idea was as appealing as trying to enjoy stale tepid beer.

Arizona had focused on healing one's thinking as much as one's body. It had made some progress in understanding happiness in general and the specifics of my particular brand of it – I had progressed from trying to hold onto air, to grasping water, yet what I desired was a solid concept to act as my guide towards a satisfied life.

They suggested an extended stay at a particular Buddhist monastery, promising it would develop the increased mental discipline and deeper wisdom that would help me define a better concept which would guide me towards contentment.

But was the monastery's promise of wisdom and understanding achievable? Was it actually possible to overwrite one's former way of seeing the world? Can we remake ourselves and start afresh? I couldn't say that I'd ever met anyone who'd successfully reinvented themselves and so feared that this next move would end up being a terrible waste of precious time.

Bursting with energy, I just wanted to get on with life but was unable to imagine it. Building up the business had been my previous reason for being. Lucas, my general manager, and the lovely Lucinda would resent any attempt for me to return, as they were running the show as good, if not better than I had. It wasn't really an option.

And thus three hour's had elapsed, bogged in futile mulling over what I didn't want. The shock of hearing the gate was open for my flight finally diverted my thoughts outwards and got me asking questions about my fellow travellers, now queueing.

Were any of them seeking a new and happier life? What goals were they hoping to achieve? That they were here was a success of sorts since they had the money to fly. Many were couples, and there were quite a few families. Hence these ordinary folk also possessed the ability to start and nurture relationships – my principal deficiency.

The lack of satisfying relationships was what bothered me most. I still harboured plenty of grand dreams and schemes and the means to achieve them, but they weren't enough. What I really desired was a person to share those dreams with. Not just any woman. She had to be the right one. The thing was, I wasn't sure I'd recognise her. To date, my dealings with the opposite sex had been a few disinterested girlfriends at university and one disastrous marriage, not yet officially nullified.

But what makes for a good relationship? Most couples I knew had relationships that defied my logic. I could never see the glue that held them together, and if you can't define it, how can you get it?

The public address system interrupted.

'Final call for Flight JA387 to Bangkok, now boarding at Gate Seven.'

The announcement jolted me back to the decision – to go or not to go. I stayed seated, stubbornly determined not to go unless I was sure it was the best way to move my life forward.

Another boarding call echoed around the now deserted lounge. This time my name was called. I was the only one left.

A few minutes later, I was again summoned by name. My resolve crumbled. I found myself standing and then walking towards the gateway to offer myself up to the forced smile of the lone hostess.

'Please stand on the line, place your hand on the square and glance at the screen; thank you.' The last words were spoken with icy clarity, her mood probably not helped by my experiment with the longhaired, bearded surfer look. The machine wasn't fooled by my disguise and the light flashed green.

'Welcome aboard, Mr Banks. This way, please, we don't have much time.' She got me moving with an insistent hand in the small of my back and together we marched down the tunnel to the plane. The glass doors behind us closed with a decisive 'click'.

Instead of being the master of my actions, I had let inertia, instinct, social pressure, or perhaps the invisible hand of fate, move me. It proved to be a non-decision that would both punish and ultimately reward.

Chapter Two

I had to walk almost the entire length of the plane to find my aisle seat, the hostess stowing my cabin bag and leaving once I was strapped in. A few minutes later, we were reversing, then turning onto the runway, and finally, the acceleration and that odd feeling of being pushed down into the seat as we whooshed into a cloudy sky.

Once we levelled off, the in-flight entertainment was available. My fellow passengers plugged in and dissolved into their zombie state, silent, still, and staring at the flickering images on the screens in front of them. A small minority, the not-quite-undead, showed signs of life with jerky jabbing and flicking as they flipped through menus in an optimistic attempt to find something interesting enough to take their minds off the eleven hours of forced incarceration.

I hoped not to join them, wanting first to sort out my rationale for continuing with my current solution. Intellectually, a sojourn at the monastery could lead to a better understanding of myself and, from there, a better feel for the nature of the relationship I hoped to have with that elusive, perfect female companion.

My head said: 'give the monastery a go', but my body remained unconvinced. Seemingly of its own accord, my left hand drifted towards my stomach, searching for the appendix scar beneath the thin material of the Hawaiian shirt. It was a silly affectation that required willpower to thwart. Once both hands were back on the armrests, I exhaled my silliness and tried to refocus.

But that scar reminded me that inconvenient truths needed to be faced and solved, not stupidly and disastrously denied. In pursuing wealth and status – the big house and trophy wife – I'd neglected my health and fooled myself that my marriage was 'normal' and not a sham. Though looking back, most of my disastrous denials were in my personal life, not in my business dealings where my logic and reason ruled. But how much logic can one apply to relationships?

The only real positive result I'd acquired in the last eighteen months was gaining the knowledge and desire to keep in good physical shape. I was thus unenthusiastic at losing all that hard-won physical fitness by committing to a year or two of gazing at my navel.

Jason, our chief facilitator at the health retreat, had countered that by pointing out the monastery offered physical training along with mental guidance. He assured me I'd be kept fit and agile by their martial arts programme, which he insisted was more rigorous than any of the karate training I'd confessed to being keen on at university.

Perhaps getting flabby wasn't the sticking point. It still boiled down to believing the monastery's promise of greater insight to recognise, heal and or accept the disappointments that all relationships are prey to.

Looking down at my open palms, I fiddled with my wedding ring. It was another unproductive habit. The plain band was scratched, its golden lustre dulled, and it now barely turned. Lucinda and I had split up and were never getting back together, so was it constructive to wear it as a reminder of the deceitful nature of women? Probably not, especially when my future happiness rested on restoring my faith in the opposite sex. But how does one restore such faith?

No answers came, so I decided to abandon thinking in favour of getting more comfortable. I had to search the overhead lockers for a cushion, got lucky, and resettled. It was only then that I fully noticed the girl beside me. She gave me a dismissive glare before returning to her task of hammering away on her keyboard, typing some sort of report. Working! I felt sorry for her.

Looking down the length of the plane, I thought of all these people jammed together but refusing to interact. What was it that brought people together? It certainly didn't seem to be proximity. We were like the contents of a gigantic metal cocktail shaker filled with multi-coloured ingredients of different densities. No amount of shaking was going to get them to intermix and stay that way.

In chemistry, we'd been taught that like dissolves like. Perhaps most of my women troubles were simply due to chasing the wrong types. What I needed to learn was the art of determining if they were made of the same stuff as me.

I considered the girl beside me. What was she made of? Did we share any of the same vital ingredients?

Twenty-six … twenty-seven … she was slim, short, and with the pale skin and auburn hair suggestive of Celtic ancestry. Mine were Anglo-Saxon, but no doubt there'd be quite a few Celtic genes lurking in my genome. Genetically, not too dissimilar.

A pleasant but rather serious and determined face, reflected in the vigour with which she attacked her laptop. Determination I understood. Another tick.

No wedding ring. Perhaps not committed to anyone at the moment, or, unlucky in love like me? Always hard to tell at a glance. Strange, because she was good-looking and was stirring my interest, though some men might be put off by her earnestness and obvious intelligence.

Her blue jeans and white T-shirt were top quality. So, she likes good things but lacks the big money it takes to travel first class. I wondered if she resented that economic necessity forced her into being an employee and one with insufficient remuneration to fly anything but "cattle class". I was here by choice, as a sort of symbolic gesture of humility – the first step on my road to enlightenment. But the more I looked at her, at her clothes, her stylishly short hair, her neatly manicured hands, free of the gaudy embellishments favoured by the poor, I became convinced she was a girl who objected to the world for not being as it should.

I smiled grimly. There was a time when I also resented the way things were until I decided no one would listen to my objections and chose to make the most of the world as I found it. Getting rich had seemed like the best first step. Money gives choices and comforts denied to the poor, and I knew all about being poor. Morality I left on the backburner. Was it such a wise choice? Maybe I did care more about making the world a better place than I had given myself credit for? I just hadn't found a successful way to do it. Perhaps we shared further common ground there too.

I turned away. Complaining about things was all too easy. What was in short supply was realistic ways of making things better, preferably ones that made money. I'd experienced the bad things that could happen when one attempted to make money in a socially and environmentally righteous way.

These unhappy thoughts were displaced by visions of my father. He had worked too long and hard to feature heavily in my memories but, as I sat staring at my dulled reflection in the screen in front of me, I again felt the cold reverberations of his words: "We all have our crosses to bear." It had been his only response to my confession of having been roughed up behind the change rooms by the schoolyard bully, chauffeur-driven Andrew Aitkens – double-A to his mates.

The next time double-A had a go at me, I thumped him back with all my pent-up anger then immediately got trounced by him and his buddies. The worst part was being disciplined by the Principal for instigating the fight. Consequently, I learned that if one is a poor scholarship boy at an expensive private school, it was best to keep one's mouth shut and run fast. That's when I'd decided that if you can't beat them, join them, and accumulating piles of money seemed the best way.

I checked the time. Nine and a half hours to go. Perhaps a nap would give my subconscious a chance to sort things out. Pushing a little more into my seat, I gained a sliver more knee room and dozed off.

And woke with a start. The girl had nudged my leg.

'Do you mind? I need to get up.'

She looked at me in a business-like manner then stood without waiting for my reply. Somewhat disconcerted, I muttered something, struggled up, moved into the aisle and enjoyed the view as she walked towards the toilets midway down the plane, her tight-fitting jeans leaving little room for the male imagination. The sight restored me to full wakefulness and instigated my own aisle wandering. It felt good to stretch and restore the circulation.

When I returned, she was sitting there, arms crossed, head slightly to one side, staring at the seat in front and probably debating whether to continue working. She ignored me as I squirmed into my spot.

The lid of her laptop was plastered with stickers of causes obviously dear to her. Two struck a chord in mine: I LOVE SHEFFIELD and SAVE THE TARKINE. I smiled. Had I really abandoned causes apart from my own reinvention? I must have smiled too long and too hard because she turned and gave me the once over, looking as though she'd just discovered doggie-do mashed into the tread of her new Nikes.

My smile became even more idiotic under her gaze.

'Sheffield, England, or Tasmania?' As a pickup line, it wasn't the greatest.

'What?' was her somewhat indignant reply.

'The sticker,' I said, pointing weakly at the laptop.

'Oh, that.'

She flipped the computer over to hide the offending slogans, then hesitated, perhaps debating the best way to stifle the impending conversation. Involuntarily, my smile grew wider.

'Don't worry about it,' I blurted. 'It's just that Sheffield Tasmania is such a lovely little town. I vowed it's the place I'd retire to one day.'

Her look softened. I waited.

'Yes, it is.'

'So ... is it still lovely? I haven't been there for a million years and then only for three weeks of bushwalking around Cradle Mountain and the forests of the Tarkine.'

'Yes. Well, it was last time.' She hesitated, a flicker of sadness briefly touching her face. 'Though I've not been back for ... over two years.'

She turned away and grew intently interested in the back of the seat in front of her. I did the same, realising how pointless it was to be chatting up a girl when I was about to become a monk.

Ten minutes later, the rattle of the food trolley became too loud to ignore and I watched with growing anticipation its slow progress. Breakfast had been meagre so by the time it arrived, I was beginning to salivate.

The petite, beautifully groomed Asian hostess announced: 'Vegan, gluten-free?'

'Over here,' I replied with a raised hand.

The girl had answered the same but a split second ahead of me. She smiled smugly, then leaned across to accept the lunch tray. The hostess tried to hide her amusement as she passed me my tray before moving on with a determined push.

The food was surprisingly good, though I suspect my

enjoyment was heightened by hunger. After the trays were collected, I put on my wraparound sunglasses, inflated my neck pillow, which I'd retrieved from my bag before sitting down, pushed my seat back and set about pretending to snooze.

The girl was still on my mind and I thought I'd learn a little more about her by a bit of surreptitious spying. But my disguise was too convincing because I dozed off again. Some hours later, my eyes popped open and took in the sight and sound of her renewed typing.

She was now editing her report, an account of the latest climate change conference in Honolulu. A journalist! My assessment of her plunged. The hatchet job they'd done on our geothermal scheme at Mount Gambier in South Australia was one I could never forget or forgive. It had been a travesty of half-truths and innuendo that had caused me needless pain and huge expense, so much so it had almost bankrupted me. For a long time afterwards, it had soured any enthusiasm for wasting my hard-won dollars on novel energy projects.

Despite my disappointment, or perhaps because of it, I continued my surveillance. She answered an email from which I found out her name was Jessica Moore. It was enough. She was no longer anonymous, no longer an indistinguishable speck in an ocean of eight billion humans. Good or bad, she had become defined as an individual.

I turned away and concentrated on wasting time.

Descending into Bangkok, I was still no nearer to fully understanding why I was going to the monastery. However, with no other strong desires, I chose to trudge the road to enlightenment until something better came along.

Chapter Three

Many months passed in the warm bosom of the Thai jungle before fate again cast her eye upon me.

One moment I was thrashing around in an unhappy dream, the next, it was eyes open, body rigid, and ears scouring the impenetrable darkness of the hut for the sound that didn't belong. Soft and secretive, a sound of someone, or something, squeezing past a bush.

After silent breathing for five wasted minutes, I gave up, exhaled my frustration then smiled to the darkness. How easily the primitive, fearful creature inside me had overwhelmed fourteen months of Buddhist teachings, meditations and rituals – my illusions of having made spiritual progress unravelled by a sound that wasn't there.

The cool night air oozing through the open window unleashed a shiver that yanked me back to reality, and the distasteful conclusion that the amorphous unease haunting my waking hours had now infiltrated my dreams. Groping around the recesses of my memory, I tried to discover when that disquiet had first made its niggling appearance.

It wasn't there during my first eight months at the monastery. Which was remarkable, considering the tremendous physical, mental, cultural and language challenges I had to survive. In fact, by the end of the first year, I was convinced, one hundred per cent, that I was on the right track to a better me.

The rot set in sometime later, after we had made our first excursion out of the monastery to the village down the road. It was the anniversary of our induction. Early that morning, the

Abbot had summoned the small group of novices, of which I was one; he told us that we were to take our first real test. We were to walk the seven kilometres to the village, there to do as we pleased until dusk, after which we were to gather back at the temple to meditate upon our experiences. We would be armed only with our saffron robes, a begging bowl and our newly found piousness. Though that last word was uttered as solemnly as the rest, looking back, I'm convinced there was the glint of amusement in his eyes when he spoke them.

The joke was on me. Two months on, and I knew a crisis of confidence had been reached., one I had to solve soon or … what? I still didn't have any firm plans of what to do next. I knew I didn't want to go back to my old life, to the old me.

An indeterminate time elapsed before I reached the conclusion that staring into the darkness wasn't getting results. The imagined sound continued to reverberate in my skull, making further sleep impossible. What I needed was the space, light and serenity of the temple.

At this early hour, around three a.m. by my body clock, it would be wonderfully deserted. Carefully I rolled myself upright, paused and again strained my ears for the mystery noise. Hearing nothing, I tossed off the cotton sheet, parted the mosquito netting, stood, reached out into the dark and plucked my robe from its hook. Dressed, I felt the tension ease in my shoulders and chuckled at my lack of enlightenment in being unable to face the dark and its unknown threats, without underpants, in a singlet insufficient to cover my maleness.

The textured touch of the robe's raw silk also bolstered my calm, presumably due to its association with the serenity of countless hours of meditating. But no sooner had a degree of calm been gained when it was lost to my marketeer's mind invading it with ridiculous images of armies of contented workers sitting at their desks wearing shirts of *Serenity Cloth*!

Grimacing, I had to squeeze my skull hard with both hands to exorcise my foolishness. Control restored, I straightened and stepped the four paces to the door. Then froze. Lurking tigers now gripped my imagination. This far from civilisation, they had occasionally been reported in the area. I grabbed my heavy wooden staff from its spot next to the door and, with unwarranted confidence in its powers, finally stepped outside.

For a moment, I stood to get my bearings, to imbibe the cool, humid air, to revel in the sense of space after the claustrophobia of the hut and, to stretch my ears in the hope of catching unwelcome sounds. All was quiet. Increasing my grip on the staff, I moved off.

The temple was a faint glow at the top of the rise about a kilometre and a half away. Silently padding along the middle of the road, staff in my right hand, poised as if to throw it, I walked slightly hunched, my body ready for action. With each step, my tension eased, strangely reassured by the cool hardness of the cobblestones under my bare feet.

All the other huts were dark and silent, apart from those few emitting the sounds of slumber. The buildings gave way to the jungle and I quickened my pace. If anything was going to happen this was where it would be. But, like most fears, nothing eventuated.

Feeling somewhat ridiculous for succumbing to childish anxiety, I paused in the welcoming light pouring from the temple's arched entrance, then, with composure fully regained, stepped inside, placed my staff in one of the large earthenware pots next to the entrance and headed across the spacious antechamber towards the washrooms on the right-hand side.

Old Somchai was in attendance. Sitting cross-legged on the dais just inside the doorway, he appeared to be a faded orange bean bag topped by a wrinkled brown melon, a melon which upon my entrance transformed into an ancient face with a toothy grin.

'Peace be with you, my brother,' he said in perfect English.

'And with you too,' I replied in my stilted Thai.

He unfolded his arms, stood up gracefully, like a man half his age, moved several paces to the cupboards behind and passed me a hand towel.

'It is commendable that your devotion moves you at this early hour,' he said with a twinkle in his inscrutable dark eyes.

As usual, I didn't quite know how to reply. I never knew whether he was laughing with me, or at me. Despite that, I really liked the fellow. He had a rapier mind and implacable logic made bearable by a mischievous sense of humour.

Bowing low, I accepted the items in silence, looked into his eyes, smiled, nodded my thanks and then strolled to the washroom. After splashing my face and washing my feet, I threw the towel into the washing basket then stalked silently through the side door to enter the main temple chamber from the right side.

The vast circular space was empty except for neat rows of red cushions on the polished granite. Dominating the far wall was the towering gilded statue of the seated Buddha whose upper parts faded into the shadows in the high domed roof. The only illumination was the warm flickering glow from a row of candles at the base of the statue.

With a certain temerity, I walked to sit in the centre of the first row, squatted down crossed-legged and prepared to meditate. As a novice, I'd only ever sat at the back of the room but hoped that by sitting in the masters' place, I would be granted greater insight. I needed it.

An hour later, I drifted back into the physical world, stood up and quickly headed back to the entrance. A subtle change had occurred and I was anxious to coax the flicker of an idea to full strength. It seemed to require open skies for its flower to fully open.

The plan was to pick up my bowl from my hut and then spend the hour or so before breakfast doing a walking meditation around the Temple's expansive vegetable gardens. I hoped that nature's bountiful harvest would inspire greater clarity of mind.

At the entrance, I picked up my staff and strode outside, only to come to a grinding halt on reaching the first step leading down to the path. The fine hairs on the back of my neck were prickling from an overactive imagination filling the darkness with lurking assassins. Tightening the grip on the staff, senses on red alert, I analysed the shadows on either side of the pathway. With only starlight as illumination, everything except the path was impenetrably dark. With no sounds to guide me, I was blind and deaf.

For what seemed a lifetime, I stood caught in the war between discretion and valour that ended suddenly with a suggestion of movement behind me, off to the right. Spinning around, I prepared to defend myself, with legs apart, slightly bent, and a tightened grip on the staff.

Out of the intense blackness on the edge of the archway materialised the smiling visage of Somchai, who ambled up to me and gently moved my staff aside.

'You have nothing to fear from me unless it is another defeat on the chessboard that troubles you.'

Letting out a huge breath, I straightened up, the tension receding as quickly as it had arisen, leaving in its wake a deep sense of embarrassment.

'You catch me in the full foolishness of the human condition.'

'The inspiration from the Abbot's cushion does not seem to have lasted long. I hope my intrusion is not the cause?'

'No, of course not. I've …' I was unwilling to talk further until I'd sorted things out.

'You have much on your mind. I will delay you no longer. Perhaps we'll meet again for a game after the evening meal?'

'Yes, that would be good. Maybe tonight the Buddha will guide my hand to victory,' I said with a confidence that surprised me.

'Perhaps I will soon experience the nobility of defeat. Until tonight then.' His reply was punctuated with a knowing grin.

Bowing low, I turned and quickly set off down the hill, all fears banished. By the time I reached the first of the huts, they were marginally more discernible, the sky on the eastern horizon greying.

On approaching my hut, I slowed; my courage suddenly waned. Changing to a two-handed grip on the staff, I cautiously made the last few paces to the door, then wasted a moment searching in the dim light for strange footprints on the damp cobblestones while squeezing the silence for threatening sounds. As before, nothing.

Exhaling, I snatched opened the door and rushed inside. Thankfully all was quiet. Pausing, I let my tension ease before taking a step to the right to my only piece of furniture, a rickety bamboo bookcase. I picked up my wooden bowl with great care, not wanting to disturb its inhabitants too much, then returned to the open doorway and gave the room one last scan – an unproductive gesture as the gloom inside was so intense I could discern little more than the white of the mosquito netting over the bed.

Placing the staff in its spot near the right-hand door frame, I stepped outside and was in the process of closing the door when two figures launched themselves at me from the bushes on my left. The bowl was my only weapon. Instinctively I tossed it and the monstrous brown cockroaches trapped within its curved sides at the closest attacker. The ploy worked. He stopped in his tracks, then erupted into a frenzy of flailing arms and cursing.

His antics barely registered. I was too busy snatching up my staff to fend off the second man rushing at me with his right hand raised, holding some sort of long pipe or cosh; in the dim light, it was hard to be sure. One thing was certain; he was going to smash me if I didn't do something fast.

I had the briefest of moments for my fear to transform into anger. That moment was enough to have me sidestepping just in time. I felt a half-hearted tug on my robes as he tried to grab me. Pivoting on my right foot, I spun around and whacked him on the skull with the staff. The iron-hard teak elicited a dull wet *thunk*, a sound that made me cringe whilst watching him collapse into an untidy heap at my feet. I prayed I hadn't overdone it.

But there was no time to consider the ramifications of that victory. The other fellow had dusted off my insect allies and, having noted the fate of his colleague, approached more cautiously. I had hoped he would give up, but his crouched approach spoke otherwise. He was small, solidly built and dressed like a peasant. Another pace closer, and he slipped his right hand over his shoulder and drew out a machete from a sheath strapped to his back. I choked.

All the moisture from my suddenly parched mouth now chose to escape from every pore in my skin. An unwelcome distraction from the silent, slow-motion dance we were now performing: the dance of death – the dance of the cobra and the mongoose.

Desperate to get room to use the staff to its fullest effect, I inched towards the middle of the path. The notion of crying out for help never occurred: this was my cross to bear.

It would finish soon, one way or the other. To survive, I needed an edge. I had to get him off balance. Feigning fear, I turned and dashed back towards the Temple. Like a blood-crazed barracuda, he raced after me. Twenty or so paces on, I pretended to sprain an ankle and sprawled forward onto my left side, keeping the staff welded to my right hand.

He was closer than I thought because as I twisted right to lash at him, he was upon me, machete raised. My staff deflected the murderous blow barely enough to save me, with the thick blade smashing the pavement millimetres from my right ear, giving off a shower of sparks, a wicked *crack* and slicing off the top of the staff.

The savagery of the blow overbalanced him, and he ended up sprawled on top of me. Momentarily winded, I lay staring at his dark silhouette, caught a whiff of garlicky breath, then head-butted him. I jabbed a glancing blow to the side of his head with the cut end of the staff and followed up with a poorly aimed knee to his groin. With a heave, I twisted free.

Thankfully he was a microsecond slower to recover. It was enough. I delivered a well-timed blow to his battered head with the bottom half of the staff. He lurched sideways and, like a marionette cut free, crumpled heavily to the cobblestones with a dull thud to become another silent pile of rags and dishevelled limbs.

Staggering back a pace, I stood hunched forward with hands on hips, immobilised by a churning mix of exhilaration from the unexpected victory and waves of fear and self-recriminations at the thought that I may have killed one or both.

Steadying my laboured breathing, I straightened up and managed to get my mind and emotions back into some semblance of normality. Why? had barely flashed into my brain when I heard the sound of running feet and cries of, 'What's going on?'

In the rapidly strengthening light, I saw two novices running towards me, the broader one's outline unmistakeably my friend, Kiet.

'You okay?' said Kiet with a reassuring arm on my shoulder.

'Who is this?' an astonished Ghulam said, pointing at my

fallen foe.

'A good question. I've no idea. There's another one over there,' I said, nodding back towards my hut. They attacked me on my way to the vegetable gardens.'

Ghulam knelt down and gingerly placed his finger on the man's neck to check for a pulse. He glanced back and grimly shook his head before jerking his hand free. There was blood on his fingertips. It sent him into a spasm of hopping from one foot to the other whilst madly rubbing his fingers on his robe, interspersed with watching our faces for an expression to emulate. After scrolling through shock, disgust, fear and bewilderment, he ended with the look of serious concern Kiet and I had settled upon.

For a minute or so, we stood mute. Kiet and Ghulam, presumably like me, occupied with some intense thinking upon the ramifications of the attack.

No matter what the circumstances, I knew that taking the life of another human was an act that incurred the greatest karmic debt. My relationships with the other novices, with Somchai, and with the Abbot were about to be pushed to breaking point.

Squaring my shoulders, I broke the silence. 'We'd better check the other fellow.' I said as calmly as I could before leading the way.

The man remained an inert untidy heap. The others would be unwilling, so I squatted down and reluctantly felt for a pulse. The skin was still warm, but nothing stirred.

Two dead. In the back of my mind, I knew I'd hit them too hard. It is one thing to use the staff in the formalised combat of the dojo but in a surprise attack, in the dark, by two unknown adversaries, fear and self-preservation lead to a heavy hand. With a feeling of intense sadness, I slowly rose to my feet and shook my head.

'Ghulam, go fetch the Abbot. The doctor from the village

will be needed, and the police will have to be informed. Kiet and I will stay to preserve the scene.'

In silence, we watched Ghulam sprinting back down the path. In his wake came the reassurance of the sun's first rays, the yang to balance the yin of the attack. The golden beams of light tentatively explored the tops of the hills on the western side of the valley then, emboldened by the lack of resistance, rushed down the slopes to return colour and warmth to the valley, to the gardens, homes and temples. But not to my two assailants.

For the furnace in the sky, it was a day like any other. For me, it was one that would be long and taxing.

Chapter Four

The day proved as arduous as I had predicted – a tortuous procession of people and trying questions. First, the doctor arrived, confirming the demise of my attackers. He concluded the first had died from my blow with the staff, whilst the second probably from banging his head on the cobblestones as he fell.

Next was the police inspector, a short, thin man wearing an oversized cap, who seemed to take up where my attackers left off. He recognised the two men – they had links to the drug trade; were Burmese refugees who lived in the UNHCR refugee camp about forty kilometres up in the hills. Inspector Phong was obviously a man who believed in guilt by association and suggested that I had killed them in a drug deal gone wrong. He was very keen to get me back to the station, so he could 'persuade' me to tell him *his* idea of the truth.

Thankfully the Abbot interceded strongly on my behalf and, after I had agreed to Phong's demands of giving a blood sample to be tested for drugs, surrendering my passport and promising not to leave the monastery grounds. Backed by the assurances of the Abbot, I was allowed to remain at the monastery.

Once the police had finished their investigation of the scene and my hut, the inspector left, and I was finally permitted to leave the Abbot's office. Walking back to my hut, it became clear that my time at the monastery was over, a decision I had pretty much arrived at before the attack, though I'd hoped to have had more time in which to work out the details of my next step. In the end, I was given that time, as it took over three weeks before the police investigation was finalised.

It was a sad time. I tried to return to my usual routine, but everything was tainted by the subtle and often blatant changes in attitude from those around me. I had become *persona non grata* – unclean because I had 'blood on my hands'. I could deal with the disdain from the novices and monks but was deeply hurt by the invisible wall that had developed between myself and the Abbot and, most disappointing of all, Somchai.

On that last morning at the monastery, the Abbot summoned me to his chambers. The room was bathed with sunlight slanting in from the tall narrow windows, giving the room a warmth that seemed to have bypassed the three inhabitants, who sat stiff and unmoving.

'Please take a seat,' said the Abbot with an indifferent wave of his hand from his secure position behind his huge ornate desk. I moved cautiously into the room and carefully sat on a rather fragile wooden chair. Perched on similar chairs was Inspector Phong on my left and Somchai on my right.

'You will be pleased to know that the police have concluded their work and have returned your passport.' The Abbot slid the offending item towards me.

'You are now free to do as you please.' Those last words escaped his lips with a peculiar mix of surface goodwill and underlying distaste. I leant forward and, with as much dignity as I could muster, retrieved my passport and sat back down. An uncomfortable silence developed. The room became stuffy.

Inspector Phong broke the impasse.

'You are free to stay here in Thailand as long as you wish. You have been completely exonerated.' I was again surprised at how well he spoke English, even if it was coloured by that accent peculiar to Thais. But most surprisingly of all was that he spoke with a degree of warmth.

His changed demeanour stunned me. I turned to have a closer look, almost expecting to see an imposter. But there he sat, with military rigidity, his face distorted by a smile hinting of one happily in possession of an embarrassing secret. I wondered what was going on and then noticed the gaudy signet ring on his right hand. It was one of ours, from a catalogue of a few years back. Perhaps he had found out who I was and, thankfully, was a satisfied customer. I returned an inane nod.

'What are your plans now, Mr Banks?' he continued.

It was a question all in the room were keen to have answered, me included. I had plenty of choices. There was my apartment in Melbourne. JTB was cruising from strength to strength under Lachlan's guidance, which left me with time for other pursuits, one of which was a business opportunity that had been hatched during my two years in Arizona – the time had not been entirely spent on green smoothies and yoga.

I'd taken time out to attend a conference in Dallas on geothermal energy where all manner of new developments in drilling technologies and progress in superconductivity at normal temperatures had been revealed. Huge new possibilities for more effectively harvesting of geothermal energy had been exposed to me. Over the last few days, all that had finally come together within me and a new geothermal project had taken form. I had a starting point. But foremost on my mind was the reason for the attack on my life.

'In some way, my plans depend upon the answer to these questions …' I paused for effect. 'Why was I attacked? Who were my assailants, and what were they after?' I held the inspector's gaze in an attempt to stress the earnestness of my requests.

His brow creased, then eased as he carefully leant back before averting his gaze and directing his answer to the Abbot.

'A curious thing. Those two were low-level thugs used by local criminals for occasional murders and the recovery of unpaid debts. Both had only recently been released from prison.'

He then turned his attention to me. 'My investigations revealed that you were targeted specifically. One of them had a recent photo of you, but who organised the hit is unclear. The impression I have is that it wasn't for local reasons, implying an overseas connection. Do you know of any reason why someone wants you out of the way?'

You don't make those kinds of enemies selling trinkets on the internet, so the only thing I could think of was an environmental extremist still yanking their dreadlocks over the Mount Gambier project. But it was almost impossible to take such a theory seriously. I shook my head.

'I've no idea. I just hope they don't try again.' It was my turn to crinkle my features, before continuing. 'So, returning to your question …' Again I paused, cruelly amused to delay telling the Abbot what he wanted to hear, '…I'll be heading back to Bangkok on the first bus and then back to Australia.'

No one spoke. Slight nods were exchanged. All accepted the wisdom of my decision, and shortly after, the three of us left the Abbot to get on with his administrative duties.

Outside on the steps overlooking the central compound of the temple complex, we paused to adjust to the intense sunshine. The inspector donned a pair of flashy glasses, which looked like ones from our Celebrity range, and then offered me a lift to Bangkok.

Turning to Somchai, I said, 'I will need to collect my suitcase from the storeroom if I am to accept the inspector's kind offer.'

He nodded solemnly, then replied, 'Give me ten minutes. I'll have it delivered to your hut.'

We parted, and I strolled back with the inspector in tow.

'You did well to defend yourself against those two. They have never failed before. I wish them a reincarnation that will allow them to do better in their next lives.'

The inspector's face was unreadable so I didn't know if the

hint of sarcasm was real or not. My understanding of Thai humour was still hit and miss and unlikely to improve.

'Yes, it surprises me also that I managed to survive. Perhaps I did so because my time here has attuned my mind and body to act in harmony.' I tried being as inscrutably ambiguous as he.

This time the inspector's smile was genuine and he placed a hand briefly on my shoulder. 'Yes, you do seem to have benefitted from your stay, but don't forget, if they try once, they will try again. You are a wealthy man, and money breeds evil in many men's minds, so remain vigilant until you find the person or persons behind the attack.'

His sobering words occupied my mind all the way back to Bangkok and beyond.

Chapter Five

Downtown Melbourne hadn't gotten any quieter. The music of the city was a shock to ears sensitised by the quiet of the monastery. They rebelled against the screeching of jammed on brakes, the squealing of tyres under hard acceleration, interspersed with staccato banging and clanging from construction sites and, as an undertone, the steady clicking and tramping of countless shoes, boots and high heels. In the past, it had been energising and exciting, but now it had me wondering if I'd made the right choice by coming back.

Rationally, I should have been rejoicing at all the noise and crowded streets, as it implied a healthy economy and hence more income flowing into JTB's coffers. But construction activity is a better measure of economic health, so I scanned the jagged horizon and noted the number of cranes in operation over the numerous half-finished high-rise developments. But not all were moving. Perhaps the economy wasn't as robust as recent statistics suggested; this was a cause for concern as I needed a swag of dollars to finance my next foray into alternative energy. I hoped the economy had the cash to spare.

I also needed a new lawyer, a trusted professional to handle the legal side of my new business escapade and, possibly advise on more personal issues, Lucinda being at the top of that list. I could have used JTB's legal team, but the new me somehow called for a fresh start, new approaches and, with luck, better outcomes.

A rather haphazard internet search had come up with a practice located in a third-floor office on Little Collins Street, where the receptionist, a demure Asian lady, Thai probably, directed me politely to have a seat before advising Mr Alwali of my presence.

Early, but not overly so, I barely had time to flip a few pages of a glossy car magazine before I was directed to his office, fourth room on the left down a thickly carpeted corridor. A silent approach, then in through the open door where I expected to see an older gent with a long white beard and turban, as seemed appropriate for someone named Ravinder Singh Alwali. Instead, I was mentally coshed to encounter a vigorous young fellow who looked like a Bollywood heartthrob with his perfect teeth, gleaming black hair, stylishly cut. He was clean-shaven and dressed to impress.

He stood smiling and, with an open palm, indicated a fancy leather chair in front of his uncluttered desk. 'How may we assist you, Mr Banks?'

Wondering if he was old enough to be up to the task, I was initially hesitant to discuss my business plans, but Ravi, as he insisted I address him, soon put my mind at ease. He appeared to be a switched-on fellow with a sharp mind that picked up on the many influences likely to impinge on my plans. He understood my reluctance to raise funds and partners here in Australia; just nodded when I mentioned the venture capitalists I'd sounded out in Dallas. Throughout, he asked many intelligent questions about the structure and funding of my proposed joint venture company.

After much tedious computer work, I became managing director and sole shareholder of a shell company called Rosewood Investments Limited.

'Perhaps a break is called for. Tea, coffee?'

I was reluctant to answer, now pondering how to broach the Lucinda problem.

'Or is this sufficient for now?' Ravi was beginning to wonder what was on my mind.

'I have another issue – on the personal side – that needs addressing.'

'Ahh. Perhaps it is best to take a break. We'll stroll to my club and have further discussions over morning tea.' His words were delivered with such smooth solicitousness, made even more entrancing by his Punjabi accent that it was impossible to say no.

The Hoffmann Club, as an institution, had always been a bit too exclusive and hidebound for my taste. I'd only been there once or twice, but Ravi seemed a regular and quickly settled us at a quiet table under a window overlooking an enclosed garden. He was a coffee and cake man. I held my resolve and settled for chamomile tea and a slice of frittata.

How does one admit to a stranger a silly reluctance to break free of the past? There is no easy way, apparently. So, after the first bites had been taken and the drinks sampled, I plunged in. 'My wife Lucinda and I have been living separate lives for … at least four years now, though in reality probably longer.'

Ravi filled in the ensuing silence, 'I'm not really a divorce specialist but can give you general advice. If the relationship is irreparable, then the best course of action is to start divorce proceedings as soon as possible. Only then can you move on with your life.'

All true, but I delayed further with a sip, then: 'But she's a Catholic, though the only time I saw her in a church was at our wedding. And the last time we spoke, which was …' My mind replayed our last meeting, in the recovery room at the hospital, '… over three years ago. She had reiterated what being a Catholic and a wife meant, so ….'

'Mr Banks, the world has moved on. The church no longer has the legal right to block a divorce even if one side objects. By forcing the issue, you may be doing her a favour.'

Perhaps he was right. Towards the end of our break, after a

bit of banter on subjects ranging from cricket, the economy and the new conservative government in Tasmania, I remembered another ramification of divorce.

'I guess I'll have to make a new will.'

'Most definitely. You will probably need time to think about it, but don't delay too long.' He gave a silent warning with a quietly raised finger and upturned eyebrows.

We strolled back to his office, mostly in silence, tidied up a few points and then agreed to meet again in a week to discuss developments with my equity partners and a progress report on the divorce proceedings, to be overseen by a lawyer friend of his.

After parting company, I decided to wander back to my unit in Carlton via the Queen Victoria Markets, for old time's sake, just to see if any of the stallholders I used to deal with would still be there. My high school weekends had been spent working for Gregorio, in his Emporium, as he grandiosely called it. There I learnt the art of understanding customers and the secrets of selling. Those skills enthused me to start my own online Emporium in my final year at school. It was the smartest thing I ever did because when the Covid-19 pandemic hit in 2020, in time for my twentieth birthday, I was able to take advantage of the surge in online buying. By the end of that year, I was making more money than the University Chancellor. Even though I persevered with my degree and an honours year, JTB Holdings ended up being immensely more profitable than anything geophysics could have offered me.

The markets were disappointingly the same: plenty of new businesses, but all fighting for the same discretionary income with the same sort of stuff to the same clientele, a mix of locals and tourists. As expected, I recognised none of the stallholders. People move on, and so must I. Suddenly appreciative of Ravi for pushing me forwards, it was well past time to get my marriage disaster behind me. I would immerse myself in my new venture, and in the process, who knows who I would meet. Life was for living, and I couldn't wait for the right girl to come along before getting started. And there was plenty of lost time to make up. I had a revolutionary idea that, handled properly, would put Australia at the forefront of clean energy production, though of course, I would have to be clever to avoid the traps that would undoubtedly be set by the incumbent energy cartels, from State electricity boards to coal and gas producers and, most probably, the media, who, having hung me out to dry with the Mount Gambier project, would undoubtedly love to do the same again.

The walk back to my unit ended in a last-minute dash as the fickle spring weather turned from sun to wind and rain. Even the weather was telling me to get a move on! Heeding the call, I spent a fruitful afternoon on the phone organising people for the new venture, an enterprise no one in Melbourne but Ravi knew anything about — which was just how I wanted to keep it for a while longer.

No one knew I was back in town, but that would have to change soon. I would have to go to head office if I was to access the cash I needed, necessitating negotiations with the major shareholders, principally Lachlan Lucas, Abernethy and Partners, and Lucinda. With sixty-two per cent of issued shares, I couldn't be outvoted, but the best outcome would be an amicable arrangement, not me running roughshod over people's feelings, even Lucinda's.

One last task for the day was a call to Higgins at *The Age*, the only journalist I had any respect for. After a bit of waiting, I was put through to his desk.

'Who's this again?'

'Julius Banks.'

His lack of recognition compelled me to jog his memory. After all, it was close to knockoff time, and the fellow undoubtedly had things to do, people to see, copy to write. 'Banks, I was involved in the Mount Gambier geothermal energy project. You covered the court case.'

'Ah, yes, Mr Banks, now I remember. A sorry affair, but ….'

'Yes, exactly. A lot of water under the bridge since, but I wonder if you have any knowledge of any of the opposing side still – 'maintaining the rage'.'

'A curious request. Why do you ask? Has something happened?'

One has to be very circumspect with reporters no matter how reasonable they appear, so I tried to choose my words with care. 'Let's just say that something I have become aware of may have some – remote – connection to the protests there.'

He hesitated for a while, presumably raking over his memory. 'Can't say I've heard anything even vaguely connected, though the better person to ask is our environment reporter, Jessica … Jessica Moore. She was the one who initially reported the protests. Worked as a junior for an Adelaide paper then. Didn't even get a byline for a story that caused such a stir, the lifeblood of journalism.'

He paused, undoubtedly sporting a wry smile, then, without prompting, went on. 'Not sure if she followed the story, as once it gained traction a more senior journalist took over. You know how it goes.'

Yes, I understood. I could have asked for more, but my mind was gummed up by the name: Jessica Moore.

Had her presence on the plane been random? Probably. But some atavistic part of me wasn't convinced; it believed in fate. Was she fated to become a part of my life and again because of an alternative energy project?

My logic recoiled at such silliness. Such things don't happen in the real world, but I was unable to resist one last question: 'Is she here in Melbourne?'

The answer was yes, and, unsolicited, he gave me her mobile number. Then we said our goodbyes.

Would I contact her, or would I have the sense to let coincidences slide?

I wouldn't have put money either way.

Chapter Six

The weekend, in hindsight, was a false dawn, everything going well and no hint of troubles to come. I made a few more calls to the States regarding financing, received encouraging responses, and also contacted the drilling company we had used in South Australia. They were a nationwide operation, reliable, and they had a few rigs available in Tasmania. So the news was all good. The rest of the time, I took it easy, going for strolls, this time armed with an umbrella as the showers were still coming through. The process of reacquainting myself with my old stamping grounds began soothing the soul.

Monday came around, and I had become so relaxed and buoyed by all the good news that I decided to put off until Tuesday my going into JTB's HQ, if a nondescript office/factory unit in Essendon warranted such a title.

There was an alternative style café a couple of blocks away that I had just discovered. So I had booked a table, thinking myself lucky they were open since most eateries have Mondays off. Perhaps emboldened by a cruisy weekend, I sent a text to Jessica, with the bare bones of information: my name, I mentioned Higgins, and Mount Gambier, and said I had a table at *La Vie En Rose* booked for 6:30 and left the rest to her.

I rationalised my actions, telling myself it was a chance to suss out the potential opposition to Tasmania. Curiosity also played a big part, as I was intrigued to see how, or if, she would respond to the bait. I was still somewhat surprised that she showed no signs of recognition on the plane, but then we had never actually met. And she would only have known me from news reports where I would have been dressed in a business suit, was chubby, clean-shaven and had short hair.

Walking to the café, I was a touch crestfallen that she had not replied and tried to think of reasons why other than that she had a life and was not interested in my doings — the sensible approach on her part. The place was pretty quiet, just as I had hoped. Busy restaurants get so noisy one can hardly have a conversation for the hissing of coffee machines and the exuberant chatter of fellow diners. I chose a table with a good view of the entrance and street outside and started studying the menu.

Having delayed overly long, I was on the verge of ordering when a taxi pulled up. A woman got out and, pursued by a sudden shower, sprinted for the entrance. And there was Jessica, on the threshold, brushing off a few raindrops and looking annoyed. The waitress tried to interest her in a menu but she was intent on checking out the clientele. Her eyes drifted past then corrected themselves to lock onto my amused gaze. Still she hesitated, her brain probably confused by my thinner face and lack of hair courtesy of my time at the monastery. Both the top of my head and beard were at the stubble stage.

Eventually, her eyes hardened, and she nudged past the waitress to walk over to my table, there to stand for a moment, presumably considering her options.

I decided to make up her mind. 'Take a seat, Jessica,' I said, indicating a vacant place opposite me. 'I won't bite, though I've yet to order.' As a final inducement, I added, 'Dinner is on me, so please ….'

My good humour did the trick. She chose the chair opposite and sat down.

She had obviously come straight from work, dressed in a knee-length dark blue skirt, matching jacket with the power shoulders, mandatory for working women, and a shiny white blouse, probably silk. She looked wonderful, spoiled only by an unfriendly demeanour, which was an aspect I was strangely keen to reverse. Strange, because we appeared to be natural enemies.

She spent an inordinate amount of time getting comfortable then, finding a spot for her rather capacious handbag, dumped it on a spare chair, after which she examined me just as she had on the plane – in silence but with growing puzzlement.

'What was the outcome of that climate conference in Hawaii?' I decided to pique her interest, keep her off-balance and hopefully force some sort of reply.

She regarded me with a mix of suspicion battling nascent recognition.

'We shared the flight to Bangkok afterwards.' I tried my warmest smile. 'I love Sheffield, remember?'

'That was you!'

'Proof that not only women can transform themselves with a new haircut and change of dress.' The haircut and my different garb, a casual jacket and a plain white shirt made her surprise totally understandable.

With recollection came a hint of a smile, which I built on by passing her the menu. 'They have quite an interesting selection, especially if you are into healthy options. If you've come straight from work, you'll need a feed.'

The meal reminded me of a session on the dojo; lots of warming up, circling around, sizing up one's opponent until, suddenly, combat is joined in earnest.

'The Mount Gambier protests … do you know if any of those involved still carry any extreme notions about the project and me in particular?'

'Mount Gambier. That was years back. The whole thing is dead and buried. Climate change and the Anthropocene are the things these days. So, why do you ask?'

As much as she was a journalist, I still couldn't help but find her attractive. Perhaps it was simply a case of being starved of feminine company, or were there other undefined forces at play? I didn't know. All I knew was that I was pleased to be having a shared meal and a conversation.

'After Bangkok, I've no idea where you went to, but I headed to a Buddhist monastery on the Burmese border and tried to become a monk!' I paused, letting her incredulity subside before I continued my story of the monastery and the attempt on my life.

'I invited you for dinner on the slim chance you could shed some light on my attackers. The police inspector's warning was that I had been targeted and that I may still be on someone's hit list.'

'Well, it can't have been anyone involved in the campaign against the drilling, that's just absurd, so I really can't help you.'

I hadn't expected any more than that but still felt deflated. I was no further in solving the mystery, and thus, the threat on my life continued – an unsatisfactory situation, but one I would have to work around.

On the way out, I offered to pay for a taxi but learned she lived only a few blocks away and not too far from my place. Thoughts stirred.

'The least I can do is walk you home. I live just around the block, and you don't have an umbrella, so there's no need to suffer.'

Hesitant at first, but outside, the cold night air and a few drops of rain convinced her to take up my offer. We had to go past my place along the way, which was an opportunity too good to miss. 'That's my building down there; we could pop in for a coffee. I'm quite an expert on the coffee machine, even though I've given up the stuff … so…?'

She stopped, made the best use of the streetlights to study my face, at first with disbelief, then, seeing nothing sinister, was on the cusp of replying when a bunch of bikers roared past, giving her a cursory glance and making speech impossible. Once they'd turned the corner, and after one last inspection, she surprised me with a measured, "Okay."

The dripping was increasing and we upped our pace accordingly. Further down in the misted lighting, three dark and bulky figures turned the corner and came marching our way. A glance at Jessica confirmed our thoughts were identical: trouble brewing.

'My place is the one with the portico. We can beat them if we get a move on.'

My heart pounded as I pressed my palm overly hard on the sensor that unlocked the heavy wooden door into the foyer. Jessica's grip on my arm added pain to the panic. The door grudgingly gave way, and I shoved her inside.

'Call the cops.' I yelled, then spun around. They were almost at the steps. There was no way I would make it inside without them following. Attack now the only option.

The leading guy, burly, black leathers and bushy black beard, was stopping and in the process of lifting a sawn-off double-barrelled shotgun. Its line of fire rapidly homed in on me. Stepping forward, I used my umbrella to force its trajectory to keep going, almost got clear of its deadly intent when the thing went off, shredding the umbrella into nothingness.

I had ducked as I had shoved, so only copped a few stings to the top of my head. The bikie hadn't been so lucky. He was staggering back and had dropped the gun in favour of keeping his bloodied and torn face together. I didn't need an invite. I dived for the gun then spun around to face them and began my 'negotiations'.

'Who's next?' The two accomplices glared back, hate in their eyes, their conversational skills muted as they looked down the wrong end of the shotgun. Their limited attention spans soon turned towards dragging their comrade away whilst keeping up their baleful obsession with me and the gun.

'Who sent you, you bastards?' I yelled at their stumbling retreat. Those lowlifes knew I wasn't the murdering type, which added more bile to the situation, especially when, after a few paces, they turned and completely ignored me as they shambled back to their bikes, which presumably were around the corner. In the movies, I would have clobbered them and had them trussed up on the pavement ready for the cops, confirming my superhero status. Instead, I staggered up the steps, got the damn door to let me in, and found a pale-faced and wide-eyed Jessica with a mobile phone still in her hand.

'Everything's okay now. They've gone – one injured, not fatally,' I hoped.

She remained gawking at me in disbelief. I guess environment reporters aren't eyewitnesses to too many attempted murders, even though Melbourne does entertain the masses with the occasional gangland execution.

Turning her towards the lifts, I selected the third floor and waited, my legs starting to feel rubbery and the rest of me unsure how long I could keep up my Hollywood hero façade.

'Jeezuz, you're bleeding,' was her only comment once the lift got moving, after which she fussed around trying to find something to stem the trickles of blood oozing down my forehead and cheeks.

We were in my apartment before she gave up, and I herded her to the bathroom, where I put her in charge of the first aid kit.

Once she had patched me up, I decided caffeine would be needed to cope with the upcoming session with the police and dusted off the coffee machine. We waited in the lounge room, opposite sides of the coffee table, on which the shotgun lay accusingly between us, its presence an embarrassment that stifled the desire to talk. Mostly, we sat immersed in separate thoughts, occasionally interrupted by unenthused sipping. Our cups were halfway gone by the time I saw, on my phone, a police car pulling up outside the building.

I dashed out to get them, afraid they'd drive off, thinking they'd been victims of a crank caller. It initially took a bit of convincing, but my bandaged face and later the shotgun, backed by Jessica's account and the feed from the cameras above the entrance finally convinced them of the grim realities of events.

In due course, they left, with the shotgun wrapped to preserve fingerprints and instructions for both of us to report to the station to make a formal statement. Their assurances that the bikers would not return were completely unconvincing, but I did my best not to show it – I just wanted them out the door.

Once we had the place to ourselves, I suggested another coffee. The answer was no. An awkward silence followed, which I broke. 'Shall I get you a taxi?' I would have driven her if I had a car.

She hesitated. 'It seems ridiculous to get a cab when I'm only a block away.'

But it also seemed not a great idea to walk.

'You could stay the night. I've two spare rooms, and you can always shove a chair under the door handle if you're worried.' The faint smile that briefly lit up her face convinced me to cancel further attempts at being witty and, after a pause, she agreed to the arrangement. Her acceptance also revealed more of her self-confidence and perhaps friendlier regard towards me.

I was unnecessarily showing her the wardrobe with the fluffy bathrobe and a spare set of my pyjamas when she touched my arm. 'What about Mrs Banks?' she said, eyeing my wedding band.

'Ah … Mrs Banks and I have been living apart for … an embarrassingly long while. She definitely won't be making a scene. I've even changed the locks, so you have nothing to worry about there. Besides, she doesn't even know I'm back. And even then, she wouldn't leave her flashy riverside apartment to slum it here with me; she likes her luxury too much.'

Reassured, we parted. I eventually heard muffled sounds of showering and, satisfied that she was getting settled, I did likewise.

Lights out, with the only sounds an occasional passing siren getting through the triple glazing, I found myself wasting an arduously long time staring at the ceiling, contemplating my fascination with Jessica. But eventually, the plasters on my forehead directed attention to the more vexed question of who was out to get me.

No answers came. At some point, sleep took hold, but one seeded with strange faces and bizarre locations that later conspired to have me fighting the bedding in nightmare battles, battles that ended with the unwelcome optimism of the rising sun when it invaded the room with bars of blazing light that forced a grumbling wakefulness. And soon after, unhappy imaginings concerning the visit to the police station, where I would have to endure another interminable session with detectives, who, with probable justification, would accost me with that wearying suspiciousness and scepticism held against anyone not a close colleague.

There was only one certainty about the day; a visit to the office was out of the question.

Chapter Seven

I was dressed and blending up a fruit and kale smoothie when Jessica emerged, looking fresh and even more alluring than the night before.

'Hope it's not too early for you,' I said after turning off the machine. 'Care to join me?' Her look of disgust at the green liquid was answer enough, but I gave her my spiel about its life-giving properties, and she hesitantly accepted a small glass.

She drank the smoothie with a "humph" of reluctant approval and consumed a small bowl of cereal, all with minimal conversation and maximum attention to her phone. Mine was still turned off.

Breakfast over, I suggested putting the police at the top of the to-do list. She considered this while casting a professional eye over me; made an indeterminate noise then phoned her boss with the news that she'd be late, followed by a very brief summary of why. Finally, she agreed to see him when she got in.

The detective in charge of our case, Liam Aberdare, would have received a report on our incident but obviously thought it worthless because he asked us to repeat our story. Afterwards, he asked the same questions of why and who, and I gave an apparently unconvincing plea of ignorance.

The only thing we did learn was that the gun had only my prints on it. My executioner wasn't totally stupid. Not only had he worn gloves but had also filed off the serial number, which, combined with the grainy quality of the camera footage and the guy's generic bikie appearance, meant the chances of identifying him were very slim. Liam tried to assure us that he had some unspecified lines of enquiry, but I wasn't holding my breath. I got the impression that Jessica's presence, and confession of being a journalist, made him less forthcoming with information than otherwise. He concluded the session with: "We'll contact you if anything turns up."

We were set free by midmorning, and, at my suggestion, we adjourned to a nearby café, enticed by the heady aroma of roasting coffee beans. Jessica had a long black – I, a herbal tea. The conversation was forced. She left in the taxi I organised.

Her mercurial nature – yesterday warming, today cool and taciturn – made it hard to understand what was going on, leaving me to conclude that maybe her mood was due to something peculiarly female, such as being put out by the prospect of going to work in the same clothes as the day before. Such chauvinist male conclusions I thought wise to keep to myself.

With a shake of my head, I dismissed further speculation, had a moment of introspection, then decided a visit to the office no longer appealed. The spring weather was behaving itself, so I chose to walk to the University, intending to do a touch more research on the best locations in Tasmania for my geothermal scheme.

A rather strange mix of emotions ensued. The pleasure of walking along familiar roads and past familiar landmarks was mixed with the bristling wariness of the hunted animal as I weaved cautiously through the intermittent stream of pedestrians. Simultaneously, I tried to keep an eye on the traffic that made spasmodic progress between the lights. A schizophrenic attitude I had to endure for a while longer it seemed.

My geology and physics professors were happy to find the time to chat about things past and present. While doing so, I managed to slip in some innocent-sounding questions regarding new geologic discoveries in Tasmania. The day reminded me of the best aspects of my time at university and also confirmed the wisdom of the locations I had chosen.

Walking back in the deepening twilight, with all senses on high alert, I felt a sense of achievement in getting back to my apartment without incident. The thought even occurred that perhaps my persecutors were running out of cash for the hiring of would-be assassins. I could only hope.

Dinner was had with my laptop, checking emails and such. Then, on a whim, I selected the local news channel, skimmed through the gossip and the usual political speculation, and was about to shut it down when I was jolted by the headline: LOCAL BUSINESSMAN ESCAPES DEATH IN GANGLAND-STYLE HIT. Eyeballs bulging, I started hitting the keys until I watched in rising disbelief the reporter's exaggerated account of Monday night's events.

Detective Aberdare was tight-lipped and managed to stick to the bare facts. But when interviewing Jessica, they really went to town. I wondered if she'd been leaned on to dramatise events because, between the reporter's questions and Jessica's replies, they certainly did a good job of doing so. How they'd got a copy of the footage from the camera over the door was beyond me. It was bizarre seeing my actions on screen. They seemed to be happening to someone who looked like me but who wasn't me. The reporter then raised my shady past regarding Mount Gambier, chopping off Jessica's reply to leave the viewer with the belief that behind the attack was a group of crazed enviro-warriors – the exact opposite of Jessica's opinion of Monday night.

Stunned and deeply disappointed, I turned off the laptop and vowed to get out of town as soon as possible to avoid any more ridiculous media attention, now more resolved than ever to pour all my energies into my plans and give the female of the species a wide berth, Jessica Moore in particular.

A restless night had me dressed and ready before dawn.

Standing at the window, a mug of lemon and ginger tea in hand and checking the sky to confirm the veracity of the weatherman's forecast, I spied a news van pulling up in the street below. A female reporter wearing a short skirt, a tight-fitting jacket with exaggerated shoulders, and made up for a gala ball stepped out, accompanied by a cameraman. They quickly located a place suitable for keeping an eye on the front door, presumably to bail me up like the bushrangers of old but armed with camera and microphone instead of guns. Their type threatened one, not with "your money or your life", rather, the making of money from trashing your life. And they had plenty of lawyers to fight defamation suits, which then became more newsfeed to keep the ratings bubbling.

Presumably, they'd been briefed about my lack of a car because they weren't covering the exit from the underground garage. They'd given me an escape route. Forgetting the planned early stroll, I threw on a light grey business suit, newly acquired since all the old ones hung on me like the flabby skin of a winner from the *Biggest Loser* reality show. With my attaché case in hand, double-checked to contain the documents needed for my visit to JTB HQ, I escaped while the going was good.

I was two blocks away before remembering I was a wanted man and began again scanning the traffic and the few early pedestrians. Unfed and not having had the time to finish my tea, I ducked into the first decent café of the many that had sprung up along the street. With a big breakfast ordered, I took up residence in a seat at the back and settled in to eat, sip and waste time.

After the rushed exit, it was a relief to saunter through a meal, dally over a pot of tea, and hide in amongst other diners also silently studying their phones. In between sips, I answered a few emails and lastly flicked through the news. They were still running my story, but it was rapidly being buried under the daily dross of gossip, sport, murders, more drug busts, and a train wreck in Bangladesh: the usual noise that passes as news. This was good because, in a day or so, the heat would be off, and I'd have more room to move, to get things happening with a minimum of fuss.

One can tarry only so long by oneself and, although it was still early, I ordered a taxi, being certain the traffic hadn't become less clogged in the intervening years. I calculated I'd probably get there just as the office staff were marching in.

There are few certainties in life, but my prediction about the traffic proved to be one of them; I arrived a few minutes after nine, having endured a gruelling crawl most of the way. The traffic had no effect on my Indian driver, who remained very jovial and talkative throughout, which was a blessing because, in all his talk, he made no mention of my escapades, boosting my hopes of anonymity.

Neither Lachlan nor Lucinda had my new mobile number or email address. Somehow my transformation required it. Hence my visit would either be a surprise or a waste of time if they weren't there. I paid for my fare with my card, for the taxman, then selected four crisp fifty-dollar notes for the cabbie to wait for me. Riffling through the new bills, I again pondered my ambivalence towards too good old cash. It was a nuisance, and like most, I hardly ever used the stuff, but when I did, it was with a growing sense of rebelliousness. Cash is anonymous – it gives governments less control over you, and they have too much of that already. Should they turn nasty, they can turn off your access to e-money, and you starve. That line of thought had me vowing to use notes more often and be a bigger part of those who endeavour to keep the surveillance state in check. A futile gesture probably, but one I was starting to warm to nonetheless.

Unmolested by such anarchic thoughts, the taxi driver

accepted my largesse and, with a lingering smile, drove in search of a shady parking spot. I turned towards Reception, having noted that the car spaces for the General Manager and Board Members were ominously vacant.

Considering I was returning to the nerve centre of the business I had created from scratch, I felt strangely disconnected from it, a feeling reinforced when I found that the faithful and efficient Mrs Reid had been replaced by a young brunette with fake eyelashes and false nails.

'How may I help you?' she said with insincerity, her head tilted slightly in the direction of a notice on prominent display on the left side of the reception bench – it stated in Arial Bold: NO HAWKERS OR CANVASSERS. ALL BUSINESS BY APPOINTMENT ONLY.

I decided to put her to the test. 'I would like to see either Mr Lucas or Mrs Banks if either is in or will be here shortly.' And I waited with barely disguised amusement for her response.

'Do you have an appointment, Mr …?' again said with that head movement towards the sign.

'I don't have an appointment, but …' My baiting of the girl was interrupted by the sound of a car entering the car park, quickly, emitting a rorty burble and scrunching the few loose stones on the bitumen. I turned in time to see a shiny black Maserati perform a rapid forward park in the General Manager's spot.

A long moment elapsed before Lachlan Lucas emerged from the driver's side, wearing a black suit and blacker sunglasses. He shut the door with a force that made me wince, then waited impatiently for Lucinda to appear. She collected her handbag and slammed the door with equal force, and aimed a wicked smile at Lachlan. He grunted his disgust, turned, and, with exaggerated strides, assaulted the few steps leading to the front entrance.

'I'm not in. Any problems, let Jackie handle it,' he said, storming past before disappearing up the stairs.

I still had my back to the receptionist when Lucinda glided in, also heading to the offices on the first floor. She was a few paces past when she stopped and, as if caught by invisible threads, slowly turned my way, took off her white-rimmed sunglasses and stared.

'Julius, darling, you should have told us you were back. My, you look … amazing! Like you were at university. No – better.' She laughed with genuine surprise, but I couldn't help thinking that her little brain was doing all sorts of self-serving calculations not revealed in her lovely face – a face that bewitched CEOs, barristers, society types and, once upon a time, me.

Grabbing my arm, she led me up the stairs and into her office, made comfortable with plush carpets and a tasteful selection of paintings, all originals by the look of them. There was a bar. She had always been fond of a drink and yet had never let it get the better of her. Through an open door were glimpses of a bathroom.

Before leaving for Arizona, I had vacated my position as an active member of the executive team. She had accepted my parting gift of fifteen per cent of the issued shares and the title of Executive Director. I had suggested a handsome salary, this office and some ill-defined duties. Lucas called the shots on paper, but I speculated Lucinda pulled the strings whenever the mood suited her.

Tossing her tiny, shiny red handbag on the polished wooden desk, she moved to the bar. 'We must celebrate your return, and one so dramatic, if one can believe the media.'

She turned from pouring liquor into two cut crystal tumblers to give me a look that suggested concern and happiness that I had survived. However, I could never be sure about her.

She walked over to where I stood in the middle of the room

and handed me my drink. I was on the point of informing her that the new me didn't drink when she intervened.

'Don't look like that. It's not poison … it's one of our new lines. It's called *Tarkine Mist*. We bought a distillery in Tassie and, after a few celebrity endorsements, it's going gangbusters. Have a sip; you'll be surprised … it's almost as good as we say it is!'

She was weaving her magic, and I found myself obeying. Taking a sip, I felt the initial bite then the smoothness, like warm honey sliding down the throat. She was right; it was top notch. My old self started wondering about profit margins and scope for expansion when the new one got a grip. Moving over to the desk, I placed the half-full glass down, along with my attaché case.

Turning, I leant back on the edge of the desk and took a moment to more fully examine my lovely Lucinda. Tall and slim, though not quite as slim as she used to be – there was a bit more to like about her buttocks and a touch more around the waist – perhaps the comfortable life was softening her body, if not her mind. She stood like a model and was pleasingly colour-coded; her black hair and dark eyes offset the white linen skirt and matching jacket, which were livened up by a red blouse and the handbag. A diamond necklace added sparkle. She held her glass in one extended arm, the other arm crossed below for support, one leg slightly extended, pointing my way. With calm neutrality, she observed me observing her. Her expression hinted of honesty, an aspect she rarely displayed, which disappeared with the return of her smile.

An ineptness took hold of me, now unsure how to broach the purpose of my visit. But I had to say something to counter her growing amusement at my indecision.

The briefcase put me back on track. 'I hope I'm not interrupting anything vital. Lachlan seemed … agitated.'

'Don't mind him. He'll get over it. He's a great innovator and very imaginative, as you know.'

I wasn't sure that her use of "imaginative" was the same as mine when applied to Lachlan. They had arrived in the same car, implying new domestic arrangements. If she was having it off with him, I was undecided whether I should feel jealousy or pity towards him. In the end, I let the issue slide.

'Some new problem?' I wanted more details in case his problems impacted my plans to cash in a significant slice of my shares.

'Oh … the China-US trade war is apparently entering a new phase. The Chinese make a lot of our stuff and buy it too, so if their economy takes a dive, so do we. I think that upsets him.'

'But not you?'

Her grin was enigmatic. 'Yes, and no.'

I waited, but she didn't elaborate, and time was moving on.

'Well, it may impact upon the reason for my visit.' I took a breath and continued. 'I would like to sell down my holdings, which would give you and Lachlan the chance to enjoy formal control of the company. To take it where you will.'

Without comment or hesitation, she put the remains of her drink on the bar, moved to the desk and established herself in the leather recliner. I made myself comfortable in the matching visitor's chair.

It was always fascinating how she could transform from charming hostess to savvy businesswomen with such instant totality. We discussed timing, numbers and current share price, the possible worsening economic impact of the US-China stoush and how much of a stake I wanted to keep. Throughout, I kept marvelling at her confidence and apparent complete disregard for Lachlan's input.

We reached a possible consensus of reducing my holdings down to forty-five per cent but left unresolved the small matter of buyers with the considerable cash needed to pay for the shares

I was selling. A knock at the door was followed by a tall leggy blonde, presumably Jackie, carrying a few items of *snail-mail*, which she delivered with a deferential nod and left.

'Excuse me a moment,' Lucinda said. She flipped through the correspondence, dismissing most until intrigued by one with the air of legality about it.

With a jewelled and rather deadly looking paper-knife, she fished out the single page and scanned its contents then, displaying no emotion, put it to one side. She glanced at the letterhead then announced in an offhand way, 'Hutchinson, Geopolis and Alwali. They're new to me, must be – shall we say – up and coming lawyers. So the new Julius not only has a new body but also wants a new marital arrangement. Divorce. It's such an ugly word, don't you think? It reeks of failure, hmm?'

Her tone goaded me. 'Yes, some relationships do stink, and there's no way to get rid of the smell but to cut one's losses and start again. Surely you don't want me hanging around your life like a pauper at a banquet.' It was a lousy analogy, but I said it with feeling.

My display of emotion appeared to amuse her, perhaps boosting her sense of control over the situation. In any event, she chose to lean back in her chair and, with restless fingers on the edge of the desk, looked skyward.

Renewing her gaze upon me, she announced in measured tones: 'Yes, perhaps what you are doing is all for the best, but we mustn't rush things. There are things to consider; money …' Her eyes lit up briefly. '… property and such, and obligations to the business.'

'There's no hurry but the sooner settled, the sooner both of us can truly move on. I would have thought the prenuptial agreement that you insisted on should make the process relatively straightforward,' I said with as much conciliation in my voice as I could muster.

She appeared to agree. 'Hmm. In theory, yes. Still have to get my accountants and lawyers to check things over. It will impact on Lachlan, and he's a bit upset at the moment; a few trifling financial developments are concerning him, which could slow things for me. But as you say it shouldn't be too difficult to arrange things. We're both adults and should be able to sort things out. Speaking of which, you really must give me your number. We should be able to communicate with each other directly.'

Reluctantly, I gave her my number and email and confirmed I was staying at my apartment in Carlton. We departed with a handshake that I found strangely surreal. Her hands were dry and her grip firm.

A few minutes later, I was waking up my driver and heading home, with the blessing of lighter traffic on the return journey. Throughout the ride, I kept hoping Lucinda would expedite both my requests and prayed she had no surprises to spring on me. She loved surprises, especially when they benefitted her.

Chapter Eight

Lucinda's mention of the trade war and Lachlan's overblown response made me curious about the financial health of the business and the economy looking forward. Both would have ramifications for my project. And what were Lachlan's personal circumstances? He seemed stressed for more reasons than just the business.

Thursday morning, on the dot at eight-thirty, I phoned Ravi and was put through quickly, making me glad he was an early starter. I filled him in on my meeting with Lucinda. He voiced his pleasure at the progress made. I then turned to my concerns regarding the trade war, JTB's finances and question marks over Lachlan. He naturally confessed ignorance in all these areas, which was fine, but I still insisted he made enquires for me, especially about the business and Lachlan. I wanted to see what his grapevine would come up with. He may uncover facts, or useful rumours, in areas I couldn't reach or would not have considered, and besides, I had other things to organise. I suggested he cast his net wide, and we agreed to discuss the findings at our meeting the next day.

The rest of the morning was spent on the laptop and phone, gathering more information on the logistics of my schemes. Later, walking a pre-lunch mug of tea around the living room, I received a call from Detective Aberdare.

'You never mentioned the attack in Thailand, Mr Banks.' Straight to the point and not sounding happy.

'I … didn't want to bias your investigation with seemingly unrelated details.'

'Hardly unrelated, Mr Banks. You'd better tell me all the details no matter how … unrelated.'

He gave me a thorough grilling that left me embarrassed and humbled but reconciled by the more conciliatory note entering his speech at the end, especially once I'd mentioned Inspector Phong, who was known to him from some prior joint operation.

On the local front, the only news he had was that they had located my *alleged* assailant but had no success in squeezing any useful information from him. They had let him go, to be followed and phone-tapped in the hope of some useable information turning up. He ended the call, again with the promise of informing me of any real progress.

There was a burst of rain around midday, the sun reappearing later in the afternoon. Feeling jaded after all the phone calls, texts and trawling through the business news for speculation and gossip, I headed outside for a jog around the park, did a few exercises and enjoyed the late afternoon sunshine.

During my long absence, I had kept one eye on JTB via their website and the annual reports. All seemed to be going well. In fact, with Lachlan and Lucinda in charge, the company was apparently going from strength to strength, the customer base now worldwide, not just in China and East Asia, and thus should weather any downturn caused by the trade war.

The most interesting snippet of news was a piece about Lachlan's association with Crown Casino. He'd recently had a big win and was pictured with a poised and glamourous Lucinda by his side. Succeeding in business requires one to be comfortable with taking risks because of the immutable law of economics: more risk, more reward, and yet understand its dark side: the greater the risk, the greater the losses. The real secret was not in making occasional huge gains but avoiding big losses. I hoped Lachlan was keeping that cardinal rule in mind in his business dealings and in his dabbling at the casino. I had no sure way of assessing his personal finances but wondered if his mood the other day was all business-related because casinos had led many to ruination. Perhaps Ravi would provide more answers.

Back at my apartment, having survived my trip to the park, though not completely unfazed as I had been spooked on several occasions by guys in black roaring past on noisy motorbikes, and there were still surprising numbers of them. Their intrusion got me speculating on what they would do once beautifully silent electric bikes took over as was definitely happening with cars.

Lachlan's Maserati certainly wasn't electric. Like them, he needed to make a statement when he moved – aural and visual – and that car did so in spades. Though it was odd that, when I'd left and given it the once over, I noted the tyres were thin on tread: not a good thing on Melbourne's often wet roads. Was he too busy to notice or was he hard up for cash? It was pointless speculating so, as a mental sorbet, I did a bit more of my workout, then yoga and half hour of meditation, all of which resulted in a good night's sleep, the first since Monday's drama.

Ravi was all smiles when he motioned me to a seat.

'Nick is handling your divorce – that's Nick junior, not Mr Geopolis senior. He's sent a copy of the prenuptial agreement to your wife at the business address and a similar letter to her lawyers. He is of the opinion that the matter can be resolved to the satisfaction of you both, but such things don't happen quickly … could be a few months, maybe more. I'm sorry if I can't be more specific.'

'That's okay, at least we've made a start. Two other things. Business first. I want you to set up a new shell company with water boring as its brief, perhaps call it *Wonderland Water Boring* or some such if that name has been taken, anything will do but it must have the words "water boring" in it.'

Ravi smiled. I confirmed his thoughts. 'Yes, I know it's a bit of subterfuge, but drilling for water is a lot more acceptable than drilling for anything else, and with my past I need as much disguising as possible.'

Ravi nodded. I then asked about the results of his enquiries re JTB and Lachlan.

'Well, as a spy I haven't been overly successful. Your company by all accounts seems to be as it is, a very successful business, above board and financially healthy. As far as Lachlan goes, the only thing to note is that he likes to take his overseas guests, especially the Chinese ones, to the casino for a good time. You know how the Chinese love to gamble. Lachlan's had a few big wins, which have made the news, but also a few big losses which haven't been so well publicised. The usual story.'

'But nothing to cause him concern?' I had to be sure.

'Hard to say, but probably no. Though he is as human as the rest of us so ....'

We were silent for a while. Ravi suggested another visit to the club but I declined, wanting to get on with the next phase.

'I plan to go to Tasmania next week to get the ball rolling. How soon can you get my water boring company set up … days or weeks?'

'A week or so should be enough. I'll email the details. You will have to sign some documentation but that doesn't have to be done here in Melbourne. The government allows you to do it electronically these days, part of its pro-business policy, which, surprisingly, doesn't extend to divorce.' We both smiled at this odd arrangement.

He continued, 'It will all be explained in the email. Once you've signed and emailed the signed copy back, I'll confirm things and you can get started. All very easy.'

We departed and I walked back, alert, but with a spring in my step. Things were starting to move. I would drop out of sight in good old Tasmania and get on with my life. But casting my eyes at the bustling crowds of downtown Melbourne, the cars crawling but motorbikes slipping in between them reminded me of how easy it is for a motorcyclist to bump someone off then dissolve into the traffic before anyone can act. No matter how many CCTV cameras are posted around the city, all a killer needs is a helmet, dark glasses and a stolen motorbike and they are invisible.

A sobering thought but one I was determined not to be intimidated by.

The weekend was mostly walks, workouts and yoga, with calls to arrange my ticket on the Bass Strait ferry, confirm the accommodation in Sheffield – my temporary base of operations – and the hire of a four-wheel drive.

Monday morning, first thing, I was at the Department of Transport renewing my driver's licence, which was on the verge of expiring. There was a moment of hesitancy over the big difference in my appearance, but passport and fingerprints convinced them.

Back at my apartment, brewing a pot of tea and wondering what to pack for Wednesday's boat trip and beyond, a surprise text rattled my phone. Jessica wanted to meet. She had style, or nerve, I wasn't sure which; she just wrote: "Dinner tonight. La Vie En Rose. 6:30", and no more.

Like her, I decided against the courtesy of a reply. I was more than annoyed. She assumed I was still in town, available and interested.

The worst of it was, she was right!

Chapter Nine

Perhaps Jessica had battered my fragile male ego more than I would have admitted at the time, because, after a thin lunch, I phoned Lucinda, perhaps seeking a way of regaining some masculine pride lost by the manner and possible intent of Jessica's summons. A churlish motivation, but such is the way of human flesh.

'Julius, how wonderful to hear from you so soon,' Lucinda purred.

I took a breath before making my reply, not wanting to appear overly keen. 'Nice to know the sound of my voice is still pleasing to you.' A bad start. I fumbled on. 'I've been thinking about our arrangements. Perhaps sentimentality is gripping me, but I'm thinking that, instead of JTB shares, as per the pre-nup, we reduce the share allocation you are owed, if such is the term, and I make up the shortfall by buying the *Tarkine Mist* distillery business from JTB, at the current valuation, in cash. The share market is falling because of the China/U.S. situation, so that cash would be a buffer to compensate for any temporary drop in the value of the JTB shares that you'll be getting. The number of JTB shares you'll receive would still make you the majority shareholder. It's just an idea.'

Her reply suffered the briefest of delays. 'An unexpected offer, but … I'll think about it. Why the interest in whisky? You were never a connoisseur. And you didn't even finish the glass I gave you.'

'Perhaps … it's to remind me of you,' I said, falsely sweet in homage to her ability to be kind and duplicitous at the same time.

'Darling! I do believe you're starting to come out of your shell. How delightful. But really, why do you want it?'

I paused sufficiently to give the impression of internal debate. 'Perhaps it's to give me something to do. I'm too young to retire, and ….'

'Yes …?'

'… it will give me an excuse to visit Tasmania.'

'You were always fond of the Apple Isle, so maybe … we'll think about it. No need for hasty decisions, is there?'

'Absolutely. Just a suggestion. I'll leave it with you.' I tried to sound as though I was doing her a favour, not me, but wasn't sure how successful I'd been. Lucinda was a canny reader of human minds.

After finishing the call, I spent a few moments firming up the rationale behind my request. It boiled down to power and water. I needed an operation that could use my geothermal power. The distillery fitted that bill. And should I strike quality water, I could either pipe it to the distillery – good water apparently one of the secrets behind a good whisky – or, if distances were too great, I could set up a Springwater bottling plant on site. My cheap electricity would enhance the profit margin, assuming I could convince enough of the buying public to believe in the water's undoubted life-enhancing qualities. Either way, for the locals, my drill rigs would be seen as a blessing, not a threat.

The rest of the afternoon was spent seeking diversion in my small collection of books. Scanning the titles was a stroll through my mental evolution. The university years: textbooks on geology, chemistry and physics, then Lucinda and the making of serious money: books on marketing, business law, economics and globalised finance, with my favourite being *The Global Minotaur* by Varoufakis, closely followed by Ann Pettifor's brilliant, *The Production of Money,* all of which explained the mechanics of how the world works.

Post appendix came the questioning of conventional wisdom and the why of things. New viewpoints and sometimes solace was found in books such as *Fooled by Randomness* by Taleb, *The Consolations of Philosophy* by de Botton, and socio-political tomes by Chomsky and others. In Arizona, I was introduced to the biology behind our decision-making processes in *The Ethical Brain* by Michael Gazzangia and *The Science of Happiness* by Stefan Klein, and broader views of how the world came to be as proffered in works by Jared Diamond and Yuval Harari.

But environment reporter Jessica had invaded my mind so I ended up reacquainting myself with a reprint of Aussie biologist Tim Low's myth buster: *The New Nature,* a book on our role in the ecology of Australia specifically, and the planet in general. It was a gift from a university friend who had hoped to green my outlook on the world. It had been read and long forgotten until Jessica – a book she, and all eco-warriors and campaigners, needed to comprehend to put their laudable efforts into a more realistic form. They would then have a much greater chance of significantly changing the way we managed the planet.

It also reminded me that understanding our place in the Earth's ecology was not the same as knowing how to put that knowledge into practice. People need convincing and logic is not enough. Jessica was a journalist and hence part of the media circus that gives us our opinions. I wondered if she realised the full extent of her contribution to that machine and its real agenda. I wondered how much control she thought she had over her life and the opinions she was allowed to express in print. Had she started questioning the way it is? Perhaps the dinner date would reveal more.

I was at the restaurant just after six and convinced the waitress to move Jessica's reserved table to that of our first encounter. The girl obliged and I spent the time toying with a glass of water and cogitating. I didn't really have a plan, having no inkling of what Jessica's motivations were, and instead tried to turn my mind to my own motivations. But all I came up with was a foggy, conflicted mess.

It had ended up being a warm day, a prelude of the summer that would officially begin on the weekend, a change reflected by Jessica when she appeared in the doorway decked out in a summery dress that exposed marginally more of her athletic freckled legs than the skirt had. After a brief exchange with the waitress, she walked over. I stood and we silently made our assessments of the other.

I hoped I came up to scratch. My beard was looking less ratty and clothes spoke of *smart-casual* – a pale yellow linen shirt and tan pleated trousers. She looked delectable. No jacket or power shoulders this time; her outfit had a much softer, conciliatory look. Was I about to receive a charm offensive to shatter my defences?

She broke the silence. 'Is this table a coincidence, or did you exercise some influence here?'

'Guilty as charged.'

She elicited a non-committal exhalation, chose a seat and didn't protest when I seated her. Two can play the charm game.

The waitress interrupted with menus and a request for drinks, with water receiving a unanimous vote. Once the water arrived, we were left to interact, which began with the menus.

I decided to let her lead the conversation, having already chosen my selections while waiting. Hence I sat back and enjoyed the view of Jessica giving serious consideration of the nourishment on offer.

She must have felt my eyes upon her. 'Not eating? I'm paying.'

I couldn't hold back a smile. 'I've already decided … on the food at least!' My grin became mischievous.

It was her turn to push back in the chair, to return a furrowed brow and indecision. A straightening and then a deep breath followed. 'Before we get off on the wrong foot, let me explain the reasons for our little get-together.'

I waited.

'Higgins has done some digging and has decided you need … following up. Dressed it up as a chance to: "deepen my skills base". To try something other than environmental issues. "It would be good for my career".'

'I see,' was all I could add, preoccupied with trying to prevent an inexplicable tickle of disappointment breaking through to the surface. Why had I hoped for more?

She continued. 'I said I had holidays booked in a fortnight's time. He said fine, but in the meantime, I was to get to know you better. So here we are, getting to know each other.' It was her turn to issue a challenging smirk.

Which had me more confused than ever because I wasn't sure if it was meant for me, her boss, or both of us. In the end, I chose to suspend judgement and try to have a good time, hopefully without revealing too much of my plans. But I had questions I wanted answered.

Over the entrée I asked the first of them. 'Saw the news report on the attack and ….'

'Sorry about that but I was ambushed. It's tricky being a journalist even for a supposedly reputable paper. All sorts of constraints are placed upon you. One's ethics get bent, leaned on, and you just have to play the game to stay in it.'

'The Nuremberg defence.'

Her puzzled look confirmed history to be a subject absent from her education. It had been one of my favourites at school and ever since. '…"I was just obeying orders" … That's the excuse many Nazis used during the war crimes trials at

Nuremburg after the Second World War.'

Her initial puzzlement soon turned to indignation, a response that had me belatedly remembering my Buddhist training, which seemed a lifetime ago. I tried again, this time attempting to be more humble in my judgement. 'I am being insensitive and unreasonable. I apologise. Sadly, reality constrains us all and pragmatism is often the best survival response.'

My pomposity didn't sit well with either of us. For me, I was being hypocritical, as my whole business life had been driven by a ruthless pragmatism. Selling whatever I could get away with, without it being illegal or too complicated, with my only consideration being to collect the cash. An attitude I was fast becoming embarrassed to have held for so long.

The intermittent silences weren't resolved until the mains arrived. I had another go at a friendly conversation. 'Assuming you survive the next two weeks at work, what are you planning for your vacation? How long have you got?'

Lifting her gaze from her plate, she accepted my genuineness; her blue eyes then drifted before returning to mine to reconfirm my state of mind. Leaning back, her shoulders eased. 'I've got four weeks due but have only been allowed two.' Her disappointment showed. 'Perhaps your reminding me of the trip from Hawaii and your pick up line: "I love Sheffield" put Tasmania in the forefront of my mind.' We both grinned. 'So that's where I'll be. Visiting the folks and just taking it easy. I need the rest.'

She used the opportunity to quiz me on my plans. Her announcement of Tasmania was an unhelpful complication. 'I've plenty to keep me busy in re-establishing my input into my business.'

'By re-establishing, don't you mean selling down and abandoning?'

My look of dismay was answer enough.

'I did mention that Higgins has been doing some digging on you. So what are you really up to?'

How much did she know? Which way should I jump?

I had to decide fast whether I could brazen it out or should I trust her with possibly too much truth.

Chapter Ten

In the end, I decided to do a bit of both. I confessed to selling down my shareholding to give JTB's management team more control but then admitted to having no plans for the considerable liquidity so generated. Not sure if she swallowed my claimed nobility of action or the idea of my leaving a pile of cash to sit idle but she didn't argue the point. As to what I was going to do next, I used the attack upon me to say I would be doing a bit of travelling and keeping a low profile until the people behind the attacks were found and dealt with. We agreed to have another dinner on Friday night, an appointment I had no intention of keeping.

When I arrived home, I called up a fellow from my flight training days and cajoled him into arranging a light plane to take me to Devonport the next day – I had to pay three times the going rate but that was fine. Then I rang to cancel the ferry crossing.

Next morning, around five, I left, hopefully unseen, and marched to the all-night burger joint around the corner, weighed down by a backpack full of clothes and a scattering of books. There I ordered a taxi for the airfield, which even at that hour was an hour's drive away. Having arrived way too early, I spent the time warming a chair in their cold and dreary waiting room, anxiously staring out the window as the rising sun struggled to burn the mist off the runway. My pilot rocked up just after seven.

It was a long day and I was having trouble concentrating on the road by the time I drove the hired Land Cruiser up the main street of Sheffield. Either the place had changed considerably since my last visit, or my memory was playing tricks because, after a bit of confused driving around, I was forced to ask for directions to find the house I'd leased. It was exactly as it appeared on the website: a well-maintained, modest, two-bedroom, pale blue weatherboard place on the west side of town – the last in a No Through Road with paddocks and the dark forested hills as its nearest neighbours.

After dumping my pack in the main bedroom, I had a quick shower then drove back to the main street for a dinner of trout and plenty of veg. The Tasmanian me was no longer vegan.

The prospect of Jessica being over here in a couple of weeks meant I had to get things happening quickly. The next morning I was up before dawn and driving down the Cradle Mountain road with the wipers on intermittent and the heater going; I had an appointment with my driller friend, Harvey, at a property about nine kilometres past the village of Moina. As much as I didn't have my water boring company organised, Harvey and his crew and machinery would be doing the actual work. All I had to arrange was the magnetic signs to attach to their rigs and support vehicles and scatter a few billboards around to placate any curious locals.

The abandoned dairy farm I'd leased, with options to buy, took close scrutiny of the GPS to locate, as the farm's entrance gate looked like all the other rusty paddock gates that occasionally broke the monotony of wooden posts and fencing wire. That it lay shrouded by the trees and bushes lining the roadside also didn't help.

The second last of my growing collection of keys was the one that coaxed the heavy padlock over to my way of thinking. I left the gate open, decorated the trees either side and the gate itself, with loads of fluoro-pink flagging tape to make the task of finding it easier, then followed the well-defined gravel track, down one slight dip, over a ridge, then down towards the farmhouse.

The home paddock was on a treeless bench, its lush knee-deep grass encroaching on the neglected white fibro house and its collection of rusty, corrugated iron outbuildings. They were a sad looking lot, and I would be doing the world a favour if I had to bulldoze them to make way for a bottling plant.

The track carried on past the house to the machinery sheds – the house protected somewhat from the encroaching grass by a wide and relatively new path of crushed quartz. Parking next to the house, I grabbed my small daypack and scrunched around the enclosed verandah to the front door. The sound made by my hiking boots seemed a sacrilegious violation of the absolute silence that reigned over this misty patch of Tasmania. I added more noise as I clumped over the creaking floorboards to unlock the entrance door.

While fiddling with the lock, a long-neglected notion from Shakespeare crept into my consciousness: that life was all sound and fury, signifying nothing. When the door finally surrendered, I paused, stopped by the sudden realisation that all my current plans were powered by a desire to prove Shakespeare wrong. My life was going to have some significance. Mission defined, like an invading general, I stepped in and took possession of the house.

With few vandals in Tassie, the place was still intact, though dusty and decorated with cobwebs. The main room, a combined living/dining and kitchen, was empty, bar a rickety wooden table and three equally ancient chairs. I checked all the rooms, flushed the loo, which was grim to behold, and tried the taps in the bathroom. They protested but produced clean water, then I made sure all the lights were working. The old gas stove in the kitchen seemed operational though the gas was either turned off or the cylinders outside were empty. All in all, the place would do the job of office, lunch room for the crew, and if worse came to worse, one could camp out in either of the two small bedrooms.

I wasn't expecting Harvey to make an appearance until mid-afternoon. The regular mobile coverage didn't extend this far out so I had to use my newly acquired satellite phone to text him about the flagging tape at the entrance. After that, the rest of the morning was taken up with checking out the sheds and having a stroll around the paddocks to get a feel for the place and develop ideas about where best to place the drill rig.

A car coming down the track woke me from a post-lunch doze on the rear seats of the Land Cruiser – *car* being a gross understatement. Harvey's mud-splattered American four-wheel-drive crew cab dwarfed the Japanese Land Cruiser, itself an overblown way of getting around. He gave me a wave before clambering out, inducing a fleeting sense of disappointment – similar to that suffered by a hungry man when served his main course at a fancy restaurant, all plate and not much food.

The moment passed. Harvey hadn't changed much; he was still short, nuggetty, wearing the usual short shorts and stained T-shirt, though his straggly hair was greyer and his skin was showing more signs of too much time in the sun.

'How ya doin'? It's been a while. You've trimmed down.'

We shook hands, which I immediately regretted. His superhuman grip had me on the verge of passing out and I was thankful to get my hand back and have it more or less functioning.

'Yeah, making a few changes to the way I do things.' I tried to sound unperturbed.

'Hope you're still paying on time!' he said with a grin that spoke of confidence in my continued honesty.

'Nothing to worry about there. How soon can you start? Any news on the first shipment of my drill rods?'

Organising shipping the rods from the supplier in Texas, I'd left to Harvey as it would distance me from the operation, for a while at least. Long ago, as a bit fun, I had set up a number of shell companies to shuffle the money around when dabbling in a bit of currency speculation, which at the time had been hugely profitable. I was using those companies again to make it easier to disguise my plans and the usual tax minimisation benefits.

'In Devonport by the end of next week, all going well.'

Nodding my appreciation, we then walked and chatted as I showed him the layout and the spot for the test hole: in the corner of one of the paddocks where the drill rig would be screened on two sides by trees and on the others by a slight ridge.

Most of his crew were from Burnie or Devonport, both of which were too far for commuting so Harvey would be bringing in a few transportables to be their home away from home during their two weeks on and one week off roster. When he left, I had a promise of setting up during the next couple of days and drilling by the end of the week.

They would use standard rods initially until a downhole logger came up with the temperature gradients at the depths I was seeking, so for the next weeks and possibly months I had little to do. Harvey didn't need me to tell him his job.

That evening, fed and nursing a big mug of lemongrass and ginger tea, I stretched out on the lounge with *The New Nature* in my lap but hadn't yet turned a page. The deep silence that had swallowed the world had got me thinking.

Back to being a man of leisure, I again had the unresolved problem of filling my days and nights with meaningful activity. Not all of my significance in the scheme of things could be carried by the geothermal project; a man also has to cultivate a personal style he could be proud of.

We are harangued in the media and in books by self-help gurus that we can be the person we want to be; we can fulfil our dreams using positive thinking or by listening to our hearts. My experience in Arizona was very much in that vein, the monastery less so, but the end results so far remained unsatisfying.

I was back to the same problems that plagued my thoughts at the airport in Hawaii. Progress had been made in doing something of personal significance – the geothermal project – but, as then, I still wanted more: that elusive thing called happiness.

Glancing at the book, its tale not of happiness but of how the natural world adapts to our desecration of ecosystems, reignited the flicker of wisdom glimpsed in the temple – the animal and plant world do not seek happiness. They chase survival. They struggle and adapt, according to their capabilities, with the boldest and most flexible generally doing the best. Bold and flexible – pragmatic if you like – were the keys to their continuing existence, which in their unconscious way could be deemed to be an animal or plant version of happiness. That's what I had to emulate.

Happiness wasn't a definable goal, like a big house in a luxury suburb, a trophy wife, or the perfect career – it was a by-product of living and, most importantly, one's attitude to what happens. Happiness was going to arise as a consequence of my doing things, from living a creative and adaptive life that exercised as many of my known and unknown abilities as possible.

Most ordinary people choose careers, friends and lovers with some thought, but not overly much. They rarely actively develop their personalities in a specific direction. Who they become is left to life's random influences. I thought I could do better. I was wrong. The man I would become and any joy encountered was going to be left to chance, to the random workings of my mind and those of fate's fickle whims.

Taking a swig of tea, I placed the mug back on the coffee table up against the sofa, then picked up the book, flipped it open to where I'd left off. Filled with a greater respect for its contents, I began to read, knowing that, in the morning, I would be going to Launceston to exercise several of my whims!

Chapter Eleven

Hobart may be Tasmania's capital and a lovely city, with Mount Wellington in the west watching over it like a taciturn older brother, and entertained in the east by the sparkling waters of the drowned valley of the Derwent River. But plain Jane Launceston is the commercial heart of the island and that's where I needed to be. The house in Sheffield would remain a weekender, a place to stay when supervising the project once it was operational, which was months, if not years, away.

At first light I set off for Launceston, arriving before eight-thirty, with my first stop a real estate agent where, sight unseen, I bought a house on Old Bridge Road in Perth, a village twenty minutes south – an executive's residence, recently vacated and semi-furnished. It was far too big for me but was well maintained and, importantly, backed onto the river, allowing me to fish or kayak from my own backyard. The airport being ten minutes away also added to its appeal. Downtown Launceston would have made more sense, but Jessica's parents lived in the city so hiding in a nearby village would lessen the odds of any unexpected meetings with her or anyone else from my Melbourne existence.

After leaving the real estate people, with their promise of the keys being available before the end of the year, I headed to the Central Library. I was beginning to feel that my electronic communications were being hacked by my unknown antagonists, so the relative anonymity of the library's internet connections would make tracking me a little harder. Journalists are infamous for their phone hacking exploits and it was a journalist I wanted to investigate. Jessica was checking up on me; thus it felt only fair to learn a bit more about her and, hopefully, get a better appreciation of her possible motivations and values.

Unfortunately, I found she was blandly normal. She'd won a prize for English at high school, went on to an Arts degree in journalism, worked at various roles for a few media companies, et cetera, et cetera. Nothing more gleaned about her character than I'd already surmised and that was annoyingly incomplete. She had an older, married sister in Melbourne and parents here in Launceston, both professionals and close to retirement. They lived in a good suburb but didn't seem to be particularly wealthy.

On the way out, I tried one last research method: a pay phone in the lobby of the library building.

Jessica took a while to pick up.

'Yes.' And nothing more.

Office sounds were a noisy backdrop, which may have explained her terseness and reminded me that, unlike myself, she was working and hence had little time to waste. Now wasn't the time for digging and yet I had to say something. 'Won't be able to make the dinner tomorrow tonight.'

Snatches of her colleagues' phone conversations filled in the silence whilst she deliberated. A sigh followed, then, 'Pity. I've just picked up some interesting information. Though it's probably the work of a fevered mind overheated from reading too many thrillers. It may have been indirectly relevant to you, but ....'

I hadn't realised how quickly the phone ate money, and my coins were running out. 'No matter how unlikely, anything would be appreciated. Look, I'm not in Melbourne and often out of mobile coverage so if you could send it via email.' I gave her the details just before the machine cut me off.

It wasn't much but I couldn't help thinking that a touch of normality had entered her voice. We were talking as equals, two humans with a shared interest. Perhaps a truce had been declared. That thought, right or wrong, bolstered my mood no end. Perhaps I was reading more into it and being foolish but I enjoyed the experience nonetheless.

On the way to the library, I'd passed an outdoors store. This time I walked in and finished up buying a kayak, wetsuit and a stack of camping gear and hiking clothes, all of which I left until I could arrange to pick them up. Tasmania is a beautiful country with plenty of rivers and I had a mind to explore both. The shop was affiliated with the local kayaking and canoe club, which advertised an excursion happening on the weekend – non-members welcome. I gave the sales guy my details and he promised to tell Karlene, the organiser, and one of their staff members. She would contact me to confirm the arrangements when she arrived for the afternoon shift.

Feeling pleased with myself and hungry, I spotted an upmarket Asian restaurant hoping for a late lunch and was lucky enough to get a seat down the back towards the kitchen and the toilets. I had made a start on my entrée when in walked Lachlan with two Asian businessmen. The headwaiter guided them to a reserved table with a view of the street. One of the Asians gave me a sideways glance before taking up his seat. After the waiter had fussed over them and left with their orders, the trio settled into quiet conversation. My main course arrived, which had me torn between studying my meal and following the waiter's return to the kitchen. In doing so, I picked up the flicker of eyes coming my way from Lachlan's table, quickly diverted once they realised they'd been caught out. Did Lachlan recognise me? And what of the other two? Who were they? Did they know me? I certainly didn't recognise them. And was Lachlan here on JTB business or for other reasons?

Dismissing further speculation on Lachlan and his guest's motives, I worked mechanically through my meal while considering the wisdom of exiting by a rear door. I wasn't keen on being confronted by any of the three. Shortly after, in the process of carefully manoeuvring overloaded chopsticks towards my mouth, the damn mobile sprang to life, over-enthusiastic and overly loud. The chopsticks ended up in the stir-fry with the phone very nearly joining them.

Lucinda! The last person I had in mind.

'You sound a bit surprised. Not expecting me. You aren't entertaining a lady, I hope?'

'No, dining alone. Had the phone on loud. To what do I owe the honour?'

'A little issue regarding our arrangements. Lachlan is unhappy about giving up *Tarkine Mist*. Insists it's an integral part of the business. He was almost upset about it.'

'A recent addition is now essential? A curious development.' I tried not to sound too eager to keep to our plan.

'Yes, most curious.'

Did she know where he was?

'Perhaps I should have a chat with him direct; face to face?'

'Not in town at the moment. Flew out early this morning in a rather unhappy mood and didn't say when he'd be back. So, a little problem to resolve, though I'm not sure if I can bring him around to giving up the distillery. Perhaps …?'

I kept my silence, hoping she would keep the interchange going and reveal more.

'You still there? How important is this to you?' My continuing silence saw a more suspicious tone enter her voice. 'Is there something else going on that you should be telling me about, husband to wife?'

The last three words hinted at anxiety, but not for me. I paused a moment longer then detoured. 'Speaking of marital arrangements, are you and Lachlan …?'

'Not that it's any of your business, but we have been seeing a lot of each other since you left, and he has intimated that our arrangements would be formalised in due course.'

'Children?'

She had never expressed any desire for kids whilst my wife but she was pushing thirty-three, a dangerous age for any woman, particularly so if a Melbourne socialite.

A rapid intake of breath as if she'd been jabbed in the ribs produced a rather truculent response. 'You'll find out soon enough. Yes … children are on the horizon.'

Maybe the waistline was a baby bump? 'Like, in less than nine months?'

Perhaps being on the phone made confession easier. She suddenly abandoned her inscrutability and, like Jessica, we began conversing as equals, not combatants. Haltingly, she revealed the whole saga. She was pregnant – had only just had it confirmed and hadn't yet told Lachlan about it. Lachlan she'd known and been involved with since senior high school, though he was a few years ahead of her. They were both from the Victorian squattocracy, old money, which inculcates a sense of entitlement to a particular lifestyle and social standing. Unfortunately, after leaving school Lachlan's finances were constrained for quite a few years, so, being a rising star and the better bet, she chose me – yet throughout our time together, she had never stopped seeing him.

One reads of these things in novels or gossip columns but, finding out that one has been on the receiving end, over the phone, in a crowded restaurant near the loos, turned her life and mine into a tawdry tale belonging to strangers, one I found impossible to digest in one sitting. Once her storytelling had run its course, my only response was numbed speechlessness.

But she needed more. 'Don't be too harsh on me. I'm worried about Lachlan. He's up to something. He's in something over his head. And …' Her voice faltered.

She wants forgiveness and pity! Why should I be so magnanimous? Her and Lachlan's fate had nothing to do with me. What did she expect of me? Staring unfocussed down the corridor that led out the back, phone to my ear, I sat like a catatonic.

'For God's sake, say something!' she yelled.

I had to jerk the phone away. Her change in mood shocked me back to life and landed me in memories of a discussion in the monastery on how fear and anger intertwine. The connection also reminded me of the values I vowed there to develop: understanding and compassion.

She was human, fallible and thus willing to lie and deceive to gain her idea of happiness. What she had done was her way of being pragmatic! – an attitude I had long considered a virtue until on the receiving end. A sarcastic smirk pained me, induced by another Buddhist truism: that everyone we meet is a Buddha incarnated to teach us a lesson, which, if unlearned, is repeated throughout life until we learn it or die. What wisdom was Lucinda forcing upon me? Perhaps a little compassion and humility.

'No need to shout. I hear your concern.' For him, not me. 'Where is he at the moment?' I still didn't know if she knew.

'That's the thing. He didn't say. He could be on the moon for all I know. But I'm sure a crisis is coming and I have no way of intervening.'

'If it's any consolation, I can see him from where I'm sitting.'

That slowed her for a nanosecond before exploding. 'You bastard! Why didn't you say so? You get a kick from my ….'

I cut her off. 'Perhaps yes. I'm as human as you are – sometimes. I have feelings too – for instance, a strong dislike to being used. So dump the indignation. Just listen.' So much for practising compassion!

For the next few minutes, I briefed her on my location and

informed her of my reasons. I told her I would be in Tassie for a while, sightseeing and checking out the distillery, wanting to know more about what I was taking on. I intimated that maybe Lachlan was here also in connection with the distillery and suggested the two Chinese were hotel owners that Lachlan was trying to woo into stocking *Tarkine Mist.*

She calmed down, even apologised – a first in all our interactions– and seemed relieved to have some explanation to cling to. I promised to let her know if I found out anything concerning Lachlan's plans. We finished on friendly terms.

Lucinda was taken in by my speculations but I wasn't. I had a niggling feeling Lachlan was up to no good. That one of the Chinese gents seemed to recognise me bothered me in an ominous way, perhaps fuelled by a growing paranoia induced by the continuing blank surrounding my unknown enemies. The thought gave me an inkling of what it felt like to be a spy in enemy territory.

Whatever Lachlan and his companions were up to, I needed some air. I called the waiter over, paid cash with a generous tip, and, when those at the table weren't looking, took my chances to find that rear exit. It turned out to be a plain metal door marked FIRE EXIT, but the numerous dents spoke of clumsy delivery men and trolleys. It wasn't locked or alarmed, and stepping outside, I was relieved to see grey skies and feel the cool dampness of a fine drizzle that had replaced the intermittent sunshine of the morning.

A few metres to my left was a white van with rear doors open, nearby, a stack of crates overflowing with vegetables. The uniformed driver was in a closeted discussion with two Chinese kitchen hands. A small white cardboard box was exchanged with an air of conspiracy. They were about to go their separate ways when the closing mechanism of the fire door banged it shut, making them aware of my presence.

Like a simpleton, I smiled, nodded then turned right and began a nonchalant stroll down the alleyway, apparently fascinated by the random clusters of wheelie bins, locked gates and deserted loading bays.

I'd never been involved in the drug scene at university, or since, but it was obvious that the war on drugs was far from won. In fact, in recent years, it had suffered many defeats, despite the publicity that major drug busts regularly got in the news media.

If people were fool enough to get involved in illicit drugs or abused prescription medications, it was their business and had nothing to do with me. But I was involved now. I was certain I'd just witnessed a drug deal going down. A tingling uneasiness developed between my shoulder blades.

The street at the end was barely visible in the drizzle and was seemingly as unreachable as a mirage in the desert. My hopes of escaping from the brick, concrete and glass canyon I found myself trapped in were fading fast. The only sounds of life were the contrived regularity of my footfalls and the diffused murmur of distant traffic.

A conscious effort was required to swallow. I hoped by keeping my breathing and walking at a brisk, even pace, I would make rapid progress without advertising my rising panic. I even tried squinting hard in a pointless bid to bring the intersection at the end closer. But insufficient headway had been made when my heart skipped a beat at the sound of an engine being mercilessly brought to life. Screwing my head around, I saw the white van do a rapid reverse, then, with a screech of tyres, it started towards me, accelerating hard.

There was nowhere to run. A long stretch of high brick walls and equally insurmountable rusty corrugated iron fences hemmed me in.

It was just me and a maniacal van driver.

Chapter Twelve

Perhaps Tim Low's conclusions about nature's winners being bold and resourceful inspired my decision to turn and face my enemy. To go down fighting.

On my side of the lane, next to the gate I'd just passed, were three overflowing wheelie bins, which could be used as a buffer to deaden the impact. That was my hope as I raced back towards them.

The driver saw my ploy and must have floored the accelerator because the van lurched. The tyres again squealed in protest as it rocketed forward, becoming a monstrous white, metal and glass hammer. He crossed over to my side of the road, intentions now beyond doubt.

I slammed into the first of the bins, catapulting it into the next until all three were sprawled over the narrow shoulder and onto the roadway, spewing out a motley assortment of plastic bags, food scraps mostly, my assessment in the split-second I had to register the fact.

The van hit the first of them and would have added me to its score had I not performed the perfect impersonation of a soccer goalie leaping to deflect a ball in a World Cup Final. Clearing the bumper by millimetres and milliseconds, I dived off to my right, hit the bitumen hard, rolled a few metres and was instantly on my feet, to the soundtrack of the van bulldozing the bins. By the time it had stopped, thirty or so metres down from the gate, I was hobbling, then sprinting back to the Golden Swan and the nearest open door I knew of. The driver jammed it into reverse with such savagery the painful clang momentarily shifted attention from my troubles to that of the poor gearbox that must have been on the verge of exploding out from under the van.

A quick turn of the head revealed the driver having trouble getting traction on the plastic bags and scraps, boosting my chances considerably and adding vigour to my pounding feet. Things improved again on seeing one of the kitchen hands wander outside to pick up the last of the crates. Muscling past him none too gently, I was momentarily aware of him falling unceremoniously on top of the crate. Then I was jogging past bewildered kitchen staff before almost taking out a waiter as I barged out into the dining area. The swing doors hit the walls on either side with a clap of thunder, adding an operatic touch to my unorthodox entrance.

Slowing, I weaved my way between the tables, unconcerned by my dishevelled and grubbied jacket and trousers. Then, impelled by a sudden recklessness, I stopped beside Lachlan's table.

'Hello, Lachlan. Long time, no see. We should get together some time. Chat about the old days, and days to come, perhaps.' I raised a finger to his incipient response. 'No need to say anything now. I'm a bit pushed for time. Goodbye, gentlemen.' I gave the two Chinese an unfriendly smirk, then turned and disappeared through the front door.

Was it a foolish case of guilt by association? But the furtive looks of Lachlan and Co. and another attempt on my life were hard to disconnect. Maybe he was in money trouble and his Chinese buddies were part of some risky scheme to solve his financial woes. If so, he was probably setting himself up for strife further down the track. All mad speculation on my part made more embarrassing once outside in the drizzle surrounded by the normality of shoppers, workers and traffic. Perhaps my parting remarks had been a case of temporary insanity.

But what's done is done. With a shake of the head, I walked

mindfully back to my rented suite at a downtown apartment hotel, constantly on the lookout for vans and other potential attackers. As an extra precaution, I went a circuitous route and entered via the garage entrance. Never had a rented apartment felt so welcoming.

After a long shower, yoga in my underpants, and then dressed in clean clothes and nursing a cup of tea, my equilibrium was eventually restored. Should I report the incident and to whom? Unless there were witnesses willing to back me, it would all seem rather far-fetched. Silence appeared the best solution for the present.

The room service dinner was spent checking emails, which added the disappointment of silence from Jessica. She'd either forgotten, decided the information not worthy, or was too busy. Plugging the phone into the charger, I lay on the sofa, then tried fifteen minutes of channel surfing before abandoning the remote in favour of *The New Nature*.

After a surprisingly good night's sleep, I handed my dirty clothes to Reception and afterwards had an unhurried breakfast in a quiet corner of the dining room. Ravi had texted to say the drilling company had been set up, saddled with my joke of a trading name: *Wonderland Water Boring* and that he would email me the documentation on Monday. Just in case he needed it, I gave him my addresses in Launceston and Sheffield. Soon to be in possession of a registered trading name, I needed a printer and, after a few false starts, I found one ready to accept my generous bonus for doing a rush job of printing up signs of varying sizes emblazoned with my new trademark. He promised all would be ready to be picked up by mid-morning on Monday.

I was on a roll, so phoned the distillery.

'*Tarkine Mist*, premium whiskies, how may I help?'

The receptionist, female, sounded energised and young, early twenties probably, and did an excellent job of being welcoming.

A good thing for any business as first impressions count. She certainly put me in a positive frame of mind. It was a good start.

'Hi, my name is Julius Banks. I'm a shareholder and wish to see your Operations Manager later today if possible.'

Not too late I hoped, as the plant was at Gowrie Park, a town halfway between Sheffield and Moina and well over an hour's drive from Launceston.

A brief pause ensued while my call was transferred, then: 'Ben McBain, General Manager. Angus Weyland, our Operations Manager, is in Scotland sizing up some new technology. Mr Banks, this is an unexpected pleasure. Mr Lucas was in on Wednesday, and ....'

'Yes, yes. I saw him in Launceston lunchtime yesterday. As you know, I've recently returned to Australia and am reacquainting myself with developments in JTB's expanded business model. I'd very much like to pop over for a visit.'

'Err – Fridays are pretty hectic. It's when much of our product is despatched but, yes, come over, anytime.'

I didn't blame him for being reticent; I probably would have felt the same way if some nosey boss was foisted onto me when busy and probably understaffed, but I had to get a feel for the legitimacy of the business I was potentially going to be more involved with. We agreed to meet just before lunch.

The dining room supplied printed copies of *The Age* and *The Financial Review*, which I skimmed through, managing to spill tea on both in the process. Usually, it's an art to glean the useful bits from the gossip and speculation, but not today. The headlines blared the big issues: namely, another Reserve Bank rate rise to support our rapidly sliding dollar and the threat of a global recession brought on by the Chinese government's unprecedented ratchetting up of their interest rates. Money markets were dumping Dollars and Euros and buying the Yuan, the Chinese currency. The Americans, Europeans and their satellite economies were also trying to stem the consequential devaluation of their currencies by similar interest rate increases. They were like gamblers determined to outbid their rivals in the final hand of a poker game.

Having failed in the last currency war, it seemed the Chinese were having another go at displacing the US as the *Global Minotaur*. Their economy was now equal to that of the US, and they had actively cultivated economic interests in all the emerging markets, significantly increasing their global economic and political clout.

The Asian superpower was like a rival bull sea elephant challenging the incumbent *beachmaster*, the US, for possession of the beach and its harem – control of the world's default trading currency, currently the US Dollar. The Chinese were obviously betting that their economy, and their grip upon their more compliant populace, would allow them to recover faster from the worldwide recession they were inducing. If so, they could then gain control over the global financial system when stability had been restored.

This development had been speculated upon for so long that it had lost its power to hold one's attention. The financial world, myself included, had become like the citizens of Pompeii, grown used to a grumbling Mount Vesuvius but now faced a full-scale eruption. I had to make sure I didn't get buried in the fallout.

The next half hour was spent in frenzied double-checking my various money market accounts and stockholdings to reach the tentative conclusion that I would be bruised but in relatively good shape to profit from either the status quo remaining or dealing with a new global financial emperor. Perhaps Lachlan was not so well placed to weather the storm. I wondered how he was coping with the news.

Racing through my finances had set loose a couple of thoughts. It reminded me of a slab of shares in a mining company working out of Savage River, less than half a day's drive from Sheffield. They would suffer in the coming recession from reduced demand and squeezed profit margins. It could possibly send them bust, which opened up the possibility of later buying the operation for a pittance. If they survived, they'd be more amenable to a cheap alternative energy provider, me, to cut their milling and processing costs. Savage River had suddenly become another destination to check out.

The other brain itch was the upsurge in drug abuse and associated crime in developed nations reported all too regularly in the media and made real to me by the Golden Swan incident. My mind was knitting fanciful new connotations into that story, so outlandish that I hardly dared dwell upon them, let alone express them, even to myself, for fear of becoming another paranoid conspiracy theorist. Shunting nonsensical ideas to one side, I chose more useful activities.

Getting up, I signed for my meal then drove to the outdoors store. After a few enquiries about the kayaking club with the fellow who sold me all my gear, he introduced me to Karlene, now working *earlies*. After a few questions to assess my abilities, she agreed to add my kayak to the rental ones she'd be taking up to the starting point: the Visitors Centre at the entrance to Cradle Mountain National Park. I promised to meet them there on Sunday at 7:30 sharp for the paddle down Ripley's River, with the finish and pickup destination being the ramp at Lake Cethana. She said we'd have a good mix of white water and smooth. Happy with the arrangements, I grabbed the rucksack I'd left the previous day, heavy now with the rest of my purchases, and said my goodbyes.

I went the long way back, via the car accessories shop, where I picked up some tie-downs and got the gents there to fit a roof rack in preparation for the kayak that I would eventually be carrying. Later, back at the apartment, having dumped my pack in a corner of my bedroom, I was checking the time on the phone when a text from Jessica pinged into existence: WHERE ARE YOU? WE NEED TO TALK.

Every time I managed to temporarily forget of her existence, she seemed to reappear in some way, a reminder that unfinished business remains unfinished until dealt with. Perhaps another phone conversation would decide things.

Again she was slow to pick up and, as before, had a cacophony of printers, ringing phones and other people's conversations playing in the background. 'We need to talk, and where the hell are you? Just give me a few seconds to find somewhere quiet.'

I had to wait more than seconds as my ears followed her passing through the office. Then came the sound of hollow footsteps, probably up a fire escape stairwell, a clanging door, until subdued traffic sounds became the dominant aural accompaniment. My guess was she was in a rooftop courtyard.

'You still with me?'

'Yeah.'

'Aberdare wants to talk to you. He called me, fishing for more info about you. It seems everyone wants me to get to know you better. So what are you actually up to? You don't seem to be in Melbourne. Where are you?'

'Is this the news you hinted at earlier? I haven't received any emails.'

There was a pause at the other end – not sure if she was still regaining her breath from climbing the stairs or was putting a lid on her frustrations.

'Look, I may be a journalist and not your idea of a desirable person to confide in, but … I've been doing my job … went all the way back to the Mount Gambier drama. This time I read all your environmental impact statements, your geological and hydrological expert opinions, checked up on similar projects overseas and ....'

'And?'

'And maybe we all got it wrong. Your scheme wasn't like the rest. You had tailored it to the specifics of the site, no fracking was needed, no chance of contaminating groundwater and ....'

'Again ... and ...?' I couldn't keep all the bitterness from my voice. '... and the geothermal project would have been more than okay. In fact, it would have provided the state with a much needed cost-effective, sustainable and reliable base load capacity. But that's all history now. So what's today's hot news?' My limited supply of understanding and forgiveness had vanished at the painful reminder of past injustice and media foolishness.

'No need to get narky. We all make mistakes ... deal with things the way we see them at the time. Look, I'm just trying to say sorry, that's all. Is that such a bad thing?'

She was right, of course. 'Sorry to bite. Perhaps unknown people trying to kill me is not showing off my better side. Had another near-death incident yesterday lunchtime.'

'What happened? Does Aberdare know?'

I stood at the window for a while, looking down at the traffic before answering. 'I'm not so happy about long conversations over the phone. Developing a certain amount of paranoia because no matter where I am, trouble seems to be waiting for me, so perhaps we should be chatting face to face. Assuming you can treat me as a good guy, not a bad guy or some sucker to be made into mincemeat for the entertainment of the uncritical reading and viewing public.'

'Can't make promises. I don't know you well enough, but I'm willing to place you in the good guy box if you can do the same for me. Okay?'

I agreed to the deal, also reserving my final opinion, then told her I was in Launceston.

'So which one of us is going to hop on a plane and when?'

'You are,' I said. 'And probably this evening. I'm paying. Pack an overnight bag and be prepared to get to Moorabbin Airport at very short notice. As soon as I have the details, I'll call.'

Hanging up, I phoned my connections and after much cajoling, arranged a private flight to leave Melbourne mid-afternoon, arriving in Launceston around five-thirty. With the transport organised, I punched in her number. She was faster picking up this time.

Still at work, she started moving to quieter areas as soon as I started speaking. I explained the details and then reassured her that I was paying for the flights and all other expenses.

'Not giving me much time to get organised. And where am I staying when I get there?'

It was a question I hadn't yet considered but, put on the spot, I chose to be bold. 'You could stay with me at my rented two-bedroom apartment? It's in the CBD. Or, you could stay with your folks.'

'You've been checking up on me.' She sounded amused, not offended, which gave cause for optimism. After a pause to weigh up the situation, she also decided to be bold, accepting my offer on the proviso of separate beds. I ended the call with the promise of picking her up at the airport but gave her my downtown address just in case.

My morning was rapidly diminishing and I'd a drive ahead of me to get to my appointment with Ben McBain. I decided to leave Aberdare for another day – today, I had to find out about the distillery.

Addictive drugs are the perfect product for repeat customers, be it caffeine, nicotine, opioids or amphetamines. And while whisky is one of the legal ones, it's hardly an ethical way of making money. Like the rest, it involves preying upon our weakness for social approval and or desire for relief from wearisome reality.

The other thing about a legitimate drug operation is that it could make it easier to conceal an illegal one. My paranoia was making me wonder if Lachlan's objection to passing *Tarkine Mist* over to me was due to some such illegal operation.

In a few hours, I hoped to clear up my suspicions one way or another.

Chapter Thirteen

Guided by the phone's female voice, I headed south on the B41 to acquaint myself with the entrance to the airport – just a drive-by – then I continued onto Perth to view my future residence. I didn't even get out of the car before telling the phone to take a southerly route to Gowrie Park via Bracknell and Golden Valley. Main highways then took me to Deloraine and a few k's north before returning to backroads to enter Gowrie Park from the Sheffield road.

Large signs directed me to the distillery, which was hidden from the road by a fence lined with huge Lombardy Poplars, old but still vigorous if their vibrant spring foliage was an indication of health. A smooth bitumen driveway curved towards a cluster of buildings with views of the river. Like my rented farm in Moina, here too, novel activities had replaced agriculture, though a few cows had been retained to keep the grass down and add that bucolic ambience loved by tourists. Unlike my dilapidated fibro farmhouse, here the house was a grand, brick and stone homestead, beautifully restored with verandahs on all sides. Signs clearly directed visitors away from the no-go production areas towards the café, the tasting room, and Administration. Visitors parking was opposite the main entrance to the homestead in the dense shade of a row of mature oaks in a similar state of rude health as the poplars.

The old stables and barn, also constructed with brick edges and stone infill, had been taken over by the distillery, creating an incongruous architecture which to my fresh eyes looked as if the outbuildings, with their protruding stainless steel tanks and turrets, had been victim to an alien fungal infection resulting in weird, parasitic, metallic growths breaking out through the corrugated iron roofs.

Parking next to another rented car, I walked in through the main door, happy with my timing: a quarter to eleven. Time for morning tea. To my left was Counter Sales, to my right, Admin. The girl at the desk was as pleasant on the eye as she had been on the ear. A few seconds later, McBain appeared, big, greying, jovial and with a hand outstretched. Introductions were made and we headed to his office, a large room overlooking the brick-paved courtyard housing the distillery. There he directed me to a couple of armchairs angled to give a view past the outbuildings, down across the paddocks to the trees hiding the river.

'Care for a coffee and a bun? Tea, or something stronger?'

'Tea and something gluten-free if available.'

He buzzed someone and placed our order.

'We've got a café attached that does a nice lunch and a decent cappuccino and cake, which should revive you from the drive. Which way did you go?'

'Went the scenic way, Perth, Bracknell, Deloraine, then through Weegena. Passed lots of poppy fields. Amelioration Australia seemed to have expanded considerably since my last visit, which admittedly was quite a few years back.'

'They are in an expanding industry, worldwide. The populations of developed nations are aging and hence demanding more and more painkillers.'

'One could be unkind and suggest we are in a similar industry. *Tarkine Mist* could be considered a painkiller of sorts.' My attempt at humour failed miserably. In fact, he flinched at the suggestion that his precious whisky was anything other than the drink served in heaven.

'Sorry to appear insulting. Sometimes I find it instructive to look on situations from all angles. You seem to be doing a great job here, built up the business, have maintained both profits and the quality, always a delicate balancing act. Though quality-wise I'm no expert; in fact, I've only had the pleasure of one glass. Found it impressively full-flavoured and beautifully smooth.'

He perked up immediately, got up and went to a glass-fronted cupboard to retrieve a bottle of *Tarkine Mist* and two tumblers. Back at his seat, he placed the glasses on the coffee table and started pouring out the drinks.

'Not too much for me, not much of a drinker, and I've got to drive back.'

He seemed a little disappointed but we toasted the operation and I put up a show of appreciating his creation. The hot drinks and cakes arrived and I won a few extra points by pouring my remaining whisky into my tea and making a display of the beneficial effects of the mixture.

Donning hard hats and white dust coats, he took me on a tour of the processing plant, from loading docks through to the fermentation tanks, then the distilling towers and finally to the bulk holding tanks and a bottling line.

Silently watching the unending army of bottles being dosed with liquid courage before being palletised and trolleyed out to the storeroom, I tried bending talk back to the opium crops I'd passed on the way.

'Can't help but be concerned about all those fields of opium poppies protected only by wire fences and a few cameras. Gets you to thinking how do they keep from losing some to the illicit drug trade? I guess you here have pretty good systems in place to keep track of your output. How do you prevent criminally-minded folk from siphoning off a few pallets to flog on the black market?'

'Can't happen. Barcodes, accurate weighing of pallets, SIM cards and a GPS transponder on each one. We know exactly where they are at any moment.'

'What about the bulk deliveries. This line surely isn't enough to service our worldwide demand. I checked the figures.'

'You're right. But a similar system does the containers sent to our bottling plants in Thailand and Spain.'

'Well, it's reassuring to know you have the security under control.'

We were now on our way back to his office.

'Security and accuracy are a big thing with us. In fact, we poached our Product and Transport manager from Amelioration Australia for his expertise in that area. Len Xiang is a top fellow and knows more about security than you can poke a stick at. So you can rest assured there'll be no product leakages sapping your profits.'

We ended up in the Sales area, which had been taken over by a busload of tourists, all silver-haired and stiff-jointed. But what they lacked in agility, they made up for in chatter. It was now too noisy for further conversation so we adjourned to his office. I couldn't find out much more being escorted around so soon made my excuses and, with a handshake, walked back to the Land Cruiser burdened with a gift box of the gold label range.

I drove north to Sheffield, had lunch at the café that was becoming a favourite, then took the main road back to Launceston for a few hours of chilling out in the apartment, checking texts and emails.

Just as well I got to the airport early because a tailwind had them arriving early. With a nod to the pilot, I bundled Jessica into the car.

'Hope you've eaten because we've a drive ahead of us.'

'Not really. I came straight from work.'

I could only grunt in reply, being too busy getting onto the main road and estimating times and distances. The semis carrying the bulk whisky would leave Gowrie Park at 7:30, according to McBain, so if I didn't delay too much, I should be able to catch them leaving and follow them all the way to Devonport, where they'd drive onto the overnight ferry to Melbourne. Jessica's patience soon wore thin.

'Where are we going? You into kidnapping now?'

After making the turn onto the B52 leaving Perth, I told her about *Tarkine Mist* and tried to suggest that behind my decision to tail the trucks was my duty as a business owner to fully understand the operational side of the distillery.

'You're trying to tell me we are driving all the way over there just to follow a truck out of a burning desire to see … what exactly?'

We were on Highway One heading towards Deloraine before I was game to voice my outlandish real reasons, but they seemed the only thing that would quell her growing annoyance.

'There's a roadhouse this side of Deloraine that hopefully serves edible food. We'll pull in and grab a bite – don't want you fainting from malnutrition.' I tried making light of her human needs and also to further delay my explanation. Her poisonous stare forced me back to rationalising our detour. 'The distillery in Gowrie Park is doing well, sales-wise. Has a global market. I checked the place over with the GM today but ….'

How does one confess to being paranoid?

'Go on,' was her unhelpful reply.

With a deep sigh, I tried to cobble together a train of logic. 'Look … yesterday lunchtime, I barely escaped death from witnessing what I'm certain was drugs being delivered to the back of the Golden Swan in Launceston. Bikie gangs are renowned for their links to illegal drugs, and the attempt on my life in Thailand was, in unspecified ways, linked to the drug trade. And all those fields of opium poppies here Tasmania, well … it's making me suspicious of everything. To put it bluntly, I fear that the *Tarkine Mist* operation is in some way hooked up to the drug trade. And Lachlan Lucas is too for that matter.'

It was her turn to cause an uncomfortable silence, which had me pondering the reasons. Did she think me mad, or was she giving some credence to my line of thinking? There was a merge up ahead so I had to concentrate on the driving.

She exhaled loudly, looked out the side window and spoke to no one in particular. 'You may not be entirely unhinged.' Turning towards me, she wore a meditative frown, as if she'd stumbled upon an unexpected thought.

'That email I never sent was all about a conspiracy theory doing the rounds, which puts the blame on the upsurge in illegal drug use, and the associated crime and social unrest, as not a simple case of drug cartels trying to improve their profits. The theory is that their increasingly successful activities, in selling and avoiding prosecution, are due to their being backed by the resources of the Chinese intelligence services. The motivation of the Chinese is apparently their desire to ... weaken the west.'

A not so ridiculous thought to my mind and one that raised a smile at the irony of the situation.

'What's so amusing?'

'Nothing really. Just nice to know I'm not alone in succumbing to conspiracy theories, though I'd not thought of that one – reversing the Opium Wars of the nineteenth century.'

'The what?' Again her ignorance of history was on display.

'In the first half of the nineteenth century, the British India Company, and other well-connected members of the British business elite, were making the most of the subjugation of the subcontinent, and one of their most lucrative earners was the drug trade, especially the exporting of opium to China. The Chinese in response to the social damage being done eventually banned the sale of opium and attempted to enforce those bans. It impacted British profits so those concerned lobbied their government to respond. England declared war on China and fought a one-sided conflict between 1840 and 1842, I think, with the result being China ceding Hong Kong to the British and lifting their ban on opium imports. Not a piece of history spoken of much in the Anglo-Saxon world, or the business world for that matter.'

'Are you saying these nutters may be right?'

'Who knows? But if you've checked the headlines, it's pretty obvious that China is flexing its economic and financial muscles. They seem to be deliberately inducing a global recession with their uncalled for interest rate rises, so perhaps they, or some factions in their government, haven't forgotten their history and are somehow encouraging drug abuse in their opponent's societies. Not only to redress a historic humiliation but also to weaken the ability of the US to respond effectively to the selloff of the greenback by currency speculators. The US, being the inheritors of the British Empire's role as global superpower and holder of the world's trading currency. A two-pronged attack. It makes sense to me.'

We travelled in silence for a while. The late afternoon sun was working its magic on the passing countryside, airbrushing amber highlights to the swaying tips of luxuriant pastures and, when backlit, its golden x-rays turned the foliage of trees into dark blades riven with glowing ribs and edges. Our silent progress had my attention split between glorying in the wonders of nature, dealing with the moderate traffic, and wondering about the wisdom of including Jessica in my mad schemes.

After the brief stop for chips and takeaway coffee and tea, we travelled for quite a few kilometres, occupied with eating and drinking, a tricky task for me. It also kept her amused and quiet. Perhaps she was trying to incorporate my historical and economic theorising into her worldview. Had a moment when she extracted the empty chip box from my lap, only to combine it with hers and the empty cups to place the lot neatly in the footwell on her side. Having restored order, she restarted the conversation.

'I still don't know how you fit into this big picture you're painting?'

We had turned off onto the narrower and more winding Weegena Road, and the light was fading so I had to be more vigilant. On a straighter section, I said, 'The short answer is I've no real idea but, being the majority owner of JTB, a company with customers worldwide, may be the link. How I don't know. Lachlan Lucas seems involved and possibly Lucinda, my soon to be ex-wife.'

'And tonight's escapade?'

'A waste of time probably but you never know. Sorry to involve you in my ….'

'No more being apologetic. In the news business, we have to run down all manner of blind alleys and waste lots of energy gathering not much. It's a pleasant drive. Just try and stay on the road!'

A sharper than expected bend had the top-heavy four-wheel-drive lurching threateningly before I eased up, somewhat embarrassed. Like most men, I've always considered myself a good driver and still had a spotless driving record as dubious proof. It was Jessica's fault, of course. The damn woman was making me confess things I'd rather not. She was getting under my skin again and distracting me by simply breathing the same air as me. I opened the windows a touch. She didn't object.

At seven-eighteen, we cruised past the distillery and I had to focus on finding a suitable place to stop, one that offered a good view of the entrance. Turning into the first street on the right, I did a five-point turn and then parked on the verge of the last house in town, hoping the residents didn't object.

We didn't have to wait long. The first of two flatbed semis emerged, each loaded with forty-foot containers, consisting of steel frameworks enclosing huge stainless steel tanks. The white prime movers were flying the *Tridee Transport* badge, a nationwide outfit and a common sight even here in Tasmania.

Keeping my distance, I delayed putting on my lights as long as possible until a forested section forced my hand. At Sheffield, they would either turn left or right, with my money on the left, as that road would have less traffic. I didn't expect them to stop as it was a straightforward run but the end truck unexpectantly turned off for the short detour via the hamlet of Lewington. An unusual move that had me following him, not the leading truck.

Increasing my distance, I was confident I wouldn't lose him as there were no turnoffs, but got a shock when I did so on the other side of town. Despite speeding up, I still couldn't catch sight of him. Just shy of the T junction back onto the B14, I slid to a stop on the shoulder.

'What's happening? Truck's got away from you?'

After doing some furious calculations, I replied, 'Going back to Lewington. He's stopped there, I'm sure. But this is most peculiar, perhaps …' I left further speculation unsaid, being too busy doing a noisy U-turn and spraying gravel into the roadside shrubbery. I did a fair bit of lurching around bends on the way back that had Jessica silently grimacing and gripping the handholds with white knuckles.

We went through to the other side of the town, turned into a side road then went back along a road running parallel to the main street, scanning the few side roads. We were behind the hotel and, as we approached, I could see their rear car park and the fenced-in beer garden. Opposite was a collection of large sheds of an engineering works. As we slowly drew nearer, in amongst the trucks and tractors parked on the gravel in front was the Tridee semi. I stopped on the side of the road a few houses down, wondering what to do next, when a fellow in a two-tone hi-vis shirt strolled out from the beer garden's rear entrance. He glanced our way, then unconcerned, walked to the truck, got in and, with a puff of unburnt diesel, headed south. All I could do was give him a bit of space and follow.

Nothing happened. We tailed him all the way to the gate onto the docks, then turned around and drove down the main highway back to Launceston with a minimum of conversation.

When we finally got back to the apartment hotel, I had to spin the story to the guy on Reception that Jessica, standing back a few paces and looking tired, was my sister down for a surprise visit, as against a tart picked up for the night. The fellow behind the desk calmly made a note of the new development on the computer and then wished us a pleasant night.

Dumping her bag on the rack in the spare bedroom, I gave her a brief rundown of the layout, suggested a hot drink, which she declined, after which I left her to it. It had been a long day for both of us. Forgoing a shower, I flopped into bed hoping Saturday would be more fruitful. Despite all the activity, the day just passed had been a disappointment.

Staring up at the ceiling, in the dim light from the neighbouring buildings, the day's events swirled around inside my skull. Global geopolitical ructions, the visit to the distillery, Jessica, and the abortive chasing of trucks. And not a grain of certainty in all of it.

Out of the whirlpool, two issues emerged that overrode the rest: what were my real reasons for bringing Jessica to Tasmania, and why had she agreed?

Chapter Fourteen

Showered, dressed, and bored, waiting for Jessica to appear, I lay sprawled across the lounge, rereading the same page of my book for the third time. I had no plans. The sun was shining, the weekend forecast was showers clearing, temperatures in the low twenties. I was getting hungry.

On the verge of banging on her door to see if she was still in the land of the living, she emerged in jeans and a white T shirt, stirring memories of the flight from Hawaii. It was strangely unsettling.

'You okay? You've a strange look about you.' She'd caught me halfway between the sofa and her bedroom.

Changing to a happy face, I hesitated before attempting conversation. 'Perhaps I'm just glad to see you?' It seemed an idiotic line and yet rang truer than I wanted to admit. I detoured. 'Don't know about you but I'm looking for breakfast. How about heading down to the dining room?'

They didn't have a great selection but what they lacked in variety we made up for in quantity. She had managed to delay the question I had been avoiding but asked it while sipping her coffee.

'So, what's happening today? This is my first kidnapping, so what's the procedure?' she said with mischief in her eyes.

'New to the game myself. Try and get the most value out of you, I suppose.' I gave her a goggling, predatory grin that ended in laughter for both of us — a marvellous moment of complete ease, which had me wanting more.

Returning to normal, I was seized by a brief spasm of unease that appeared to be passing through Jessica as well. What were the implications of that unexpected moment of – friendship, connection, warm regard? I couldn't put a name to it but it felt dangerously seductive. I broke the spell with a confession.

'I'm afraid I got you over here on false pretences. I don't think I really have anything so important to say that couldn't have been said in an email or a text.'

She was sitting back, her now serious face studying mine with an intense fascination that had me wondering if she was enjoying my lack of direction or was she silently sharing similar uncertainty. Either way, I gave up on speech, just leaned back, stroked my chin to encourage the stubble and imply deep thought. I capitulated with a shrug, flopped my hands on the table, palms up, hoping that doing so might encourage some telepathic method to solve the confusion in my brain.

Jessica provided a solution. 'Since you're not suggesting a next move, it's up to me.' My silence ended with her declaring that we should take advantage of our hearty breakfast and the increasing sunshine to go for a stroll. Cataract Park was suggested. I'd been there once but had limited recollections of the place. In Jessica's company, it would be much more memorable. So I agreed. After she had a final sip of coffee, we headed for the door.

We drove the short distance to the park and chose one of the walks that followed the river up through the forest to the lower of the series of waterfalls that defined the park. As if by silent agreement, we talked of everything but ourselves and our possible motives for being there. We stopped to observe interesting aspects of the vegetation, the delicacy of some of the flowers, the roughness of the bark on trees, the dappling light, and the delightful splashing of the water's energetic bouncing over and around the rocks.

At one stage, the track grew muddy and narrow, forcing me

to give her a steadying hand while she concentrated on placing her feet. I kept hold of her until we reached drier ground where the track returned to being wide enough to travel side by side. I found myself reluctant to release her and she seemed in no hurry to break away.

But after a few more metres, 'Perhaps you'd better give me my hand back before you get … other ideas.'

She said it with humour and a smile, but I couldn't help remembering those lectures in Arizona on the pretzel-like workings of the unconscious mind, one of which confirmed the old adage that many a truth is revealed in jest. How much of her attempted humour was a declaration of intent? I dared not hope for too much – needed a few more clues, not just to her intentions but also the motivations behind them, a much trickier task. I also had to be sure I wasn't suffering from wishful thinking and seeing things and emotions restricted to my imagination only.

We crossed a short bridge to the other side of the river then followed the trail downhill to eventually break out of the forest into the grassed area that formed a manicured park in a natural bowl in which the swimming pool, public facilities and the cafés were scattered. The walk had taken longer than expected, and the café on our side looked the better one so we tramped in and ordered an early lunch.

The place was at near capacity, service was slow, leaving us plenty of time for conversation. It had barely started when Jessica's phone pinged. 'Leave it … please.'

She was on the cusp of indignation, saw my expression, probably a mix of annoyance and unspecified hope, before she slowly retrieved the device and made a show of turning it off and sliding it back into her hip pocket – a tight squeeze.

'Thanks. I'm not really a control freak. It's just nice, no … therapeutic … to give the world out there a break sometimes.

To enjoy the moment. A clichéd line but ….'

'No need to get upset. You're right. Relax.'

We both smiled at my petulance. The air cleared. Soon after, a bottle of water arrived but no food, the waitress disappearing without a word. It was pretty clear they were under the pump and lunch would not be such an early one after all. We sat in silence, enjoying a long sunny break. I was intrigued by the swiftly moving river, its surface fractured into infinitely changing combinations of liquid valleys and hills that either painfully flashed back the sun's rays or zoomed past in metallic greys.

A few minutes of squinting at the river soon shouldered Sunday's trip to the front of the queue. 'I've booked myself on a kayaking trip tomorrow.' My face found it difficult to hold an appropriate expression.

'And?'

'And if you're worried about getting back to Melbourne, you've a ticket on a flight leaving eight-thirty tomorrow night. '

'And?' She added an irreverent twinkle to her reply that had me smiling and decisive.

'And do you want to go kayaking tomorrow or not? The group leaves from the entrance to the Cradle Mountains National Park at seven-thirty a.m., which would mean a very early start from Launceston but a later one from Sheffield or … Moina.' I mumbled the last word, then immediately regretted the evidence of an urge to confess more of my plans. After all, she was still a reporter, even if an enchanting one.

'You haven't asked if I can swim or have any experience as a paddler. The rivers up there can be very demanding. And you haven't asked if I have other plans.'

'I reveal myself a lousy kidnapper. Not only have I planned your release without payment of any kind. So far, that is.' I gave her an amused expression, hiding unspecified hopes. 'Now I'm offering a day of excitement and wonder, admittedly based on the assumption you have the capabilities and ….'

'Yes, yes, enough!' Her eyes were gleaming. 'I would love to go. I represented my school at the state swimming finals and did plenty of kayaking at university but not much since. I know my body will regret this later, but I've been told life is filled with suffering as well as joy.'

Decision made, I dug out my phone, turned it on, then called Karlene, explained the situation and reminded her that my kayak was a two-man one. After a hesitation, she assented and sternly repeated the start time and place. The call over, I turned the phone off.

Lunch eventually arrived and was consumed in haste from hunger and my desire to get to the outdoors store before it closed at four. I had to organise some gear for Jessica and the extra food and drink to take with us. By three-forty, we were back at the apartment, at either end of the sofa, feet on the coffee table nursing mugs of chamomile.

Though mostly thinking of Sunday's trip, a big slice of me was pondering the contents of the missed calls and texts I'd received. One was from detective Aberdare, another from Higgins, Jessica's boss. Later, I'd see what they were about. At that moment, I was determined to be living in the here and now.

'If we start from here, it's going to be a very early start. There's another option.'

Turning towards me, mug to her lips, her face showed curiosity and amusement.

'I've rented a two-bedroom house in Sheffield. There's a rather nice restaurant in town that wasn't there years back, so how about we shift camp?'

'Fine with me.'

Saturday night is usually the big night in most towns, but I was glad we got to Sheffield early because I was certain my restaurant wouldn't be open much past eight. Her eyebrows lifted when I ordered the trout. I explained by saying the wilderness was forcing me to go paleo, to get in touch with my Neolithic side.

The trout was perfection. She seemed happy with her veggie stack with nut cheese.

Back at the house, occupying opposing armchairs, sipping herb tea, we were faced with the task of filling in the hour or so before bed. She occasionally glanced through the open door of her bedroom, not suggesting romance I was sure, but almost certainly suffering mobile phone withdrawals. I knew how she felt.

'I know it's hard, but let the phones rest 'til morning. There's no coverage here anyway.' Not totally true, it was intermittent, but she probably didn't know it. 'I've a few books; you can try one if you like.'

Without waiting for a reply, I dashed into my room then lined up my limited collection on the coffee table, in the neutral zone between us. She pushed a few around then picked up *The New Nature*, noting the bookmark. 'Any good?'

'More than good. If you're a greenie and still rational, it will change the way you think for the better. Unless you're one of the many who can't handle views other than their own.'

'Quite a challenge!' she said with a boldness I found encouraging.

'Higgins reckons I can learn a lot about a person by finding out what they read.' Leaning forward, she picked it up, sat back and flipped it open at my bookmark and started reading.

She kept going, leaving me content to watch her, sip my tea and contemplate truth, especially why it was that I, and everyone else on the planet, had such a hard time engaging with it. Not the truth of material things and their *rules of engagement* – few of us argue over the laws of physics and chemistry, almost all our troubles stem from biology – the ways we organic beings interact with other organic beings on a large scale, which is ecology and human history, but more importantly for most, myself included, how we get along with the rest of humanity on the smaller scale. And especially how we understand and cope with our interpersonal behaviours and the meanings we assign to them.

For instance: was Jessica ignoring me for the book, the work of another man, a rival male, one could say? Was her behaviour a slight to my fragile ego, or was she enjoying the book I had presented to her, indicating a similarity of thinking and offering hope that we may be on the same wavelength and destined for closer and happier interactions in the future? There were no objective measurements available to solve such conundrums. All I, like other males, had to rely on was instinct in judging the mood of strangers – our gut feelings.

The train of thought raised a smile of humility that had my left hand moving up to rest on my stomach in a gesture of respect and reassurance. I decided to give my digestive system the time needed to inform me of Jessica's mood.

But it wasn't long before I doubted the primacy of instinct over logic and evidence. Memories stirred of a lively, almost heated debate I witnessed at the retreat in Arizona.

We were on what they called a *rapport ramble*, a bushwalk in normal speak, and had reached a Y junction in the trail, one not marked on the rather crude maps we were all given at the start. The majority were for the left fork, but a stubborn minority argued for the right. A few of us were undecided.

My reading was that either would get us to our destination, a log cabin where we were to spend the night. The leader of the *lefters* finally declared to all of us, with an intensity I'd not expected: "You're either with us or against us." He herded his followers left and moved them off, leaving the rest to decide. An older, philosophical gent, one of the undecided, muttered into my ear, "Just like President Bush in September 2001 when announcing his decision to invade Iraq. The same ridiculous notion of either/or."

He'd obviously taken on board the Buddhist teachings of seeking the middle path. I also had a distaste for assuming there was only one way of seeing a problem and hence the solutions to it. My reply was that either way was okay but, to be controversial, we joined the rebels on the right fork and had a good laugh when we beat the others to the cabin.

But my philosophical companion had forgotten that life is replete with situations of either/or. And it was that summation I increasingly applied to Jessica. Was she for me or against me? On one level, I knew she was a complex person with a history, dreams and complicated emotions, but I couldn't stop seeing her as a Yes or a No.

After another sip of tea, I decided tomorrow's trip down the river might provide some irrefutable evidence of her attitude towards me. The warmth of the liquid seeping into my core stoked an impatient, fervent hope that Sunday would be the decider.

Chapter Fifteen

When I dragged myself into the living room, Jessica surprised me by being first up. The alarm had wrenched me from a deep sleep; thus, I felt like an aging heavyweight, on the ropes, legs about to fold, and with all the lights blazing, even my half-open eyes were taking a merciless battering.

'We forgot to bring lemons for the herb tea, so this will have to do,' was her opening remark as she handled me a mug.

Somehow I latched onto it without dropping it, grunted and then sat down heavily, propped elbows on the dining table to support my head while I concentrated on breathing in the steam. It was black tea and smelled like the stuff that came with the house. Lipton's probably and stronger than I normally liked and too hot, but its caffeine content was exactly what was needed to rev me up. Not that I wanted to make a habit of it.

As I sipped and grew increasingly alive, I watched Jessica busy at the stove. She seemed to be cooking up a big omelette and had something else steaming away in a pot. In less than fifteen minutes, she had dished up our very early breakfast that I hoped my stomach was up to. We faced off across the table.

'Don't look at it as if it's going to kill you. You and I both need plenty of fuel to cope with a day's paddling.'

'You've got me all wrong. It looks fantastic, veggie omelette on a bed of rice, but ….'

'But what?' She stared back accusingly.

'But I thought you were a vegan … no eggs.'

'Never said I was a vegan. I just like healthy and ethical food.

These eggs are pasture-raised free-range, and the rice is Doongara and low G.I. If pushed, I'll eat most things – within reason, of course.'

'Fine. Thanks. Bon appetit.'

We ate slowly to be kind to our digestion, cleaned up and then packed a simple but calorie-dense lunch with plenty of snacks, energy-rich paleo bars and a handful of apples, along with stainless steel flasks of water. With the food and drink divided equally into two day-packs, we locked up but left the outside light on so as not to break a leg trying to locate the car in the predawn darkness. After a last mental check of my list of the things we needed, I started the car and, with lights blazing, drove through the quiet streets of Sheffield.

Shortly after entering the National Park, as instructed, I headed for the camping grounds past the visitors centre. They were starting to show some signs of life, though not much since the sun had yet to climb above the ridges, and the temperature was barely above freezing thanks to a clear sky. But the vegetation was wet, and scattered puddles in the car park suggested a dose of rain, one that had bypassed Sheffield.

Our group was easy to spot, all wearing beanies and huddled around the minibus towing a trailer filled with kayaks on racks. Mine was unmistakable, by its length and its mottled blue, amongst the single-seaters in monochrome yellow.

We were the last to arrive. The rest had camped there overnight. After introductions were made and our day packs stowed away on the bus, we were directed to the amenities block. I needed a loo stop, and both of us had to put on our wetsuits if we were to survive the cold water. A short time later, suited up and sporting matching water-resistant, fleecy sleeveless jackets and beanies, we took our seats on the bus and survived a rather short but bumpy ride down to the launching area, a small lake crowded in by thick forest and rocky slopes.

Once the bus and trailer were unloaded and our packs stowed in the kayaks, which had been lined up along the pebbled shore, Karlene gathered us for a pep talk.

'Now you all claim to be competent swimmers and old hands at kayaking, but …' She paused to give us a sweet but doubting smile. '… we're going to do a few exercises here first just to make sure. During the trip to Lake Cethana, I'll be in the lead, showing you the best lines to take. Please follow, or you may get into unnecessary strife. Roget here …' She rested a hand on the shoulder of a tall, lean fellow with a dark complexion suggestive of mixed ancestry. '… will be in the rear to help any stragglers. By the way, if Roget is a bit hard to pronounce, he's happy with Roger.'

Roger let a hint of a smile play briefly across his face but remained silent. Though not a talker, deep down, he must have possessed a sense of humour if the big skull and crossed bones flag sewn onto his lifejacket was any indication. Mind you, none of us looked particularly dignified standing around similarly garbed in black wetsuits, orange lifejackets and yellow helmets. It was the sort of get-up that requires a sense of the absurd as well as the practical.

The first task we were given was a short swim, in pairs, out to Karlene and Roger in their kayaks. Surviving that, we launched our craft and did some basic paddling manoeuvres then beached for a final talk before moving off.

The driver, who had stayed on the bus throughout our preparations, drove off once assured we were all going, presumably to meet us at Lake Cethana. I wasn't worried too much if he decided to abandon us because the lake wasn't far from Moina, and I could always dig out my satellite phone from the aft storage pod and get Harvey to rescue us.

Finally moving off, we were last in line bar Roger, keeping a respectful distance behind. It was all rather enjoyable gliding over the calm waters of the lake after all the busyness of our preparations.

'Beautiful isn't it,' Jessica murmured behind me.

For a second, I'd forgotten she was there. She was in sync with my rhythm so the kayak handled as if I alone were doing the paddling – another moment of harmony to add to my mental scoreboard.

'Yes. It's good to finally be moving and wonderful to feel a bit of the sun's warmth. This little lake may be beautiful, but the water's damn cold!'

'Not wrong there, so let's try and stay out of it.'

She'd read my mind. The others in front were disappearing through a notch in the low ridge that held back the waters. Adjusting our line to that of the guy in front, I experienced a tremor of excitement. The fun was about to begin.

The river's escape was dark and narrow. The geology squeezed us, and the vegetation scratched and grabbed at us like a horde of beggars desperate for coins. We paddled frantically to get sufficient speed to steer in waters turbulent and invigorated by the overnight rain. Karlene had said this section was called *Threading the Needle*. It was a gross understatement.

Surviving that, the walls and shrubbery drew back. The stream widened and calmed itself into irregular bends, with the water's depth varying, making the ride both rough and smooth with no discernible pattern – it forced me to remain paranoid of hitting submerged rocks or snags. A quick glance rearward revealed Roger looking confident and maintaining his distance, and more heart-warming, the cheery vision of Jessica with rosy cheeks and excited eyes.

'Okay back there?' I managed to snap before pushing a surfacing log with my paddle.

'Fine. Just stay away from those logs. They scare me.'

There was no need to reply. I had my job: to get us safely

home and still have a good time. Trying to keep the kayak in front of us in sight proved a taxing full-time occupation. He was constantly disappearing around bends and swerving like a lunatic around rocks and semi-submerged branches.

The river raced us, and we kept up. Time passed until it became a contradiction: it ceased to exist and yet seemed to go on forever. It was like entering a meditative state, one of physical experiences devoid of thought other than the automated ones of paddling, observing the guy in front, the water, spotting the ambushes laid by trees and rocks and feeling your body pulsing with life. You are alive and obsessed with only one goal: that of staying alive.

Thus it came as quite a shock when, shooting out from a tight bend where the rocks and forest had once more closed ranks in another attempt to grind us to a pulp, we found the river suddenly wider and briefly straight. Revealed also was our group beached or beaching at a landing backed by a small grassy area that held at bay the dark menace of the forest.

One of the others, an Italian from the few snatches of conversation I'd overheard during our preparations, gave us a hand to drag our craft ashore, then left without a word to join his friend who had a thermos and two mugs. No one needed to tell us this was our mid-morning refuelling stop.

Jessica, after wandering in a circle, stretching her legs and shoulders, came back to where I sat on the grass, unbundling our food.

'How come you didn't think of bringing a thermos?' she said, not entirely in jest.

'Eat this and stop complaining.'

The sandwich stopped a retort, and a few minutes later, all complaints were forgotten when Karlene came over with the offer of tea or coffee. She departed with our orders.

'That's why I didn't bring a thermos.' I crowed, hoping

Jessica hadn't seen my surprise at Karlene's unexpected offer.

The break was longer than I would have thought necessary but the rationale became clear when Karlene and Roger came around and told us to pack up and get ready. Again we stood around lined up in front of our kayaks ready for Karlene to explain the next section.

'We've had a nice long rest, recharged our batteries and are in top shape, I hope. We'll need to be because before we get to the calm waters of Lake Cethana, we'll be going through the *Washing Machine*.' She paused, enjoying her showmanship. 'The first obstacle is *The Soaker*, where the river goes over a small ridge and becomes braided. We take the central one and get well and truly dumped upon by the others, so make sure your seating is properly sealed.

'A little later, we'll enter *The Agitator*, a long series of rapids, a real slalom requiring fast reflexes and constant and often harsh directional changes to avoid the worst of the rocks and the foam holes where you'll sink because the water is so aerated you'll have no buoyancy. You must avoid those at all costs. Follow my line, and if anyone gets in strife, keep paddling, the next kayak will rescue them. Got that. The guy behind rescues the one in front. Things will be happening too fast for you to turn back.'

Worried looks rapidly spread amongst many of those gathered, myself and Jessica included.

Karlene gave us all a big smile. 'Don't panic, I've been taking groups down here for over four years and lost no one yet. If you keep your heads, stick to the line, you'll find the adrenaline will keep you safe, as will the lifejackets and helmets. Don't forget, Roger will always there to come to the rescue. So have fun, enjoy the buzz but respect mother nature – she can bite!

'An easier section follows, then another drop off where you'll get another soaking, though not as bad as the first. That's "the rinse". A longer reprieve before the last hurdle, *The Spin Cycle* –

the best or worst depending on your viewpoint. You'll come around a group of huge rounded boulders and enter a large pool. Keep right and you'll avoid the whirlpool left of centre. If you do feel its pull paddle harder, don't linger. It gets harder to escape the later you leave it. After the main whirlpool is a series of much smaller, milder ones before the valley widens; the bends then increase in radius, and you eventually enter Lake Cethana for a cruisy paddle to the finish.' She paused to let her words sink in before continuing.

'Hundreds before have conquered it, and I don't see anyone here who looks like they can't do the same, but if I've described something you feel unhappy about, don't do it. There are plenty easier experiences to be had here in Tassie. If you don't feel up to it, let me know and I'll arrange a pick up from here. There's no loss of pride in being realistic. In fact, it's a badge of maturity. I'll give you all a couple of minutes to think things over, then off we go, assuming, of course, I get any takers!'

She turned back to confer with Roger, who was packing up the mini stove and stowing it in his kayak. Coldly sober, we broke up into ones and twos.

'Well? What do you reckon?' Jessica's face had creases I'd never seen before – worry lines. I probably had them too.

'I thought some of the stuff we've been through already was pretty hard-core. What she's describing doesn't seem much worse than what we've done so far. I'm game if you are. How's the body holding out?'

'I feel great, though I'm sure I won't be saying that tomorrow, or the next day,' she said, staring intently up at me.

For what seemed an inordinate time, we stood studying each other's face, eyes locked. It was a strange moment. Pledging your life to another in front of a priest at the altar seemed a paltry commitment compared to this. Here I couldn't realistically proceed without her, and if we did go, we were physically placing our lives in the other's hands.

I kept silent, not wanting to persuade her either way. She had to decide. Karlene had started moving shoreward. Jessica blinked, placed her hands on my shoulders, then pushed up and quickly pecked me on the lips. 'We're going. Don't let me down.'

Before I could respond, she was putting on her seat sealing, passing mine to me along with my paddle, and that was that.

Everyone had decided to go, and a current of raw energy ran through us. The decision we had all just made was akin to soldiers joyfully *going over the top*, eager for the battle ahead.

Live or die, this was going to be an experience we'd never forget.

Chapter Sixteen

There was no chatter when we paddled off in the same order as before. I know I felt a certain trepidation when the straight section gave way to the first bend and the forest closed in again. But Jessica and I were now a team and paddled with strength and a unified purpose that made our silent progress like a stroll in the park. Almost too easy. The first series of bends held no challenges, the ride bumpy but not overly so. Perhaps Karlene had been winding us up.

A sense of disappointment started to develop. But it didn't last long.

One minute the river was defined and in front of us, then it scattered as if frightened by the sight of the land disappearing. The individual streams then became possessed of a suicidal mania and threw themselves over the boulder-strewn edge. The guy in front was a flash of orange and yellow mid-stream shooting over the lip, then, like lemmings, we followed. If I hadn't known it was survivable, I would have had a heart attack. As it was, it felt as if the bottom of the river had dropped out from under us. Temporarily airborne, we re-joined the water with a whoosh, to be pounded under by a thousand firehoses on full bore as the other streamlets coalesced back into one. We went under briefly but madly kept paddling, keeping our heads down. I assumed Jessica was doing the same. In a few strokes, we had escaped to the foam and fury of normal rapids.

My only thought then was that Karlene was into understatement, not overstatement!

I managed to shout a quick, 'You okay?', received a shouted

affirmative that sounded more excited than scared, and kept paddling at a slightly reduced intensity.

'The agitator is next. See any signs yet?' was Jessica's next shouted communication.

I delayed answering until a bend revealed a boulder-littered staircase that the river slithered over and around in a messy scramble to get to more level ground hidden by the forest further down. The kayaks in front followed a vaguely defined central stream that roamed from side to side in a crazy dance with the rocks and the trees.

'Slow down. We need to give the guy in front a little more room.'

Instantly she was back paddling with me, which gave me the time to select the best line. Then, committed, it was down the chute, furiously digging our oars in, twisting and wriggling the kayak, trying to keep to the deeper water, all the while fending off the rocks that were keen to taste our blood. The ride down was an adrenaline-soaked blur that I had to shake from my head to be rid of once the river flattened out, temporarily satiated.

'The rinse – is next,' Jessica announced between ragged breaths.

'Need to slow up again,' I said after a quick glance to see how Jessica was travelling and to make sure Roger was still in the game. He was roughly the same distance back as before and sat with a relaxed posture. I hoped he wasn't being overconfident. Rivers, and life in general, have a way of punishing hubris. But the philosophic moment didn't last long enough for me to rate my own abilities – I was too busy surviving.

Our period of relative ease ended with another decline, where the river once again split forces, going over the edge as individuals to become one again at the bottom. The rinse wasn't as bad as the soaker but was bad enough, and we both copped mouthfuls of gritty, near-frozen water that set the teeth on edge.

'Swallow much?' I said once I'd spat out most of the grit, and things had quieted down a touch.

Jessica just shook her head. Like me, she was trying to spit out sand grains without taking her hands from the paddles.

Perhaps the grit distracted me. Perhaps I thought we had a longer respite before the final challenge – whatever the reason, we were again getting too close to the guy in front. Before I knew it, he was sliding past a huge rounded boulder; we followed and saw its bulky brothers, five monstrous rocks like trolls hunched around a swirling pool of swift-moving glassy water that exited by squeezing between the two largest boulders to continue its flight down the valley.

We were entering *The Spin Cycle*, travelling too close on water frantic to take us into the oblivion of the whirlpool's gaping maw.

The fellow in front obeyed instructions, kept right, but overdid it, or underestimated the speed of the water. Either way, he overcooked it and ended up ramming one of the boulders standing guard on the right, stopping him briefly until the spinning water turned him, blocking our path. I had only one option: a more central line.

The immense tug of the current caught us and started slowly to draw us towards the spiralling throat. Adrenaline pumping, we paddled for our lives – missed spearing the other kayak by millimetres – glimpsed freedom before the current hurled us into the boulder forming the exit's left portal. Out of the corner of my eye, I saw the other fellow free himself and shoot through the gap. The water was now dragging us backwards with increasing force, trying to suck us under. Roger zoomed past too late to react to us drifting anticlockwise on the wrong side of the pool. I saw him glance our way and attempt to back paddle before he disappeared, and we were back to fighting for survival.

The kayak was slowly turned and pulled backwards despite

our best efforts to break free.

'What are we going to do?' Jessica screamed. 'I can't last much longer.'

'Can't fight it. We have to use it. Full strength on the right paddle we're going to reverse out at full speed, go in the same direction as the current, do a circuit and let it slingshot us out of its grip.'

She was silent. Risking a glance back, I noted her feverish paddling than the fear in her eyes and yelled: 'It's the only way. Roger's gone past. It's now or never.'

Seeing my resolve, she squeezed incipient tears from the corners of her eyes. Her face hardened, and a fierceness to survive took over. 'That's my girl! Now full reverse. Go! Go! Go!' Turning, I instantly pushed my fear into my arms and dug the blade of the paddle deep into the water and heaved.

No longer fighting the current, we shot backward, which was almost as terrifying as the glistening, black funnel waiting to claim us. But what I had hoped for happened. We climbed up the edge of the whirlpool and broke free, running blind, full speed in reverse and struck the rock that had caught the previous kayak, thankfully not so hard that it broke the hull, but enough to turn us the right way around.

The clutches of the whirling monster renewed its cloying embrace, but I could see the exit. Like demons, we launched ourselves through the gap. My arms and shoulders seemed possessed of superhuman strength so that when we entered the next pool again, we were too fast but in our pumped-up state were even faster to correct and contemptuously broke free of the undersized whirlpool's attempts to swallow us. We powered around it and then on through the next swirling pool and finally squeezed past the last of them. The river regained some semblance of normality, and I backed off, suddenly mindful of Jessica's existence and that she may be close to exhaustion.

'You okay back there?' I shouted, not taking my eyes from the frothing waters of another rapid further down, which proved to be the last of the white water.

'Fine. Just glad the worst is over,' she said while paddling with moderated power.

A short time later, we encountered Roger paddling manfully against the fast-flowing current in a valiant effort to come to our rescue. We shot past him, giving him the thumbs up in passing.

The river kept us engaged for a while longer with a few twists and turns, but the fight had gone out of it. Minutes later, the valley suddenly opened up, the trees backed off, and we entered the calm waters at the upper end of the lake.

Thoughts of safety turned my arms to lead, and I gave up paddling, leaned heavily into my backrest and sat aware of only two things: my laboured breathing and the desire to say something.

'We made it!' I said turning, my voice sounding as gravelly as a chain smoker who'd run a marathon. A superfluous remark but it was all I could come up with.

It was a while before Jessica responded, prompting me to turn fully around to check how she was. She also was leaning back, her head tilted skyward, her hands on the paddle resting crosswise in her lap, breathing slow and hard. Eventually, she straightened up, caught my eye and calmly proclaimed: 'Not there yet. Keep paddling.'

A moment later, Roger pulled alongside, looked us over briefly, nodded, then, without uttering a word, drifted back to follow at his usual distance until we made landfall and joined the rest.

Both of us were kept busy explaining what had happened. Karlene and Roger both praised our levelheadedness, but I'm sure were secretly reassessing the river as a suitable venue for even experienced kayakers. I know I was.

A barbeque lunch, overseen by the driver, was in progress. It included not just the usual steak and sausages but grilled trout, and there were plenty of vegies and salads. But Jessica and I were only half interested, still a little shell shocked by our experience and confined our eating to plates lightly loaded.

Neither of us was much in the mood for talking, just concentrated on recovering physically and mentally. I was beginning to fret about what would happen next. Had I overdone our bonding experience, which I came to realise was the deeper rationale behind the kayaking. Perhaps she thought I was too reckless, too much of a risk-taker. She could have died twice in my company; by shotgun in Melbourne or drowning here in Tassie.

She wasn't talking, so I didn't know whether to broach the subject of risk and reward as far as our "relationship" went. I was being optimistic in my definition of the term.

Before I could resolve my impasse, Karlene was giving us all the heads up to pack up and to get back on the bus.

Barely a word had been exchanged by the time I had strapped my kayak onto the Land Cruiser, and, having said our farewells to the other paddlers, we were driving back towards Sheffield.

I took it easy, not wanting to upset her further with sloppy driving. Something had to be said.

'Are we still talking? You've been a bit preoccupied since we survived the ride down the river. I'm sorry if it proved more …' I had to pause to find a neutral word. '… challenging than I'd first thought, but ….'

I was going to spout some guff about life being filled with challenges that reward us by building up our character but couldn't. I gave up and concentrated on driving and put a large slice of my mind to sweating on which way to go. Part of me was hoping she would say she didn't want to fly back to Melbourne, in which case we could spend the night in Sheffield.

But with the continuing silence, that fantasy grew weaker and weaker. At the outskirts of Sheffield, it died.

'We'll pop into the rental house to pick up the rest of our stuff, then it's back to Launceston to catch your flight.'

'Fine. I'd forgotten about all that.'

And that's about all she said until her flight was called and I walked her to the departure gate.

'Will I be hearing from you?' It sounded pathetic but was all I could manage when we joined the short queue at the gate.

She turned, gave me a weak smile and replied in a pained voice, 'Yes. Sorry. Haven't been very good company … just have a lot on my mind. Work and …' Her face softened. '… you.'

We were blocking the line. I could feel the growing heat from the big guy in the business suit behind us. I nudged us forward.

'Jessica, I …'

'Boarding passes, please,' the uniformed fellow said, hand outstretched. Jessica obeyed. He did what he had to do and she started to move through.

'I'll call you,' I said to her before stepping aside, noting the glare of the businessman moving into my space, and watched briefly Jessica's retreating form until she was gone. It felt as though a door had closed and shut out the light.

Somehow I drove back to my apartment in town, parked the car and made it inside. Closing the door behind me, I dumped my day pack on the floor and stood scanning the room as if for the first time. The place had gone from airy and welcoming to empty and clinical. It did a job efficiently but without enthusiasm or warmth. But it wasn't the room that had changed. It was me.

From such hopeful beginnings: the bushwalk, the hands held and the reluctance to part, the little jokes seemingly full of meaning, the kiss, tentative and brief but still a kiss, our working as a team to survive the river, all that and the day had ended in … what exactly? How much, if anything, had been achieved in clarifying Jessica's regard for me? For that matter, where did I stand? Was she the girl for me?

The question shocked me. Not because I didn't know the answer but because I did. For the first time in a long, long time, I'd stumbled on someone I felt I could live with and love, genuinely and fearlessly. I might be wrong, but at some stage, you have to stop studying the form and place your bets. I realised I'd just made mine and had a lot riding on it. For unknowable reasons, I felt sure Jessica was going to be a winner.

Lucinda had dazzled me, fed my ego, and ultimately deceived me. I couldn't imagine Jessica doing that. If we had problems, I reckoned she'd tell me to my face.

So why was she so reluctant to admit she was attracted to me, despite all the little hints she'd given that were definitely not just my fevered imagination? That was the thing that stumped me.

The only answer that sprang to mind was that her love life had been as bad, if not worse than mine, and thus she was scared of getting hurt again. That thought gave room for hope. All I had to do was convince her that she loved me too. Such an easy task!

At least I had a way forward, just wasn't overly confident about my chances of succeeding. But standing around wasn't going to do much, so I headed for the shower to revive the body as a starter.

Later, propped up in the bed, I briefly tried channel surfing then abandoned the remote, turned off the lights and set my hopes on the curative properties of sleep and the unknown opportunities sure to surface in the days ahead.

We would be separated tomorrow and the next four days, but she would be coming back to Tasmania, on holidays, on the weekend. Leaving five days to sort myself out and come up with a scheme to win her over.

I had faced worse tasks and won.

Chapter Seventeen

One can avoid the world for so long but not forever. Monday morning, I had breakfast brought up to the room. The meal eaten, tea in a mug, I was ready to turn the phone on and see what needed to be done.

I always felt better in the mornings, something to do with a rising sun whose rays were flooding in through the window. The weather, at least, was off to a good start. First thing, I waded through the emails and texts queued up on my phone and received the reassuring news that my partners in the States weren't getting spooked by the worsening global economy. China had announced another rate rise for spurious reasons that the US and other developed nation raucously protested.

Firing up my laptop, I put my electronic signature to the Memorandum of Incorporation for *Wonderland Water Boring Limited* and sent it back to Ravi, who also reported that the divorce proceeding had bogged down, presumably in response to Lachlan's displeasure over *Tarkine Mist*. It wasn't anything to worry over. More concerning were the emails from Detective Aberdare. The first to say that further reports from Thailand had added weight to the drug trade theory regarding the attempt on my life, though still not being specific about who and why. Sort of news without being news. More ominous was the second email that simply stated that he had been asked to share all he knew on the case with the AFP. He was still in charge but they wanted to be kept informed of any developments. He expected they would contact me at some stage. In the meantime, he wanted me to keep him in the loop and fully informed.

Why was the Federal Police getting involved? I doubted Aberdare had asked for their help, which raised the question of how they had found out about my troubles? Perhaps Higgins at *The Age* had started asking the wrong people the wrong questions. If there was a story with international perspectives, he wouldn't have blabbed it to anyone until he'd nailed the story down, so he seemed an unlikely source for putting the AFP directly on my case. Anyway, his two messages were about trying to locate Jessica, who had disappeared offline, which in this age of connectedness was just about headline material by itself.

My mind kept turning back to the incident in the Golden Swan, *Tarkine Mist*, Lachlan and the two Chinese businessmen. The AFP's interest seemed to confirm their involvement in some international intrigue or drug dealing, and I was getting roped in through JTB and my association to Lachlan and from there to the two Chinese and the distillery.

But if the AFP had become interested in me, I certainly couldn't do much about it, or could I? Those guys were big on surveillance and subterfuge if one can believe what's implied about them in the media and give credence to my own Big Brother fears. They would have access to anything that went through my mobile, the regular one, but less so the satellite phone, which was hired through one of the shell companies I used for my currency speculation. It would be hard to trace it back to me because of my connection to those companies, all registered in Luxemburg, each hidden behind by several other holding companies, all designed to quarantine my risky currency trading from bringing down JTB. And if they did connect the dots, they'd have to break the encryption I'd paid for on all communications to and from them.

My laptop also had plenty of anti-spyware, and all work on it was done using a removable hard drive, so again the AFP was going to find lots of blanks when checking me out. A boost for my ego but not so good long term as it would fuel any suspicions they harboured against me. I probably should have told Aberdare about the Golden Swan incident, but again, it was a rather tenuous link between any of the previous attacks. Just another drug-induced incident with purely domestic implications. If anyone needed telling, it was the local police, but where was the evidence? It would be an unnecessary waste of my time and theirs.

All of a sudden, life was becoming too complicated.

After finishing the tea, despite kayaking-induced aches, I did a few yoga stretches and a mini workout to clear my mind. Aberdare and the AFP could do what they liked. I was going to get on with my plans, though being more circumspect in the way I did things as I wanted to appear less worthy of their suspicion while keeping my longer-term plans as opaque as possible.

A text from the printers announced the signs were ready. That's what I like, a supplier who promises less and delivers more. When I got back, I left the signs in the back of the Land Cruiser, returning to my rooms a little happier knowing I had one less job to do.

Next on the agenda was to check my currency position to make sure my bets covered all possibilities, then a peek at the stock market and my shares portfolio. Then I did a bit more digging into the other shareholders in the Savage River mine and got the run-around trying to find out who was actually in control. Glowang Equities' majority shareholding had them calling the shots at Savage River, but who ruled them? They looked suspiciously like a front for the Chinese government keen to control the resources needed to fuel their enormous economy. It wasn't such a big deal. I would do the same in their position, but strategic interest from the Chinese made Savage River a better bet, so I increased my holdings to a touch under eight per cent, enough to have influence but not too much to cause concern to Glowang Equities. I paid a bargain price but knew the shares would slide further before hopefully recovering. At least I now had enough to make a visit to the mine a justifiable one, should the urge arise.

Back outside, I walked around the block back to the outdoors store, bought a tiny foldup stove, a bit more camping gear and a bundle of maps covering the course of the Savage River and the surrounding Tarkine Wilderness Zone. I wanted to get to know my patch of Tasmania a little better.

Karlene was with another customer but glanced my way on occasions then came over when her customer departed. I was in the process of filling my daypack with my latest purchases.

'Coming back for more white water?'

'No. Might stick to walking for a while,' I answered, rolling my shoulders as I settled the daypack into place.

'A shame. You and your girlfriend seem pretty competent in the rough stuff, although you did give Roger a turn.'

'Not as much of a turn as we had.' I tried making light of our narrow escape.

She could see I wasn't interested in another paddling trip but lingered, possibly from a sense of guilt. Her continued presence sparked an enquiry.

'Which airlines are flying in and out of Waratah? They have an airfield according to one of the maps I just bought?'

'McCurdy's and Latham's are the only two I know of, and they're not overly regular in their services, in more ways than one, if you get my drift.'

'Thanks. I guess their numbers are easy to find?'

She told me to wait, went around behind the counter and, after a bit of rummaging around, produced two business cards. I said my thanks, left, returned to the apartment, retrieved the car and drove to the airport.

After learning that Latham's had Mondays off, I fortified

myself with air-fried chips from the airport cafeteria and, armed with directions to McCurdy's office, strolled to the big blue hangar down the back that housed the small operators. In amongst the aircraft was a tiny prefab office in front of a container. Its open doors revealed racks of spare parts and a solidly build, silver-haired fellow in blue overalls.

'Mr McCurdy?'

'Who's asking?'

'Julius Banks, and I'm not from the taxman or the FAA.'

He grinned, put down the metallic contraption he'd been cleaning, wiped a bit more grease from his hands then came over to share some of it via a firm handshake.

I was glad I was wearing jeans and a checked shirt, not my best suit. 'Any chance of a flight soon?'

'How soon? How far? And how many?'

'Right now. Waratah then Savage River and back here. One passenger, me.'

He had a think. I munched a few more chips and offered him some. He accepted and seemed to enjoy the extra taste provided by his greasy fingers.

'It'll cost you a packet.'

He mentioned a number. I didn't flinch, which resulted in him ambling into his office, where he made a few phone calls and consulted his computer. He printed out an invoice. I used one of my Luxemburg accounts, to which his EFTPOS machine answered: "Okay". The machine's response elicited a wolfish grin that I found strangely appealing. To me, he was a pirate but a likeable one.

And so he turned out to be. The plane was a twin-engine turboprop Cessna with room for seven passengers if one sat in the co-pilot's seat as I did. It was slow going so we had plenty of time to chat over the intercom, which cut out the aircraft noise. I asked lots of questions and tried to get him to do the talking, especially about the various mining operations west of Waratah. The plane had pontoons, allowing us to land on the Pieman River for tea and sandwiches at the village of Corinna. We got back to Launceston with the sun a red ball falling to the horizon through a sky made murky by high cloud and an unseasonal bushfire somewhere in the southwest.

He noted my laboured movements when exiting the plane.

'You look a bit past it for football.'

'Not football, kayaking.'

'Ahh! Hence all the questions about rivers.'

'No flies on you,' I answered with a smile.

He accompanied me back to the car park, which had me wondering if he was going to invite himself to my place for dinner.

'Into mining too?' he said as I opened the driver's door.

I gave a non-committal tilt of the head.

'Done a stack of aerial surveying work for various mining companies, though it's dropped off these days. Been replaced by drones. That's progress for you. But if you need another look around, the pontoons give me access to areas the others can't go, so don't hesitate to call, anytime, you hear.'

I heard. I seemed to have made a friend, though he may not have appreciated my part in his declining survey work. JTB had investigated drones and made money on the drone racing side and even more when we branched into mining surveys. But I held my tongue, said my goodbyes and drove back a little wiser about the country I could be dealing with if my geo-thermal system became a success and was called upon by miners and other remote operators. It was a rugged, unpopulated wilderness, one in which a body could easily wander in and never return.

That wilderness and my lingering stiffness, insulted by hours in a poorly designed chair, rocketed Jessica to the forefront of my mind after a day of keeping her on the back burner. I decided to have dinner with her, vicariously. Ordering a room service meal, I made a start, then, with the phone on speaker, I selected her number.

It rang for so long I was amazed I hadn't been fobbed off to voicemail and was on the verge of cancelling when she finally picked up.

'Hello, Julius.' Her tone was hard to read, but at least she wasn't at work – no office sounds. Instead, classical music played somewhere in another room.

'How's the body holding out? Thought I was pretty fit but my shoulders and abs say otherwise.'

'My vocabulary doesn't extend to describing all the parts protesting. But …'

'Survive work okay? Higgins seemed put out. Left a few messages on my phone.'

'Rang in sick. Spent the day doing not much. Higgins will probably chew me out tomorrow,' she lamented, with a sigh thrown in for good measure.

'Err … I've been thinking ….'

'Do you think that a wise thing to do?' A little bit of spark had thankfully entered her voice.

'Probably not when it comes to ….' I was floundering again. '… to you.'

She kept breathing but that was it. She wasn't making it easy for me.

'You're still supposed to be getting to know me so …?'

'But I know so much more about you now. How much more is there?'

'Plenty!'

She cut me off again. 'So … is the rest of you worth knowing? I'm sure Higgins probably has other things for me now. Probably changed his mind. He's like that.'

I don't mind playing games, but I've a limit. 'Damn Higgins and the rest of them, you're the one I'm interested in and I reckon I'm not totally repulsive to you too, so …'

'Yes?'

'So quit fooling around and tell Higgins you need to start your holidays early. Come back to Tassie, there's things for you and me to do over here.'

'Not another kidnapping?'

'Too right! This time I'm not giving you up, leastways not until I get a decent ransom, or should I be thinking: dowry!'

Did I hear a chuckle? There was a pause then she spoke the fateful words: 'Okay. I'm willing to take my chances. When?'

'Soon as I can book a flight. I'll text. Pack a few extra bags this time. Bye. I ….'

'Please, don't say anything. Not yet.' She spoke with unexpected seriousness, or was it fear?

'Okay. But … can I at least say that I like you. Is that permitted?'

'That's fine. I like you too. Bye.'

I was almost out of the woods and into the open. Jessica still had to be coaxed from some dark forest of painful memories. That's how it sounded to me.

Now I had a new story to write, this time with a: "they lived happily ever after' included. But like most things, it was easier said than done. There was still a lot of unknowns to deal with: the AFP, Lachlan and Co, and the people intent on reading my obituary.

I had to maintain my vigilance. More than ever, I needed to get things right.

Chapter Eighteen

As soon as the call had finished, I was on the net checking flights; found one with QANTAS, business class, which would please her after having shared the cabin with freight on the first trip over. Leaving Tullamarine, Thursday at five, it gave her time to get ready and time for a celebratory dinner once back in Launceston, at a decent restaurant – anyplace but the Golden Swan.

Having texted Jessica the flight number and times, I tracked down the contact details for the Savage River mine and sent an email to their Launceston Office, using my Jaeger Investments letterhead. It explained my increased shareholding and desire to inspect the mine site. Hopefully, they would oblige.

With so much going on in my mind, I was up early on Tuesday morning and soon afterwards was heading up the highway to Sheffield, where, having checked over the cottage, I had breakfast at 'my restaurant', as I was starting to call the Blue Wren Café.

I was glad I'd put the flagging tape around the gates into the farm; otherwise, I would have missed the entrance. Driving past the house and sheds now involved weaving past the dongas, a forty-foot container, a fuel truck and assorted four-wheel drives before following the wheel tracks down to the drill site.

They were hard at it. Harvey came over and we walked up the slope until we could have a conversation without shouting.

'How far down?'

'Three hundred plus metres and making good progress. Will

soon switch over to laser drilling and the first of the new rods.'

'The forty-foot container near the shed?'

'Yeah. Arrived yesterday. Things will speed up now.'

We chatted about the target depth and when to start using the temperature probe.

'Any mineralisation?'

'Not that I can see. Just rock to me.'

'You're not fooling me. You've been in the game too long. You know what the interesting stuff looks like. Unlikely to hit any ore deposits around here, according to the geological maps, but you never know. On the way out, I'll have a quick look at the cores, presumably in the old hay shed.'

Harvey nodded.

'Much water?'

'Nope. The little encountered so far is being fed through a filter bed then into the river. Nice and clean. Don't want to upset the natives.'

'When you get a chance, put the signs on the rig and the billboards out the front. I'll leave them on the verandah. If you do strike a decent quantity of water, get to sampling as we agreed. I reckon if nothing eventuates heat-wise, at least I'll make something from the groundwater.'

The day had plenty left in it, except for sunshine, which had been smothered by clouds bunching up into a lumpy blue-grey ceiling. With a full tank of diesel to burn, I set my sights on lunch in Waratah. Then, time permitting, a preliminary look around the village of Savage River and the river itself, if I could gain access.

As much as the kayaking trip had been an ordeal, it had also been a peak experience, and life tastes immeasurably better when reminded how quickly it can be stolen from you. What with surviving my appendix's attempt to kill me, fighting off machete-wielding hitmen, shotgun-wielding bikies and a lunatic drug dealing van driver, I was verging on addiction to near-death experiences. Maybe my subconscious was starting to give too much credence to Mordaunt's idea that: "one crowded hour of glorious life is worth an age without name". Living for a glorious now and to hell with tomorrow. Such dreams have resonated through the centuries in many a Y chromosome, stirring heroic deeds and disastrous follies.

Dangerous thoughts I knew, but ones I found unable, or unwilling, to entirely disregard. The very name, Savage River, was the problem. It had an aura about it that challenged male pride. I wanted to ride that river and conquer it. It was blindly stupid but surely there was no harm in just looking. Was there? Leastways that was the rationale that kept me on the road until Waratah came into view a surprisingly short time later.

Waratah had all the makings of a small town, much more so than the smaller settlement of Savage River would be able to offer and, with lunch approaching, I decided the Bischoff Hotel was the place to be.

Parking out the front, I wandered in to check their dining room; had to walk through the public bar to get there and received interesting looks from the handful of older gents nursing beers. They exuded the comfortable assurance of regulars until my entrance, when the mood instantly changed to one of confused mistrust. Confusion I suspect imparted by my outfit: the same as the day before, with the addition of the sleeveless jacket worn in response to the cloud, which had drained the warmth as well as the light from the day. The locals found it difficult to determine if I was a miner, a logger, a tourist or a greenie. The only certainty was that I was an out-of-towner.

The dining room was pleasantly deserted. Meals were from twelve until two. Being ten minutes early, I sat down at a table overlooking the street to study the menu's scanty options. On the dot of twelve, a short, dark-haired waitress came in to take my order: trout and vegies, no gravy, and a pot of tea, no milk. My exclusions prompted a distrustful glance before a shrug and she moved off to disappear behind the small bar that served the dining area.

A couple of pensioners wandered in to take up another table with a view to the street, leaving plenty of room between us. The waitress rushed in to take their order, the usual apparently, then disappeared and returned shortly after with a basket of bread and a bottle of water – for them, I had to wait a while longer before I received the same.

The next piece of entertainment came from the street when a white four-by-four pulled up bearing government number plates and parked next to my car. A young fellow in drill shirt and trousers got out and was in the process of heading inside when accosted by a scruffy fellow of a similar age, who berated the other with much arm waving before stomping off. The victim shook his head, then a moment later appeared in the dining room from a side door. He stood close enough to allow me to read the Department of Environment logo on his shirt. It was an opportunity too good to miss.

'Why not join me for lunch. You'll find me better company than your scruffy friend outside.'

After checking me out, he decided to take the risk and took up the chair opposite.

'Name's Julius Banks. Don't expect quick service unless you were born here, but I think they'll eventually feed us. I hope. This is my first time in Waratah, so what I just said is merely an educated guess. You a local?'

'No, based in Burnie, though been here often enough to be semi-acceptable.'

We exchanged smiles, shoulders relaxed, and both of us got more comfortable in our chairs.

'Amir Ranjanii. With the department ....' He pointed to the

logo on his shirt. '… checking up on water quality in the rivers hereabouts.'

'Ah. Got bureaucrats, miners, farmers and greenies on your case. Must be nice to be popular.'

More smiles. The waitress arrived, gave us both puzzled looks, then took Amir's order and left.

'Help yourself to the bread. I only eat gluten-free stuff, which is too hard to explain out here so …'

He must have had a thin breakfast or none because it didn't take much convincing before he got stuck into buttering the buns and scattering crumbs over the tabletop.

'I'm into water quality too.' His eyebrows startled. 'Into kayaking. You parked next to my car, the one with the kayak on the rack. Savage River has a name that intrigues me so I'm here to investigate. Is it also one of those you monitor?'

Suspicion entered his gaze but subsided after a moment of consideration. 'Yes, it is one of those the department has me keeping an eye on. Some say the mining operation at Savage River is polluting the river with heavy metals and sulphates, sulfuric acid really. They are being blamed for the occasional fish kills further down at Pieman's River. The department has set up monitoring stations and also supervises those put in by the mining companies. And …'

I interrupted, '… your friend in the street?'

'Josh Bantling. Head of the local green group. Not happy we are still allowing the mining. Not interested in the facts as we presently know them, which …' Amir paused, probably unsure how much to divulge to a stranger.

'No need to go into details. Wouldn't want you to get into trouble. Only thing I'm interested in is whether the river will provide good paddling and that the water is safe to drink.'

'Water quality varies slightly with the season but is well within World Health Organisation guidelines. As for paddling, I've no idea. It's pretty forbidding country so I reckon you'd have to be extra careful.'

The meals arrived, and, between mouthfuls, I turned the conversation to general subjects before trying for more information about the mine. He chose his words carefully but did let slip that the workforce was worried about the mine closing. Overtime had been canned, presumably feeding their fears. Amir implied that the men were blaming government interference and pressure from green groups.

I found it interesting that the Chinese-induced recession and subsequent economic uncertainty was not being linked to management's cost-cutting. It was either a case of deliberate misdirection by management or people wanting to believe what they wanted, without much reference to the facts, the broader picture or a range of views – all depressingly normal.

When buying my stake in the mining company, I never really considered the pollution aspect, just assumed governments here were more enlightened than in developing nations and were enforcing decent environmental standards. But all standards can be massaged, if not broken, and governments the world over allocate minimal resources towards environmental issues. It got me wondering.

'Before coming out here, I tapped into Google Earth and it seems most of the mining is below the village of Savage River so I guess that's where you do your monitoring?'

Amir finished a morsel of trout before answering. 'It's no secret. But we've recently put some in upstream, either side of a proposed new mine further along Baretop Ridge. Got to establish the baseline conditions first.'

'What about naturally produced sulphuric acid from oxidising of iron pyrites in soils.'

Amir stopped eating, leaned back and renewed the suspicious demeanour he'd initially given me.

'Did geology and geophysics at uni, a long time ago,' I said in answer to his unspoken questions. 'And … I've an eight per cent stake in the Savage River mine. So I am hoping they are doing the right thing, not just for us shareholders, but for the environment too. By the way, that kayak on my car is not just for decoration. I am genuinely interested in the sport as well as the bigger issues. Visiting town to do a bit of incognito snooping on both aspects.' I added a good-natured smile to my confession.

It didn't elicit much response from Amir. He concentrated on finishing his meal, then called the waitress over for the bill. She returned with an EFTPOS machine, upon which he waved his departmental card, pocketed the receipt and then shortly after stood up to go.

'Nice to meet you, Mr Banks. Have a nice day.'

Before he could escape: 'Nice to meet you too, Amir. You seem like a straight shooter, which gives me confidence that there are no corners being cut in regard to water quality. But if you ever do get suspicions about Savage River, I'd appreciate a call. You can leave a message with *Wonderland Water Boring*. They're a sideline of mine.' I handed him a crisp new business card. 'A text is all it would take, nothing specific, don't want to get you in trouble with your bosses. Just say you are interested in buying my kayak. If I get that message, I'll make moves to investigate Savage River to ensure they are behaving. If you don't trust me, check me out. Julius Tiberius Banks.'

He pocketed the card, nodded non-committedly and left.

I was not sure who was taking the greater risk: Amir if he did send me the coded message in response to uncovering something dodgy, something he was afraid to tell his higher-ups, or me, for trusting a lowly paid public servant who could be in the pocket of unscrupulous miners. Miners who may decide I was an unacceptable risk to their profit margin. Time would tell.

After paying cash for my meal, I wandered back to my car, which was dimpled with droplets from a light drizzle that looked like it was settling in for the day. I would have to take it easy along the forty-three kilometres of winding mountain roads I had to negotiate before Savage River could reveal any of its secrets. If there were any to uncover.

The whole journey would probably turn out to be another wild goose chase, like tailing the semi to Devonport, just another foolish errand of a foolish mind. But I had the time, and what else would I be doing?

Chapter Nineteen

My low expectations of Savage River weren't improved by the soaking rain that formed its welcoming committee. The village itself, what I could see of it through the downpour, was a scattering of unappealing buildings that included the usual: a service station, a café, a general store, a hotel, a school, a few government buildings, some engineering businesses and aging houses suffering from too much damp. There was a central park with a rivulet going through it, but no river. The village should have been called Whyte River as it was considerably closer than Savage River, which was five or more kilometres on the northern side of the ridge separating the two.

The park contained a noticeboard with a map of the town and the surrounding shire, which I found useful in orienting myself and provided me with my first destination: the lookout point for the mine.

Garwinia Holdings proudly announced itself as the company in charge of operations on the noticeboards in the caged-in viewing area, on a knoll overlooking the main pit. The display boards explained the orebody's placement, the history of the mine and trumpeted how the local community and the state benefitted from its continued existence. As expected, there wasn't much said about possible downsides apart from a bald statement declaring that they used state of the art environmental practices.

A gravel road led further up the long slope of Baretop Ridge that confined the two rivers into roughly parallel courses running from the northeast to the southwest. Both terminated in the Pieman River on either side of the hamlet of Corinna, my tea stop of the previous day.

The road had been well maintained up to the lookout but, after following it further upslope for a few more kilometres, it deteriorated abruptly, became a washed-out goat track on a ridge that ominously sharpened into a rock-strewn knife edge. It couldn't be the way to the new mining area Amir mentioned. By the time I'd reached that conclusion, the track had become so narrow I couldn't turn around. The only solution left was to reverse out.

The day may have been cold but I was sweating buckets by the time I'd reversed an agonising distance to a slightly broader spot sufficient enough to permit a grunting fifty-point turn. A task that involved much wrestling of the steering wheel and battering of the vegetation by the car's bull-bars and both ends of the kayak.

There is nothing like a change of context to alter one's view. Upon returning to the village, I suddenly grew appreciative of its charms, principal of which was the café and its promise of a hot cup of tea. Daylight was on the wane so I also had to consider whether to try my luck with a room at the hotel or drive back to Waratah where accommodation was more abundant.

The café had only one other customer, an older woman in close conversation with a lady who appeared to be the proprietor. She was slightly less mature than her customer, well rounded, with shortish, wavy salt and pepper hair. After a minute or so, she came over.

'What have you decided?' she said, noting the menu in my hand. A genuine smile advertised a friendly demeanour and brightened my mood considerably.

'Says here the soup is gluten-free and gluten-free toast is available.'

'Have to cater for everyone these days. Besides, my daughter is a coeliac.'

I ordered both. She left me to study a few brochures of the region that I'd picked up from a stand just inside the entrance. Five or so minutes later, she returned with my meal.

'Travelling around? Or into pruning trees?' was her comment as she stood for a moment, having glanced through the window at my car parked outside, garlanded with twigs and bits of vegetation.

'Nosing around and getting stuck mostly. Looking for new rivers to conquer and was hoping to check out Savage River, but access seems a well-kept secret.'

As we chatted, her other customer left with a departing nod to my host. It was quarter to three, and they closed at four so they were unlikely to be swamped with more traffic.

'Never heard of anyone travelling down Savage River. Whyte River yes, much easier to access. There's a spot where the B23 crosses it this side of Luina, or here in town at the end of Mends Street.'

Sounds of dishes being washed and stacked came intermittently from the kitchen. She remained hovering over me, either keen to talk or trying to encourage me to eat up so she could go home. If she was a talker, she might have some interesting local gossip about the mine or the river.

'Why not take a seat? You could tell me about the town and the river whilst I get stuck into this marvellous soup of yours.'

'Can't do any harm to keep a customer company.' she said, sliding out a chair.

The soup was hot so I had to sip with a lot of blowing. In between, I plied her with general questions about the town's history, the mine and the tourist trade. Towards the end, I tried questions of a more specific nature.

'How's the mine travelling these days? I guess its health is critical for the town. I read somewhere that the Chinese have taken a controlling interest. Always had my doubts about some of their, shall we say, different ways of doing things. Has it had much impact on the workers?'

'Initially no change at all, but of late, I hear grumbling about the lack of overtime and an increased obsession with productivity. Makes me glad I'm not a miner. But maybe it's all part of the general slowdown, not the new managers. There are less tourists too. Mind you, it's still early in the season. Summer's barely started.'

'You call this summer!' I said, tilting my head towards the picture window and the street outside, hardly discernible through the sheeting rain.

We both shared a chuckle.

'May be wet today, but we're still receiving less rain than we did twenty or thirty years back. That's not just an old wives tale. The weather bureau tells us so.'

'I guess I shouldn't complain because it'll make for better kayaking. If I ever do find out how to get to that elusive river of yours.'

She was quiet for a while, then appeared to conclude an internal debate. Looking around, she then leaned forward and spoke in a conspiratorial tone. 'One of my regulars, Jimmy Bronte, since he retired has taken up fishing and prospecting, leastways that's what he tells me, though I don't believe half of what he says. He's never produced any nuggets, but a couple of months back, maybe more, he came in with this beautiful big trout that he reckoned he'd caught in the Savage River.'

She used her hands in the time-honoured tradition of fisherfolk when exaggerating the size of their catch. 'Wanted me to cook it up for him. It turned out a treat. Anyway, when I said there was no access to the river, he told me, in strictest confidence, so don't go blabbing, that there's a spot about eight k out of town back towards Luina, where a track comes off the B23. It heads up the hill to an old fire tower, long abandoned. Seems, way back, the bored fire watchers made a track down to the river, laid traps and always got a feed. One of them told Jimmy's dad. Been a family secret ever since. But Jimmy's not the best with secrets so I guess my telling you shouldn't cause too much concern. So find that track and launch your boat, just don't upset any fisher folk and don't mention me either.'

'Mum's the word. I much appreciate your help, though it still seems like quite a tricky business best left for a sunny day, not …' I said with a wave towards the street.

'How was the soup?'

I was mopping up the dregs with the last scrap of toast. 'Worth the trip. You've put Savage River on the map for me!'

She was most pleased and started to gather up my plates when I interrupted, 'I'm heading back to Waratah. Can you recommend any of the accommodation? I know there is a hotel and also a guesthouse. Any others?'

'Know the lady running the guesthouse. Just mention my name, Zoe, and she'll make you nice and comfortable. Her place is the best in town. If you like, I can give her a call?'

Not one to knock back special treatment, I assented and a few minutes later made a dash for the car, though not fast enough to stay completely dry. Trying to ignore the water streaming off my rain jacket, the cold, clammy embrace of wet denim on my legs and the water creeping into my socks, I strapped in, then cautiously moved off, with the fan, heater, air-con and wipers all going full blast.

Down the main street, I saw the sign for Mends Street, noted its location for future reference, then turned down a side road and around the block back to the main street, this time heading back towards Waratah. I reset the car's trip metre going past the Post Office, hoping that Zoe's eight kilometres was an accurate figure. It was going to be a difficult task to find a sidetrack in the rain.

In the end, the rain made it easy. Approaching the ten kilometre mark, the bitumen became awash with a baby poo yellow slurry coming down from Jimmy Bronte's secret track. Turning into it, I stopped to select four-wheel drive, then moved off, wondering how far I'd get with the road-biased tyres the car came with.

I got further than expected. The track was not as bad as first thought; in fact, it showed evidence that someone was maintaining it. Washaways had been filled and it had benefited from a recent grading. That there was a mystery benefactor was confirmed towards the top of the ridge when rounding another hairpin bend appeared a newly posted billboard threatening prosecution for trespassers, though by persons unknown. I kept going, figuring no one would be mad enough to use the track in this weather, and if spy cameras had been set up, they'd be useless in the pouring rain.

At the top, I slowed to a crawl, dropped into first gear, low range, to do a circuit around a broken concrete pad that was the only evidence left of the fire tower. On the second go-around, I noted a diagonal break in the shrubbery that might be the alleged trail down to the river. There was only one way to confirm my suspicions. Donning the baseball cap that came with the kayak and adjusting the hood of my jacket, I stepped outside, locked up and trudged through the unceasing deluge to the trailhead. I followed it down through numerous switchbacks for fifteen minutes until convinced it led to the river, then trudged back. One thing about those who made it, they did a good job; they had cleared the timber so that progress was relatively easy despite a few bushes and saplings beginning to encroach upon it.

Back at the car, I contemplated following the road further up, just to see how far it was to the new mining lease, the one Amir had mentioned, but thought better of it. Another time, and armed with a valid excuse. To find the place again, I dug out my satellite phone, turned it on and activated the record function. The descent was made with ease in low range descent mode but it was still a huge relief to reach the bitumen unscathed. Selecting two-wheel drive high range, I headed back to Waratah.

Mrs Wetherby was gushingly helpful when I turned up sodden on the doorstep of her guesthouse and mentioned the magic words: "Zoe sent me." The room was very civilised, and as a bonus, she offered to wash and dry my jeans and socks. I'd grabbed a takeaway before arriving so, after watching a bit of TV in the lounge with the other guests, I retired early for a good night's sleep.

In clean, dry clothes and refuelled by an earlyish breakfast in the dining room, I paid my host and promised to return. Mrs Wetherby's goodwill towards me seemed evidence of how important personal connections are, especially for country folk. And it was pleasant knowing I would be welcomed back if and when I returned.

The excursion to Savage River had been relatively successful, probably more than I really could have hoped for. I'd seen the mine and located access to the river, of a sort, and possibly made a few friends.

But I needed to get back to Launceston as there were still a few more enquiries to make, but my first stop was the house in Sheffield to retrieve my laptop and a few other bits and pieces. Reaching Sheffield, I couldn't resist a half-hour tea break at the Blue Wren.

When I eventually approached the house, it appeared exactly as I'd left it – better actually, as a burst of morning sun had it and the surrounding countryside sparkling as though newly minted.

Things weren't so wonderful on the inside though. The place had been turned over, but after a quick check, it seemed the only thing missing was the laptop. A strange type of burglary, with no signs of a forced entry and the wardrobe, hardly touched. My Rolex, which I was strangely embarrassed to wear and yet unhappy to part with, was still in the pocket of my spare jacket. The break-in left the impression that once they'd found the laptop, under the spare towels in the linen cupboard, they'd upped and left.

It raised two questions in my mind: was it the work of my unseen persecutors or perhaps the AFP doing a bit of unauthorised evidence gathering?

After pocketing the watch, I locked up, more for appearances than anything else, then drove off deep in thought about what to expect when I got back to Launceston. Would the AFP make an official appearance, or would they keep tabs on me by other means? If they had requisitioned my laptop, what would they learn from it? If it was the other mob, what good would it do them?

There were too many unknowns, and yet I had the feeling things were coming to a head, without having the slightest idea of what that entailed. All I could do was get on with my life with extra care, especially now Jessica was getting more deeply involved. Was it such a great idea bringing her into it? She was involved anyway, thanks to her boss. At least getting her over here meant I had better prospects of shielding her from any dramas — dramas she would be exposed to because of me. Another burden for me to carry.

A karmic train of action and reaction was in progress: Destination unknown. And we were both riding it. I just hoped we'd be there at the end, when, and where ever that might be.

Chapter Twenty

Parking the car in the basement car park, I went straight up to the apartment. The first thing I noticed was that the linen and towels had been changed, as expected. But a subsequent inspection produced suspicions that my carefully arranged underwear and socks had been riffled through, similarly the few clothes in the wardrobe and the few books I'd left near the television.

I called Reception and asked to be moved to another suite, citing the desire for a change of view. There was a slight hesitation, but after I rejected their first choice, I agreed to the second, on the top floor, overlooking the alley behind the building but on the same floor as the pool and spa.

It took the better part of an hour to shift and carefully arrange my few belongings. Before I left, I scattered on the floor some of the brochures taken from the café in Savage River, a couple in front of the sliding door leading to the balcony and others in front of the door accessing the corridor. With the curtains drawn, the room would be dark so any uninvited intruders would either slip up on my paper traps or, in dislodging them, leave some evidence of their passing. My usual phone that had been turned off for the past two days, I left beside my bed and turned on. After a quick scan of who the messages were from, I resisted the tremendous urge to deal with them, bolstering my resolve with the logic that, having waited a day or so, a few more hours wouldn't hurt. The phone appeared suspiciously to be the way my unknown antagonists were keeping tabs on my movements. Unlike my satellite phone, distanced from me by five layers of shell companies, it was registered to me personally and hence was a neon sign flashing out my location to those who knew about technology. Hopefully, they would conclude I was snoozing.

Putting on my daypack, containing my removable drive, satellite phone and a folding umbrella, I pulled the door shut, placed the Do Not Disturb sign on the handle and then headed for the stairs, wanting the exercise and the greater anonymity it provided.

The stroll to the library didn't require the umbrella, for which I was thankful. Their lobby was underpopulated so I took possession of the payphone, this time with a fully cashed up phone card.

Judging by the background noises, Jessica was back at work, and picked up without delay, perhaps curious about the identity of her mystery caller. 'Hello, Environment Desk, who's speaking?'

'An anonymous admirer.'

'Where the hell have you been? I've been getting voicemail since Tuesday morning.'

No "Hello, how are you? Nice to hear your voice."

I paused, debating whether to be indignant or not – chose not to, having realised I should be happy she wanted to make contact and knowing too how frustrating it is to be cut off when we're all addicted to instantaneous communication. And I had deliberately committed the gravest of all modern sins: guilty of wilfully having my phone turned off.

'And how come I don't have this number?'

An answer of some type was required. 'Nice to hear you're back to normal. This number is a payphone in Launceston Central library so probably one not worth saving. Been out of mobile range the last couple of days. Sorry about that.'

'Humph. Okay, let's forget reasons. I contacted Detective Aberdare. He'd left messages. Seems he's sharing you with the AFP now, though he didn't say why. He'd been trying to contact you apparently and having as much luck as me. He didn't have much more to report. He asked me what I knew, and I couldn't help mentioning your incident at the Golden Swan. Thought somebody in the police should know, it might help them track down your ….'

'Yes. Okay. Fine. Look apart from wanting to hear your voice … for some bizarre reason … there is another thing: I had my laptop stolen from the place in Sheffield. And I'm certain someone has gone through the apartment here in Launceston – not thieves before you ask.'

'You sure?'

'They left behind a very pricey Rolex and no forced entry.'

'What's your conclusion?'

'It's either my unknown enemies or the AFP, who hopefully aren't one and the same. Which brings me to a little bit of research you could help me with.'

I explained my suspicions regarding my phone, gave her the satellite phone number on the proviso she used it only for emergencies, and advised her it was mostly turned off. I suggested she store the number under a bogus name, such as *Al's Handyman Services*. I also mentioned that not much about me could be gleaned from the laptop as I used a removable drive before finally spelling out the job I had for her.

'I still haven't given up on Lachlan and the Chinese connection. Remember that photo of Lachlan and Co. at Crown Casino, his big win? Could you use your undoubted abilities and try and track down the names and business connections of the Chinese gents in that photo, especially the shy looking one on the periphery, on the left? He reminds me of one of those at the Golden Swan. If you can get some better photos of them, that would be good. That fellow, in particular, may be a crucial element in my dramas. I have to assume my usual phone is either being hacked or in some way compromised because where ever it is, trouble tracks me down.'

'Shouldn't you be telling all this to Aberdare or the AFP?'

'Maybe, but for some reason, the AFP haven't contacted me directly.'

I paused, uncertain what to say next because it would sound like more paranoia, yet it had to be aired just in case my unknown enemies proved successful. 'I think the Feds are using my stumbling around to entice my opposition into the open, into doing something overtly criminal, presumably in the hope of getting the evidence for a successful prosecution. I'm their bait. And I still think those out to get me are involved with Lachlan and indirectly in the Chinese government's global machinations. Just don't ask me how.'

'Haven't been reading too many thrillers, have you?' She tried to be flippant, but I felt an undercurrent of belief.

A frustrated sigh was my only answer.

'Don't fret. I believe you and …' She paused, worry edged into her voice. '… and, will see you on Thursday night. Make sure you're there, or I'll call the cops. Don't want …' she faltered.

'Everything will be okay. No need to fret. I'm quite a resilient fellow, as you must have figured out by now. I'll be careful. Just make sure you do the same. If you can trust Higgins, put him in the picture, but don't tell him everything just in case he sees the story, not the lives at stake, mine and possibly yours. If anything horrible happens, we don't want the opposition getting away with it. But nothing is going to happen if we are discreet. So, think you can dig up that info and stay out of trouble?'

'Yeah. No problem. I am a seasoned journalist, you know. You be careful. Okay?'

Before we disconnected, 'One last thing. If I am in trouble, or you are for that matter and in Tassie, there is a fellow, Harvey, a driller who I'd trust my life with. Call Harvey at any time. In fact, he'd be insulted if you didn't. But only if you deem the situation requires it.' I gave her the number and explained the bare bones of the drilling operation out from Moina.

She was silent for a while after my confession of another geothermal scheme.

'My, you are full of surprises. Anything else up your sleeve?'

'Plenty. But for now, just remember how the Mount Gambier project turned out to be legit, environmentally and economically. You'll just have to trust me when I say this latest energy scheme is even more so. Look, haven't you figured out yet that if you want to save the planet, you just can't go on reporting how bad things are or criticising how useless and short-sighted politicians are? The people who control and benefit from the status quo aren't going to give things up. There are other ways. What I hope to do is one of them. It's leadership from the bottom. Hopefully, those controlling governmental opinion won't realise what's going on with my cheap renewable energy until it's too big to stop. If it gets to that stage, watch them suddenly get on board and try and claim the credit. But I'm not in it for the glory. It's my hope to make a positive impact on the planet and make money doing so. If it can be shown that being green can make cash, then ….'

'Okay, okay. I'm convinced. See you tomorrow night. Bye.'

After hanging up, the lobby filled with silence and became uninviting. After a brief pause to gather my thoughts, I went in, settled myself at one of their terminals and hooked into the internet to start my own enquiries regarding the ownership and control of Amelioration Australia, Glowang Equities, and Garwinia Holdings. I even checked out the engineering place in Lewington.

Unfortunately, the globalised economy makes it difficult to pin down national influences, but nothing I'd learned refuted my conviction that the Chinese had controlling stakes in those businesses, with the probable exception of the engineering shop in Lewington. But whether those interests were for purposes other than commerce was impossible to discern.

When I got back, my brochure traps remained undisturbed, which was reassuring. I spent the rest of the day, and much of Thursday morning, checking texts and emails, reading, exercising and setting up the replacement laptop I'd bought on the way back from the library. Just after lunch, Harvey rang.

'Julius.Got some good news, I suppose. We've struck a substantial aquifer, sandstone by the look of it, but I'm no expert. The water's warm and drinkable. Tested quite a few samples, even had a swig of the stuff. Tastes alright. So it looks like your signs have paid off.'

'Hmm. That is good news. How warm?'

'Around twenty-seven Celsius.'

'Well, keep drilling. It's heat we're really after. Water is just icing on the cake, a lousy analogy but you get my drift. I'll come over in the next few days. Any problems?'

'Nope. The boys are happy, the rig's powering through and all's right with the world, so I reckon I'd better send you another invoice: the next progress payment. Just to keep your feet on the ground. Have a nice day!' Harvey chuckled before disconnecting.

With a few hours in hand before the drive to the airport, I had time for a bit of thinking. Did I really need the distillery? A water bottling plant would do as well, and it could be placed on-site, hence lower transportation costs. And if the water was suitable for whisky-making, it offered the possibility of setting up my own distillery. With the right staff, technical expertise and my marketing skills, I was fairly confident I could make a distillery pay. It was a crowded market, admittedly but …

By this time, I was horizontal on the lounge, with the timer on the phone set at forty minutes. I dozed off dreaming of water and whisky and woke a few minutes ahead of the buzzer. Rolling vertical, I then phoned Lucinda. A slight change of plan was called for.

'Hello Julius.'

She sounded tired, and the background noises suggested she was at home.

'You okay? You sound hungover, which would be a first.'

'No. According to my doctor, I've just had my first bout of morning sickness. Can't recommend it.'

'You at home I take it. Lachlan back at the office?'

'Yeah. He got back last night. And not too communicative. Still got something on his mind that … anyway, nothing to concern you. Why the call?'

'The divorce settlement. Just want it off my plate. So to speed things up, how about we forget the *Tarkine Mist* distillery swap. You can keep it as part of JTB if doing so moves things along. What do you say?'

After a lull, she spoke in a neutral tone. 'The cash would have been handy, but if retaining the distillery sweetens Lachlan, he'll be a lot easier to live with.' She paused, then continued. 'So, okay, we'll keep things simple and stick with the agreement. I'll contact my solicitors. Anything else?'

'No. Nothing really. But …' I hesitated to go on, unsure of the wisdom of giving her some unsolicited health advice, most likely to be ignored, but also carrying the risk of insult by the implication of ignorance in the receiver. '… don't want to seem to be interfering but if your doctor hasn't mentioned it, I read somewhere that morning sickness is aggravated by too much meat in the diet. If nothing else works, it's worth a try. Anyway, take it easy. Bye.'

'Thanks, Julius. Bye.'

It felt strange having such an amicable conversation with someone I was divorcing, but as she had said, we were both adults and being civil and realistic should be within our capabilities.

Shaking my head, I chased the conversation from my mind, completing the process with an overly long shower. Before dressing, I rang Ravi to mention the new arrangements with Lucinda and then spruced myself up, dressing in my powder grey suit with the pink tie. Standing in front of the mirror before heading for the door, I felt like a teenager going to the final year ball. It was idiotic, but I guess that's what happens when the heart starts to rule the head, a situation I wasn't complaining about; in fact, it had put a bounce into my step.

Carefully resetting the brochure trap, I closed the door and headed for the lifts.

Hopefully, a new phase with Jessica was about to begin.

Chapter Twenty One

Having spied me in the crush around the Arrivals gate, Jessica came to an abrupt halt. Her eyebrows startled skywards before rapidly settling back, after which she weaved her way through the mingling passengers and well-wishers to where I stood at the back of the pack.

'You're looking good. Going to a wedding?' she said, before briefly infiltrating my personal space to bestow an ever so light touch of her lips on mine. I wanted more but didn't feel comfortable putting on too much of a performance for the herd of strangers rubbing past us.

'Err … not at the moment. But you never know. It's good to get in some practice before it does happen again. Only had the one go so far, and that was years back.'

'Right.' She stretched the word, in tune with her disbelief. 'Anyway, there's more important things to do, namely luggage to collect and dinner to be had. You are beginning to develop a habit of interrupting my mealtimes; well, not tonight. If you can't come up with a decent restaurant, I'll phone my mum. She'll feed me.'

'Don't panic, everything's organised. Speaking of your folks … you staying with me, or them?' I held my breath.

She said nothing, just grinned and turned me in the direction of the baggage carousel. It wasn't until I had put on her overfull trekker's backpack and was lugging her two battered suitcases — loaded with her favourite bags of cement — that she announced she'd be lodging at my apartment for the time being.

Dinner was in the apartment hotel's dining room on the first floor. They put on a good spread and she seemed happy with her selections. Afterwards, back at the apartment, she left to organise her things, disappointingly in the spare bedroom, whilst I distracted myself by brewing some tea. When she emerged, she came over, took a seat at the dining table and placed a folder on it.

Joining her, I placed our mugs out of harm's way as she opened the folder and passed me a typed page containing a list of corporations and associated personnel that summarised who they were and what they did. The third on the list was the man I was interested in. I pulled out the grainy enlargement of him taken from the casino photo.

'Is that the fellow?' she asked.

'Yep. He was one of the guys with Lachlan at the Golden Swan.'

'Mr Zhou Chiang, economic adviser with the Chinese embassy in Canberra, here to encourage trade with his homeland. But when you read his biography, it's confined to a very generic background of education and overseas postings. That's all I could find out, unfortunately.'

'Done better than me. Not sure how it will help us, apart from feeding my favourite Chinese conspiracy theory.'

We were silent for a while, both concentrating on our tea and, for me, what happens next. Jessica must have read my mind.

'So what happens now? Tomorrow and after?'

'Hmm.'

Suddenly stumped by the realisation that once I'd solved the mystery of finding my murderous antagonists, the future, one hopefully with Jessica in it, was a blank canvas. But how can it be anything else with human relationships? Or was I being overly pessimistic? With the right person, it should be …

'You still there?

'Yeah. Just thinking.'

'Thought you were falling asleep on me, which wasn't very flattering for my ego. Anyway, what were you thinking? Hmm?' There was mischief in her voice.

'Apart from our little investigation, which by the way involves a visit to Savage River tomorrow – I hope you're coming along?'

After a brief moment of thinking, evidenced by strange facial muscle exercises, she nodded an affirmative, confirmed by: 'Okay.'

I continued. 'What troubles me is not tomorrow but what happens in the days and weeks ahead.' I glanced towards her bedroom then back to her. 'The sleeping arrangements for one.'

It was her turn to be reticent.

When she eventually did respond, it was to begin a long sad tale of an abusive previous boyfriend, who had been all sweetness and light at first, then morphed into a bullying control freak once they'd started living together. It was an experience that had shattered her self-confidence and poisoned the idea of ever trusting another man. Disillusionment had of late also invaded her career. The high hopes and idealism she'd started with had, after six years in the game, withered to the point she was left wondering what she was accomplishing by persevering. Basically, she was stuck in an unhappy and uncertain place.

How does one cure another's unhappiness? I wasn't doing too well with my own. So what could I say or do? Words appeared an inadequate medium to convey any measure of understanding enough to instil hope, and I wasn't sure that a hug was going to be such a great move either. In the end, I just leant back and released my indecision with a long, drawn-out sigh.

She removed her gaze from the tabletop. 'Sorry to unburden my troubles onto you; you have been so ... decent. So ...' She stretched out a hand, rested it upon mine. '... so patient and understanding. You give me something to hope for.' Then, glancing towards the bedrooms. 'But I'm not ready for that next step – not yet. I hope you understand.'

'I know something of your hurt. Lucinda really … never mind. Just take your time. Do whatever you feel comfortable with and we'll see what happens. Right now, all I can do is restate that I really like you and hope one day you'll like me enough to forget your past and maybe find a better future – a future I'm hoping to play an especially large part in. But for now, if we're going to Savage River tomorrow, then it's an early start, so I suggest you have a shower and head to bed – whichever you choose.' I couldn't resist a wicked grin and leery eyes.

'That's what I like about you, Julius. Come here,' she said, getting up.

I was happy to obey. Once in range, she threw her arms around me and squeezed me with surprising power. When she'd had enough, she disengaged and, with colour in her cheeks, said, "Goodnight." Then she placed a kiss on my cheek and departed for her bedroom, leaving me chuffed and content to engage in the motion meditation of cleaning the tea things, all the while clinging to the silent mantra that her actions meant what I hoped they meant.

Lying in bed, lights out, trying to discern details in the ceiling cornices and mouldings, I realised that I had no real understanding of what was going on in Jessica's skull. I'd just have to be content to simply enjoy her company while it lasted. My only hope was that it would be a long, long time.

On Friday morning, my internal alarm failed me. It was the frenetic rattling of the phone's alarm that kicked me from a confusing dream into an equally confusing consciousness. Groaning, I rose, stumbled around in the shower until fully awake, then wandered into the kitchen to prepare an early breakfast. On the way, I banged on Jessica's door until an annoyed utterance indicated life.

Leaving Launceston, the rising sun took up most of my rear mirror; conversation didn't fully start until our tea break in Sheffield.

'We'll stop at the farm on the way through to show you the setup and to introduce you to Harvey. Then we'll try our luck with lunch at the hotel in Savage River. Don't get overly optimistic – you know how it is – the smaller the town, the poorer the choices. The mine manager is expecting us around one-thirty.'

'Never did get to examine close up the drilling at your Mount Gambier project, so this should be educational,' she said before busying herself with finishing her tea. A short time later, we were back on the road.

'The paddocks look good, but the buildings are pretty rundown,' was her summation as we approached the farmhouse.

'Yeah. Anyway, this isn't about resurrecting a farm past its use-by date. It concerns building a different and hopefully better future.'

As we drew closer, the full decrepitude of the buildings registered on Jessica's face.

'Yeah. It doesn't get better close up. But I've asked Harvey to bring in some handymen to give the house the once over. From that painter's van over there, it looks like they're working on the insides first. Anyway, forget the house and sheds; I'll park with the rest of them and then walk you down to the drill rig. It's not far now.'

I slotted in next to Harvey's four-wheeled beast, then escorted Jessica down the wheel tracks past the sheds, getting our shoes muddy thanks to the morning rain that had finally petered out. A few patches of sun breathed life into a scene dominated by sombre dark greens and greys.

Harvey met us halfway up the rise leading down to the rig.

'G'day Julius, who's your lady friend?'

'Jessica. Jessica Moore. She's …'

'She's very pleased to meet you, Mr Harvey.' Jessica extended her hand. Harvey wiped a grubby hand on his T-shirt, to little effect, then tried his best not to inflict too much pain. Jessica grimaced a little but, to her credit, didn't squeak. Once she had her hand back, she asked about the drilling, got an enthusiastic response from Harvey and together they wandered off towards the drill rig, leaving me stunned and searching for something to do and somewhere to do it.

Around twenty minutes later, they caught up with me near the support truck where I'd been chatting to Stanko, one of the drillers on an early lunch break.

'Jessica here is a gem. Asked me loads of questions and put up a good impression of being interested in the answers.' Harvey grinned with humorous insolence. 'Seems to have a head on her shoulders judging by what she asked. So, you'd better keep this one, if you can handle her, that is!'

'Yeah. Right. Well, she's certainly smart enough and a definite pleasure on the eye. And I'm working on the last bit.'

'What is it with you two? Is this how you talk about all the girls in their presence or is this for me in particular?'

Harvey said nothing, just shrugged and kept on smiling, putting the spotlight on me. I considered the situation.

She could have been indignant but she wasn't. She appeared more amused than anything else, amusement that filled me with pride and hope.

In an age of growing consciousness to male insensitivity and relational inadequacy, unaccompanied by an expansion in the understanding of the structural biases behind said inadequacies, many women had lost much of their sense of humour to male behaviours. Having heard Jessica's tale of abuse from her last lover, I was encouraged to see her smiling at our feigned rudeness.

There had been the odd occasion where I'd overheard women gossiping, passing equally unadorned judgements between themselves – actually, much worse – about the men in their lives. And they probably had considerable justification from the details of their accusations. That, and other dealings with the fairer sex, had left me thinking that men and women were different species – if judged by their often divergent ways of seeing and doing things. For undoubtedly ingrained biological reasons, us fellows habitually needled each other, unconsciously testing each other's strength and resilience in an unceasing and stupid point scoring game. When interesting women were present, this braggadocio could easily get out of hand.

My time in Arizona and at the monastery had made me considerably more aware of such unconscious behaviours, and yet I still found myself falling into them. But such is human fallibility. At least I knew I had limitations and was prepared to recognise them, most times at least, and in doing so was trying to be more lenient on myself and others. That Jessica also had the generosity to grant men a bit of slack would make living with her a hell of a lot easier. But I had been silent too long.

'Only women of high esteem get the honest treatment. And we both agree that, Jessica, you're a star. You've tamed the old rogue, and I'm hoping, in turn, he's convinced you that I wasn't lying about this operation. That everything is above board.'

'Rest assured, Harvey's done a good job of selling your scheme. I'm convinced. Okay? Happy now?'

'Very much so.' I then turned towards Harvey. 'One last thing: I was talking to Stanko and he mentioned the Savage River mine, which is where we are headed after this. He reckons the new mob are mongrels to work for. What's your opinion? Had much to do with them?'

'Tight-fisted bastard's more's the point. Gotta short-term contract with them a few years back. They screwed the price down so much I was practically doing the job gratis, and then they added insult to injury by paying like I was robbing their grandmother. Most of the drilling contracts are now done by a firm they partly own, Wizdean Contracting. And you wouldn't wanna work for that mob no matter how desperate. That answer your question?'

'Yes. Thanks.'

We said our goodbyes, shook hands, with Jessica adding a kiss on Harvey's bristled cheek.

Back in the car, I couldn't help commenting: 'He'll probably never wash his face again after that kiss. Wow, you really know how to charm them when you put your mind to it. I'm jealous now.' I pouted half in jest and half in truth.

'If he's to come to my rescue, I thought it wise to give him a reason to do so.'

What could I say to that awesome piece of womanly wisdom? Silence prevailed for most of the drive to Savage River.

I turned at the first road sign indicating the mine site then pulled over onto the shoulder. Not sure how to play the visit to the mine, I now had to make up my mind. Her adroitness in handling Harvey provided a direction.

'With an eight per cent stake in the mine, I'm sure the manager will try to impress me and show me the good side of the operation. I'm hoping you are willing to assist by playing the role of personal assistant, who I'll leave to have a chat with the secretary and then ....'

'Yes?'

'Well, it's hard to say what I'm hoping for. They have a canteen. It would be good if you could go there and have a chat with some of the workers, anyone – just try and get a feel as to whether there are any irregularities going on. Any gossip, anything other than the official line. Like tailing that truck to Devonport, this is a fishing expedition, with equally small hopes of discovering anything.'

An hour and a half later, we were driving back through the gates, leaving the ugly scar on the landscape behind us. I was disappointed that I wasn't any the wiser regarding the legitimacy of its operational side.

Turning left onto the B23, I aired my conclusions. 'The manager did an excellent job on me. It was like being walked through their glossy Annual Report but in three-D, full technicolour and surround sound, all showing a profitable, well-run mining operation. Did you find out anything?'

'I convinced the secretary to drop me at the canteen but most of the workers were more interested in eating than chatting me up. So it seems my charms are not as great as you and Harvey imply.' She gave a sad face then continued. 'Managed a brief chat with the cook. She'd been there a long time and was none too happy with the new management's cost-cutting. It's giving her headaches trying to keep in budget and still produce something edible. It's taken all the fun out of the place, she reckons. Her hubby was working on the new tailings dam, but that was postponed, and now he's only working half the hours he used to. So, nothing really.'

A short time later, we caught up with the Tridee Transport B-double that had left the mine a few minutes ahead of us. It still had the Ammonium Nitrate Class 1 Explosives signs on the back, which puzzled me initially because it was presumably empty, having delivered its load to the mine's explosives store. Then I remembered the manager's spiel about how cost-efficient they were with explosives: getting it cheap from Melbourne, via Devonport, then backloading the empty containers with water, which was shipped to Melbourne to be sold to an Agrichemical company as the basis of a cut-price liquid fertiliser. On that return journey, it would still be classed as explosives until reclassified at the fertiliser plant.

The truck made for slow going. We were still following it as we drove through Waratah.

'Thought we were going to spend the night in Waratah?'

'Change of plans. There's still plenty of light so we should be able to make it to Sheffield. The house offers more privacy than the guesthouse in Waratah.'

'Privacy for what?'

What indeed? I gave a sheepish grin in reply. But my libidinous mind was soon side-tracked when we reached the A10 intersection. The truck should have gone straight, the shortest route to Devonport. Instead, it turned right as we were doing. Where was he going? Sheffield? And why?

I kept driving. He was easy to follow.

Chapter Twenty Two

There were a couple of chances to overtake on the A10 that I deliberately rejected and none on the Cradle Mountain road so we got to see a lot of that truck's rear end. Finally, I let him go when we got to the farm by doing a rather sharp turn in through the gates, which raised Jessica's ire.

'What's going on now?' she said with daggers in her eyes.

After the tedious drive, she was probably as jaded as I was, so her anger was understandable. 'Sorry about that, but I want to change cars.'

Her unspoken reply would have curdled milk.

Harvey was at the house chatting to the painter, who looked to be in the process of packing up.

'Okay if I borrow your beast for a couple of days? I've ….'

'Yeah, no problem, just fill'er up on the way back. Not going to be too long I hope. I'm rather attached to the old girl. You heading for the rough stuff or what?'

I said I'd explain once I'd parked next to his beast. There I asked Jessica to give me a hand to transfer our stuff, what there was of it, into the backseats of Harvey's monster truck. By then, Harvey had joined us to remove a few bits and pieces of his own. Once the transfer was done, I explained that I wanted to do a bit of surreptitious truck spotting and that my car was too conspicuous with the kayak still strapped on top. Jessica groaned at the news.

After one last look around, we exchanged keys and clambered into Harvey's machine. I fired it up, grimacing at the volume coming from the three-inch exhaust pipes, then waved goodbye,

Harvey looking like a mother sending her only son off to war.

Having turned right leaving Moina and passing the signposts showing distances to Sheffield and Devonport, Jessica broke her silence. 'Another trip to Devonport, is it?' She didn't sound happy.

'Not that far, hopefully. I suspect we'll catch up with the truck at Lewington. You with me?'

'Lewington?'

'Yep. I reckon there's something going on at that engineering place that connects the mine and the distillery, and who knows what else. How I don't know. Sorry about the …'

'Oh, forget it. I'm just a bit tired. But you could tell me what's going on in that head of yours before you spring any more surprises. It's all getting a bit unnerving.'

'Yeah. Sorry. I am being rude. Too focussed on my concerns. Forgetting you're there. How is that possible?' A pathetic smile was all I could manage, puzzled and a little shocked at how easily someone I held in such high regard could be taken for granted, driven out by my monomania with the mystery enmeshing my life. 'Not letting you know what's going on, you must be wondering …' I paused, not liking the implications of my thinking and unsure how to save myself.

'Yes?'

'Don't like to say this, but maybe you're starting to think I'll end up as uncaring and bossy as that former boyfriend of yours.'

She took her time to answer, studying me as I concentrated on a series of bends.

'No, you're different. You are …' She stopped, gazed skyward, obviously searching for the right expression, but as the silence extended, I felt a growing sense of disquiet.

'I could suggest a few adjectives if you like.'

'Don't rush me. There! That's it. You're too impatient. Too much in a rush to do things, too …'

She must have seen the increasing surprise building up in my face.

'And … too interesting to be ignored.'

She relaxed. The moment of tension faded, and the rest of the journey sped by in amicable speculation of what we would find and what it would mean. On the outskirts of Lewington, I stopped at the roadside information bay to consider my planned visit to the engineering works.

'It's past five and a Friday, so they may be closed, but if not, I'll pull in and ask for some help, complain of a noise in the motor, or some such. While waiting, perhaps you could stretch your legs and keep your eyes open for anything unusual. Again we're probably wasting our time but ….'

'If they are closed?'

'I'll still pull up … get out and have a poke around under the car as if something is wrong, and again you hop out and have a brief wander.'

The place was open. The Tridee truck from the mine was parked out the back, so we put Plan A into operation. There were only a couple of guys in overalls hanging around. Neither seemed overly keen to help, so I had to go into the workshop to ask for their assistance.

The shorter, younger one was given the task of dealing with my strange intake sound. I popped the bonnet and he went through the motions as I turned it on and tried to explain about the noises emanating from the engine bay. He checked various things and ended up adjusting a belt that was marginally tight. I couldn't detect much difference but nonetheless thanked him enthusiastically. Jessica, by this time, had climbed back in and, having vehemently refused my offer of payment, we waved him goodbye and headed off north towards Devonport, the mechanic's surly image quickly shrinking in the overly large left side mirror.

At the B14, I turned right for the short trip to Sheffield, admitting to finding out nothing from the mechanic. Jessica's only comment was that they seemed to have installed two new underground fuel storage tanks in a fenced-off area sporting breather pipes and newly laid gravel but as yet no bitumen sealing. We both agreed it seemed strange considering they only had two bowsers, diesel only, especially when combined with the size of the village and the growing trend towards electric vehicles. I added that they didn't have any recharging stands for electric cars, which, for a small business, was a custom they could ill afford to shun. She countered by pointing out that the transport industry was still around seventy per cent diesel-powered, and they seemed heavily involved with trucks rather than passenger cars. Our observations and speculations provided little in the way of clarity, resulting in our conversation lapsing into self-contained silences for the remainder of the trip back to Sheffield.

I parked a few doors down from the Blue Wren café. After ordering our meal, Jessica retrieved her phone and I, my new laptop. Together, we acted like a long-married couple, sitting close but interacting with people in cyberspace.

After the food was served, Jessica put her phone away. 'I thought you said there was no coverage in Sheffield?'

'In town is fine but not so at the cottage,' I replied, spoon in hand, poised over a generous bowl of pumpkin and ginger soup.

'I hope there are no further surprises tonight?'

'None I've planned. Must be your turn,' I said with flickering eyebrows that Jessica refused to acknowledge.

After the meal and back at the cottage, I went in first, anxious to see if another break-in had occurred, and was pleased to find all appeared as it should. We dumped our bags in our respective rooms, then, nursing mugs of tea, watched a movie Jessica had selected. It wouldn't have been my first choice, but it proved fun. It was nice to be sharing some laughter after a disappointing day.

Around eleven on Saturday morning, we were back at the apartment in Launceston sprawled at either end of the lounge, our luggage stowed and both at a loose end. Too late for tea, too early for lunch and neither of us was inclined to play further with our communication devices, having given them the once over when we first arrived.

'How about a swim?' Jessica said after a quick glance at her phone.

Less than ten minutes later, we were doing laps, and I forgot everything but the business of swimming and turning at each end of the twenty-five-metre pool, a pleasantly hypnotic process that was brought to an abrupt end when I saw Jessica clambering out, looking marvellous in her flowery red one-piece.

After checking the clock above the door, she said, once I'd reached her end of the pool, 'See you back at the apartment.' Then she turned and left, her abrupt departure sending a ripple of disquiet sprinting up my spine. Something was amiss. But what?

When I reached the apartment, she was still in the bathroom, leaving me to hang around wrapped in a towel and smelling of chlorine. She emerged shortly after, smiled and then disappeared into her room.

By the time I was showered and dressed sufficiently to face the public, I was thinking of a well-deserved lunch. Jessica was still in her room. The door was half-open.

'You interested in lunch?' I said through the gap.

'No. Got other plans. Come in.'

On the bed were her suitcases and backpack. She had her back to me and was pulling tight the last of the straps on the backpack. Picking up her phone lying on the bed, she checked its display, pocketed it and then turned to me.

'Be a darling and grab the suitcases. My mum is waiting downstairs.'

She hefted the pack onto her shoulders and, pointing to the cases, eased past me, heading for the door, where she stood while I, in robot mode, followed with the suitcases. Pulling the swipe card from its cradle near the door, she pushed it open and led the way to the lifts.

Halfway down, she handed me the swipe card. 'Here, you'd better have this, or you won't get back in.'

Still on automatic, I pocketed the card. On entering the lobby, I finally managed to find my voice. 'So … what's going on?'

'Going to spend some time with my folks. That was the original idea behind these two weeks off. Remember?'

Her face was unreadable, to me at least. I had no idea how, or if, I had offended her or that she was even upset with me. She appeared calm and unconcerned. Was it a façade hiding all manner of things? All I knew was that I had a hollow feeling in the pit of my stomach, which wasn't hunger, and my legs felt like lead.

In the lobby were luggage trolleys, one of which she took and onto which she directed me to put the cases, having already loaded it with her backpack. There was a clock above the Reception desk that she checked before turning her attention to me.

'Well, Julius, it's been fun, but ….'

'But what's going on? I thought ….'

'That's the thing, "I thought", not enough, "we thought", not enough …' Her frowning faltered, a sad tenderness surfaced in the wake of a deep exhalation. Placing her hands on my shoulders, she met my gaze, seemed to have a hard time swallowing, just like I was, and then suddenly, she hugged me with a strange fierceness. Equally abruptly, she broke away, planted a kiss on my cheek, then turned and pushed the trolley out through the front doors where I glimpsed a white sedan and two dark shapes, who helped her put her luggage into the boot. They drove off.

Looking like an idiot, I stood where she'd left me until I grew aware of puzzled glances from passing guests. I turned and plodded back to the lifts.

Doors opened and closed, opened and closed, people got in, people got out.

Eventually, I found myself alone in the apartment staring at the furniture, my mind as blank as the ceiling.

Chapter Twenty Three

I must have dozed off because I woke stretched out on the lounge, momentarily wondering how I'd gotten there. Everything came back with a rush, but nothing seemed to make sense. All my plans regarding Jessica, vague as they'd been, were shredded and burned, leaving nothing but confused memories. What of the future? Again the blank canvas.

Time passed. My body decided that, since my stymied brain wasn't giving directions, it was going to. A growling stomach commanded a late lunch in the dining room downstairs. The brain revived considerably once the stomach was happy, which resulted in a conscious decision to get some fresh air in the hope of furthering the mental recovery. Stepping outside, I faced another moment of choice. Left or right?

The weather was iffy, cool, with ugly grey clouds closing ranks as though spoiling for a fight. Ignoring their blustering winds and threats of rain, I chose right, on the logic that if the rain did arrive, I could always find shelter in the library, a short distance in that direction.

Other pedestrians walked past with determined strides, wrapped in their own concerns and mindful of the weather. They parted around me, aware of my existence but giving me no notice. There are times when being thus ignored can be liberating. Ignored and anonymous can open up the possibility of doing what one wants to do without censure. But no such positive notions touched me. I continued in my fog of confusion and disappointment, though the gloom lessened with each step

I took.

A couple of blocks past the library was a small park that the weather had made wonderfully deserted. Selecting a bench, I distracted myself by watching the antics of a bunch of pigeons near an overfull bin. They were mostly pecking away at scraps but one male kept interrupting his foraging to puff himself up and strut around the females, who ignored him, being too busy fighting over a crust of bread, all this to a soundtrack of complaints from a bunch of crows hidden in one of the nearby pines. How very human it all was.

The birds soured my mood further but rather than bellyaching like the crows, I decided a useful task was called for, no matter how small. A trivial but doable job made its presence felt, distracting me from my malaise, which fled to the shadows once I reached the apartment.

Stuffing my daypack with laptop, hard-drive, phones and a couple of bottles of *Tarkine Mist,* all padded by a few changes of underclothes, I put it on, then grabbed a suit bag from the wardrobe and headed to the basement. Minutes later, I was muscling into the traffic on my way out of town, back to Moina. My mission: to return Harvey's diesel guzzling monster toy and repossess my rental car and the kayak.

'Where's the little lady?' Harvey said as I stepped out onto the wet gravel of the yard behind the farmhouse, which had all lights blazing even though the setting sun had yet to kiss the horizon. Mine was the only other vehicle there; the drill crew's cars were gone, presumably at the start of their week off.

'Back in Launceston.' After which, we busied ourselves transferring gear between the cars, with me reluctant to meet his enquiring gaze. The job didn't take long. I was mumbling my goodbye and turning to hop into my car when Harvey's iron grip on my shoulder pulled me up short.

'When you say back in Launceston, under what

circumstances? She's a fine girl, better than that Lucinda by a mile. You'd be a fool to let her slip.'

'What makes you think …?'

'Look, I wasn't born yesterday. Julius, I know something's happened, so what gives?'

Harvey may be a driller and a tough guy, but he also has a heart, which is probably why I liked and trusted him. He deserved an honest answer. I had to start at the beginning, from when I encountered Jessica on the plane. He also insisted on the full version of events, forcing me into confessing everything that had happened, from Thailand to Melbourne, as well as the incidents here in Tasmania. He even extracted from me the Chinese currency war with the US and my suspicions they were somehow linked to Lachlan, the Chinese gents at the Golden Swan and possibly the mine at Savage River and the engineering workshop in Lewington.

By the time I'd finished, we were in the house, sitting at the dented but now clean dining table in a newly painted kitchen/living room. We were sipping tea, laced with *Tarkine Mist Gold Label* from one of the bottles I'd intended for celebrations of milestones in the drilling operation, not embarrassing moments in my stumbling love life.

Harvey added another dollop of whisky to his tea, took a swig; he seemed happy with the extra fortification and then spoke. 'You certainly spin a story. Who'd have thought?'

He paused, sipped again then caught my eye. 'Looks like you have two problems: Jessica, and these people out to get you. As far as Jessica goes, don't sweat too much, let her be for a few days then contact her, in person or over the phone but none of this texting rubbish.' He waved his hands to add weight to his judgement. 'As far as the other bit goes, Lucinda would appear the obvious suspect – spouses are fond of killing each other, especially when lots of money is concerned, but somehow that doesn't fit with me. Anyone else benefit moneywise, if you drop off the perch?'

'None that I can think of.'

Harvey had another taste of whisky-tea. 'What about that copper fella in Melbourne, Aberdare? Can you trust him? Maybe you should sound him out. Tell him your theories, what you've been up to. Maybe …'

'What about the AFP?'

'Forget 'em. They don't seem overly concerned what happens. Aberdare seems the better bet. You gave me the impression that he is a straight shooter, so tell him what you suspect. Perhaps doing so might shake things up enough to get things happening. Get a resolution.'

'Or, stir up the opposition enough to have a proper go at me. You trying to get me bumped off!'

He paused, screwed up his face as if considering the pros and cons of the idea, then delivered his verdict. 'Nah. You're too valuable alive. I've got bills to pay, wages, insurances, and you're the one who's gonna pay them! Just be careful, that's all.'

It was my turn to sip before answering. 'Okay. I'll chat to Aberdare, give Jessica a few days, and I'll be extra careful.'

We clinked our mugs to seal the deal.

One other thing I did before heading off was to remove the kayak from the car and stacked it out of harm's way in the shed. I wouldn't need it for a while and it made the car a touch too noticeable.

In the driver's seat, engine on, Harvey asked me one last question, curious about my plans over the next few days, which, apart from a call to Aberdare, consisted of staying a few nights in Hobart because there were some architects I wanted to consult there. He didn't ask for more but did volunteer to check out Lewington during the coming week. My parting remarks were that his truck had been seen there before, so he'd best find some less conspicuous transport if he did visit, and that he should keep his nosing around as low profile as possible.

I spent the night in Sheffield, then, after a leisurely and lonesome breakfast, headed back to Launceston to pick up a few things before the long drive down Highway One to Hobart. On a whim, I'd booked into the Wrest Point Casino overlooking Sandy Bay. Their accommodation was top class, dining rooms too, and, in the evenings, I planned to study the bizarre behaviours of the gambling public.

Whoever claimed there was nothing deader than Canberra on a Sunday night had never been to Hobart, or so I concluded after driving through the CBD, then up past Battery Point where the Salamanca markets were winding up, before getting to the casino/hotel complex. After settling in, I took an evening stroll out along the bay back towards the markets, half thinking of trying one of the restaurants that looked out over the waterfront. But the few that were open were booked out, and closed early, so I tramped back to the casino dreaming of food.

The lower dining area was packed, but the mezzanine – the premium a la carte restaurant – had room for me. Dressed in my grey suit to remind myself of Jessica in a happy mood, I followed the waitress to a vacant table for two on the back wall but lagged behind as the girl was in a hurry, having a queue of other diners waiting. Scanning the room, I noticed a woman standing and waving from a crowded table near the low wall that looked over the dining hall below.

It was Lucinda! Beside her sat Lachlan, looking embarrassed. They were at the head of a table of guests, all fascinated by Lucinda's unrefined behaviour. All I could do was offer a half-hearted wave in return and stumble after the waitress who'd already reached my table and was wondering what had become of me. She seated me then zoomed off so briskly I was left gasping by her haste to be rid of me.

Either way, I was suffering from too many surprises. The menu I held open in front of my eyes was just white parchment with incomprehensible lines of black scribble. The food choices lay in front of me, but my thoughts grappled with the reasons behind Lucinda and Lachlan being here. Was it coincidence or some quirk of providence?

My stunned attention spun in neutral, then jolted into gear by a light tap on my shoulder, followed immediately by Lucinda's glowing features filling my view then flowing with rapid grace into the chair opposite me.

'What a wonderful surprise to see you here. We are having a double celebration: Lachlan has landed a big contract with a hotel chain, and I've …' She stopped, her eyes glinting like black diamonds. Apparently, she wanted me to guess what it was she had to announce. Not having a clue, I sat with flapping hands and shaking head, hoping to encourage her to end my agony.

She relented and, in barely contained excitement, continued her story. 'My lawyers rang today to say they've managed an expedited hearing with the court on the 24th, as in Christmas Eve, to grant the divorce as per our agreement. Isn't that truly wonderful news? A marvellous Christmas present for us both. On Christmas day, no more Mrs Banks, and you can toss away that ring you're still wearing.'

She raised her left hand. Her wedding band was gone, and another had taken its place, gold with three chunky diamonds winking unashamedly at me.

'Lachlan sprung that on me only hours after we got the news. We're engaged and hope to tie the knot in early January. Don't look so glum. It's what you wanted, isn't it?'

Her peeved expression jolted me into responding. 'Not glum, just a little shocked at the pace of events. Always thought these things took months, not weeks. No. You're right. It is the best of news. I hope you and Lachlan have a happy life together.' I ran out of words, and could only sit back and look comatose.

She turned, glanced towards her table, then back to me. 'Better go or Lachlan will fret that we might reconcile, and we wouldn't want that would we. Just kidding! Suddenly everything is turning out right. Got to go. Bye, Julius.'

I watched her glide through the tables as if the air was barely displaced in her passing. The wine waiter then ambushed me with a request for drinks. Blinking stupidly, I'd not even considered the wine list. He hovered expectantly.

'Do you stock *Tarkine Mist Gold Label?*'

The answer was yes, so I ordered a double, on the rocks. Somehow it seemed the appropriate thing to do.

Chapter Twenty Four

Whisky and wine with dinner meant Monday morning waking with the first hangover I'd experienced in decades. It was a condition I swore never to repeat. I'd vowed similar in the distant past but hoped – with little reason – that this one would have a longer use-by date. To revive, I took an overlong shower, had a light breakfast of items selected to be easy on the digestion and brain. Once fully functioning, the day disappeared in meetings with architects on several building developments I had in mind. The building projects were to keep me busy while Harvey ran the drilling operation. From my internet searches, Hobart appeared to have a greater concentration of architectural practices, suggesting the council could think outside the box, had some enthusiasm for environmentally friendly designs that were practical pleasing to the eye.

Lunch, in a quiet corner of a restaurant in the city, was spent on the phone with Aberdare. He wasn't impressed by my tardiness in reporting the Golden Swan incident but surprisingly didn't suggest I seek psychiatric help when I mentioned all my theories regarding the reasons behind recent events in my life.

Towards the end, he warned that he would have to report our conversation to the Feds. In reply, I raised my concerns about their motives and doubts over their regard for my safety. He was noncommittal regarding AFP's reasoning, simply finished by reiterating his previous insistence that I report as soon as possible any new developments. I said yes, though we both knew the chances of me complying weren't high.

I returned to Wrest Point around four-thirty, pleased with my progress – having clicked with the culture of the last set of architects on my list of probables. My job now was to sharpen up the specifics of what I wanted and clarify the overarching rationale behind my design parameters. I was so enthused that in the brief interval before dinner, I managed a jog along the beach and a brief splash in the freezing waters of Sandy Bay. The hunger so generated added zest to the enjoyment of my meal, a meal thankfully uninterrupted by Lucinda or anyone else. It allowed me to further postpone dwelling on the central ramification of Lucinda's announcement: the drastically shortened time frame to my becoming legally single again. Instead, I kept wondering what Jessica was doing?

It seemed too brief an interlude had passed to be calling her. So, with my pleasantly full stomach and free of the influence of alcohol, I decided to visit the gaming rooms as I'd promised myself.

The ground floor appeared reserved for the average punters, some of whom seemed to be having a good time. But others, often pensioners by the look of them, were like mindless battery hens pecking away at their poker machines, maniacal in their hope of a reward, which, when it arrived, often failed to elicit much excitement or a desire to stop. It was sad to watch.

After wandering for a bit, I discovered there were rooms upstairs with a more exclusive clientele, judged initially by the clothing and confirmed by the size of the bets. These people probably considered themselves sophisticated compared to the common folk downstairs. They were *gaming*, not gambling, but the end result was the same, and equally sad in my mind.

I needed a bit of fresh air, so walked off down the corridor towards the balcony that overlooked the bay. According to the brochure in my room, it had a bar and a coffee shop but, more importantly, was open to the night sky.

With a pot of tea and a table shielded from the scattering of other patrons, I tried mulling over my architectural dreams, but thoughts of Jessica kept interrupting. I heard a conversation slowly approaching. As the two voices drew closer, my ears tingled. It was Lucinda and Lachlan, arguing.

Keeping rigid for fear of being noticed, I glued my ears to their words.

Lucinda was doing most of the talking.

'Please don't go back. That Mr Chiang is a mechanic. He's fleecing you blind.'

'Look, I know, but with the Chinese, it's ….'

She cut him off. 'Rubbish! He's a shark, and he's taking you for a ride. You've signed the agreement, just make an excuse. You could convince him of your concern that I'm not feeling well, which is all too true.' She groaned to add weight to her argument.

They were almost at the door, so I only caught the first part of Lachlan's reply, 'Okay, darling. I'll see what I can do. But they are very influential, and China is a huge market …' after which the closing door ended my glimpse into their world.

Their conversation injected new memories to mind, this time, one of the talks I'd attended at the Arizona retreat. To grab our attention, the guy had started with that apparently famous line from the writer Jean-Paul Satré: "hell is other people". He then went on to try and persuade us that other people can also create our heaven on earth once we practise better, more truthful and often more forgiving ways of looking upon said people and our relationships with them.

His talk had resonated deeply in me. It seemed to summarise what I'd been struggling to achieve since surviving my ruptured appendix – finding contentment through a better understanding of myself and, from there, a better appreciation of the capabilities of others. But in my desire for a truer and more humble understanding of myself, I seemed to have overlooked the second half of that road to enlightenment: my interactions with those I shared the road with. And one person in particular: Jessica. I had allowed my sense of urgency in building a new way of being to divert me from her part in that dream. It was an error I was determined to put right.

I would call Jessica the following evening in the hope of …

I drew breath trying to clarify my desire, which I boiled down to giving her a better understanding of my motivations and my deep regard for her.

At some level, we all know that you can't force someone to like you. What I had to do was to try and explain the context, past and present, of my behaviours and hope she could understand me more fully and, in doing so, more fully appreciate what it is I had to offer. Which, of course, I felt was plenty! Tomorrow would tell.

With that plan in mind, I returned to my room and slept like the just. Skipping breakfast, I checked out early and was on the road just in time to catch the start of the rush hour. But I soon escaped its clutches and headed north on Highway One: destination Launceston.

Back at the apartment, my brochure traps remained undisturbed, which set up a pleasant afternoon of checking emails and texts, reading a few more pages of *The New Nature*. Tiring, I then stretched out on the lounge to commune with Beethoven via my earbuds. I dozed off at some stage and was woken by the phone alarm at seven, a time I'd calculated to be suitable for an uninterrupted chat.

Her phone rang for quite a while. Then it surprised me with an unknown female voice answering. 'Hello, Mr Banks, I've heard so much about you, I …' which was interrupted by Jessica yelling from another room, 'Mother! Just tell him I'll call back.'

She reluctantly complied, and I was left wondering and waiting, and waiting, and waiting. At seven forty-six, the phone broke its silence.

'Sorry for the delay. I was giving Mother a break from her domestic goddess duties – cooked them a vegetarian paella, which was pretty good even if I say so myself. Had no complaints anyway. So what have you been up to?'

I had to take a moment to unscramble my brain. 'Err … this and that. I could say, pining for you, but then you'd probably think I was being pathetic or who knows what. I just …'

'Before you say too much more, I've been thinking.'

'Thinking? That can be a problem sometimes. Leastways it is with me – especially when I do too much of it with too little to go on.'

'Shoosh! Just listen. Firstly, where are you now?'

'At the apartment in Launceston. Why?'

She held her breath before answering. 'Well … why not come over for a cup of tea? My folks …'

'Wow!'

'Wow, what?' she responded with a hint of indignation.

'Wow, as in wonderful. I'll be over in fifteen minutes. What's the address again?'

Suburbia looks different in the dark, kind of washed out, the vegetation only seeming alive in the splashes of light provided by the street lights. Their place was on a hill; the street trees were well established as was their garden, very neat and probably lovely in full sun. The house, with lights blazing, was a normal brick and tile number, probably a four by two. All very civilised and nice and yet, after locking the car, I found my feet slowed, my mind filled with images of a moth drawing ever nearer to a candle's flame, confused by the light but unable to resist its call.

The door opened as I stepped onto the short portico, revealing Jessica resplendent in a red mohair jumper and a long, bone coloured, pleated skirt. Most welcoming of all was the smile on her face and the laughter in her eyes.

'Come in, you're letting the cold air in. Come on,' she summoned with impatient hands.

She led me down a short corridor, through a door on the right and into a comfortably furnished lounge room that had a fireplace, with a fake fire burning, that provided a focus for the room, which I usurped upon entering. Jessica's mum and dad, occupying high-backed wing chairs on either side of the fire, stood up, wearing kindly and amused expressions induced by their daughter's struggle to coax me further into their inner sanctum.

Introductions were made, and handshakes exchanged, after which I was directed to a two-seater that matched her parent's chairs. Jessica left to bring in the tea things. I'd only had a couple of job interviews in my life, long forgotten until that moment, when all their anxiety and awkwardness suddenly resurfaced. For a successful businessman, I was humbled to find myself not handling the situation as well as I should.

Mrs Moore eased the tension. 'Jessica tells me you like water – kayaking on it and drilling for it, apparently. Though here in Tasmania, I'd have thought we had enough of it lying around not to have to dig for it?'

'Not sure how much Jessica has told you about me or my little projects, but you are right. I am interested in water. It's an intriguing substance in many ways and so pervasive in our lives that most take it for granted.' I smiled weakly, not sure how much further to push the subject.

Mr Moore chimed in. 'When I asked what it is that you do, Jessica was most reluctant to say at first. Said you used to sell things at the markets, but you'd given that away to become a part-time driller's offsider, out the back of Moina. I'm afraid it wasn't a very encouraging start.'

Mrs Moore finished for him. 'But we gradually got a more accurate picture from her, and may I say we are very pleased to meet you: her mystery man revealed at last.'

'Honestly, Mother, Dad, you'll be making Julius blush if you carry on with more of that.' Jessica had arrived with a tray of fine china which she placed on the coffee table in the centre of the room.

Once Jessica had poured out and distributed the various cups, coffee for her parents, tea for us, and had taken up residence next to me on the sofa, the rest of the evening went smoothly and with much humour. Though there was a dip when Jessica's father twiddled his wedding ring and looked enquiringly in my direction. I had to announce the news of the court hearing on Christmas Eve, after which we all did a bit of synchronised sipping of our drinks to imbibe the news more so than to quench our thirsts. But afterwards, the conversation resumed where it had left off.

Both her parents were still working so the tea session wasn't prolonged. A little over an hour later, I bid her parents good night in the lounge room, and to Jessica on the steps leading down from the portico.

'I hope we can talk soon. I've …'

'Yes, I know. I've got things to say too, and we have other things to sort out. But there's no need to be apprehensive. It's not as bad as you're thinking. In fact …' Abandoning words, she grabbed me and kissed me full on the lips, after which little else needed saying.

'How about lunch tomorrow at your apartment, say … twelve-thirty. We can have it sent up,' she suggested, and I agreed.

One last kiss, then somehow I managed not to tumble down the steps as I turned to walk back to the car. Waiting on the portico, bathed in light, Jessica looked like a goddess in modern guise. She waved as I drove off down the street. A prettier sight I could not imagine.

Chapter Twenty Five

Wednesday morning, I woke early. Too early. Four-thirty-seven, according to the clock on the bedside chest of drawers. Then I had the brilliant idea of retrieving the kayak and suggesting to Jessica a post-lunch romantic cruise down one of the quieter streams, specifically the one going past my soon to be residence in Perth. The forecast was sunshine with a maximum temperature of around twenty-four. Perfect. I just needed the kayak, which was at the farm.

The drive there and back was record-breaking and proof that he travels fastest who travels alone. I arrived back a bit after eleven, had a quick shower, changed into blue pleated pants, white shirt and a red V necked jumper. The mirror's reflected image reminded me of a politician dressed for the cameras, enamouring himself with the voters by proudly associating himself with the colours of the flag. I was hoping for similar, being after Jessica's vote. To steady my ridiculously shaky nerves, I brewed a cup of chamomile and ginger tea.

From eleven-thirty, I was on the balcony, sipping tea and studying the passing parade of trucks and delivery vans in the laneway behind the hotel. There was a surprising number of them, kept busy supplying the apartment building with who knew what. Their unceasing scurrying held my interest so much that it was a shock to hear the phone sound its twelve-twenty alarm. A few quick strides and I was presiding over the dining table, flipping through the lunch menu and pondering how fast room service was in the lunch hour.

But a menu can be studied alone for only so long. Twelve thirty-five: I moved to the sofa, picked up my book and attempted to read. My brain seemed intent on experimenting with imbibing the page as an entirety, rather than the inefficient word by word, line by line process, and naturally got nowhere. I was going nowhere. Twelve-fifty: still no sign or message from Jessica. By then, my skull was swarming with a long list of plausible explanations – all plausible but none convincing.

At one-thirteen, I called her mobile, waited the agonising moments before it went to voicemail, then left a "Where are you?" before hanging up. At one thirty-five, an internet search produced her parent's landline number. I added it to my contacts list and pressed "call".

'Hello?' Mrs Moore answered cautiously to my unknown mobile number.

'Julius Banks here, Mrs Moore. I'm wondering what's happened to Jessica. We had arranged lunch at my hotel for twelve-thirty. She hasn't responded to my voice message, so …?'

'She hasn't arrived! But she left around quarter past twelve. It doesn't take more than ten minutes to get into town and, even if parking was a problem, you should have seen her well before now.'

'Perhaps the car broke down, and she's having trouble either getting it going or ….'

'Unlikely. She took my car, a red Prius. It's all electric; has full batteries, and has never let me down. And it's such a short distance. And anyway, I'm sure she would have called you, or me.'

I then asked which way she would have gone and offered to drive the route to check on her whereabouts. In the meantime, she was to send me a text, or phone me if she had any news of Jessica.

The call over, I scooped up my wallet and car keys and was

at the door, but went back and picked up my daypack, stuffed it with my laptop, phones and a weatherproof jacket, spare jeans and a checked shirt – unsure of my reasoning. Perhaps I was driven by grim thoughts and the desire to be prepared for every eventuality.

Mrs Moore had described the most logical way to the hotel, which I followed with maddening slowness for those unfortunates behind me. I copped a few beeping horns and unfriendly hand gestures that failed totally in distracting me from my careful study of the oncoming traffic and cars parked on the side of the road. By the time I had come to a halt in her parents' driveway, I was suffering the discord of tightness around the chest, fighting to hold in a wave of rising anger. If my unknown antagonist had targeted Jessica, they had crossed a line that would see a more primitive and unforgiving me.

Mrs Moore, who worked from home, met me on the front portico. 'Well? Any sign of her?'

My presence and unhappy look should have been answer enough, but the words still had to be said. 'I'm afraid not. She's just plain vanished, and I reckon we should call the police straight away.'

'She's only been gone an hour or so. She could have gone shopping?'

We both knew that was highly unlikely. She sighed and continued. 'Do you think the police will take much notice?' Her expression held as much hope as I had of the answer being yes.

'Phone them anyway. I hate to say this, but she may have been abducted as a way of getting at me. I can explain later. The sooner we get the police looking for her, the better. I'd rather we made fools of ourselves than regret things later on.'

She ushered me inside, down the hallway into a room on the left that served as an office. Once seated at the desk, she phoned the police. I stepped out into the hall and called Detective

Aberdare.

Shunted around at first, I finally managed to cajole a sergeant into disturbing Aberdare at lunch in the canteen.

'Aberdare. This had better be good.'

'Julius Banks here. My friend Jessica Moore has gone missing. I think she's been kidnapped, though her parents, nor I, have yet received any confirmation to that effect. I'm not trying to …'

'When and where?'

I explained the situation and my efforts to find her so far, inadequate as they had been. He was silent for a while – I heard him munch something, then take a slurp of a drink before he gave his verdict.

'Okay. We can't do much until you or the parents are contacted. You say the local police have been informed?'

'Yes, but I doubt they'll give it much priority. I wonder if you could have a persuasive word.'

More munching and sipping in a background of muffled conversations in a hollow-sounding room.

'I'll inform the AFP boys. If they think it significant, they can get more action happening than I can from Melbourne. I'll send you a text with the developments and you do the same from your end, got it!'

'Yeah. I got it. One other thing: I have two other numbers you can use to contact me on, apart from that of Jessica's parents. One's a satellite phone registered to Jaeger Investments, incorporated in Luxemburg and encrypted, so you'll have a hard time trying to hack into it, but it will have the best reach and probably the one to use. The other is for a fellow called Harvey. He's a driller doing some work for me in Moina. He has my complete confidence and is a straight shooter, like you, so you can trust him. He won't blab any of your secrets.'

I gave him all the numbers and then ended the call. Mrs Moore was still on the phone trying to convince the local police to take her seriously. I listened in for a few minutes until she ended the call, clearly frustrated and having trouble containing her ire. She turned, saw me in the doorway, then, after a brief pause, suggested a cup of tea.

Sitting at the kitchen table, I watched her busy herself with the kettle and cups and wondered what else I could do. There were only two other persons on the island that I knew enough to ask for assistance: Lucinda, an unlikely source and probably on the way back to Melbourne, and Harvey.

I punched in Harvey's number and waited. The call went to voicemail: I left the briefest of messages. He phoned just when I'd taken a sip of tea to wash down a too big a bite of the sandwich Mrs Moore had kindly made, having realised I'd missed lunch.

'What gives?'

I gave Harvey a brief rundown of recent events and what measures had been taken, after which he was silent for a bit, allowing puzzling background noises to penetrate.

'Where are you?'

'At the pub in Lewington, in the beer garden, having lunch with Stanko. He's getting the guys at your engineering works to fix two punctures for him.'

'Two?'

'Yeah, one wouldn't have seemed enough to get us to pull in. Had to ruin two good tyres but I told Stanko that we'd pay. By which I mean you pay … capiche.'

'Yep. No problem. Just put it on the next invoice. But getting back to Jessica, if you hear or see anything, like a red Toyota Prius for instance … anything, just let us know. Okay?'

'Sure. By the way, you still interested in our impressions of the engineering …'

'Yes of course. Anything dodgy?'

'Nothing much really. Asked the waitress what it was like

living in Lewington, as a way of sussing out the general vibe – is that the right word? Anyway, she was a local and said it was a great little town, mostly. She and the more established residents weren't too keen on the new people who'd taken over the engineering works and the farm behind it. They had staffed it with a mixed bunch of immigrants to do the picking and planting, but disappointingly they rarely came into town to spend their money. All the mechanics are blow-ins too. On the upside, the new owners had funded lots of renovations around the town and had tarted up the pub, which they half-owned.'

He drew breath, had a sip of something, then continued. 'More specifically, I did notice that the ventilation pipes over the new underground fuel tanks seem overly large and more numerous than I would have thought necessary. Could simply be them obeying new regulations. Then, after ordering our lunch and finding a spot in the beer garden, one that gave a view of the fellows working on Stanko's *fourbie* – that big yellow Patrol you would have seen parked up in the shed. Not that you can see much of the yellow because Stanko believes in protecting his paint with a thick layer of mud and grime. Isn't that right, Stanko?'

After a brief pause filled with the clink of glasses and a muted reply, Harvey got back to his story. 'Anyway, we were just getting stuck into our steaks when the head guy – leastways that's who we assumed he was by the way he walked – he comes out, phone stuck in his ear, grabs one of the mechanics – the shortish fellow – gives him some instructions then heads back to his office, which must be out the back somewhere. The mechanic drops everything, goes out the back and soon after, we hear the sound of a car start up, possibly a four-wheel drive. It made a fast exit, but didn't go past us so must have headed south. Could have been some emergency callout or ….'

'Yeah. As usual nothing really specific to go on. That's been the problem ever since Thailand. I'm continually fighting shadows, leastways the people behind the … Sorry, Harvey, I shouldn't burden you. Anyway, thanks for your efforts. Thank Stanko too for interrupting his week off.'

'Not a problem. Stanko often pops into the pub for a meal, or a coldie, on the way home from four-wheel driving. Got a house, wife and kids in Devonport. He's a good man, a "dobar čovek", isn't that right Stanko!'

I couldn't hear Stanko's muffled reply because I was too busy telling Harvey that I'd given Aberdare his mobile number.

Once I'd pocketed my phone, Mrs Moore asked for an update, what there was of it, after which we continued to sip tea and sweat internally. I had to use everything at my disposal and so extracted the phone and sent a text to Lucinda asking for her location on the pretext of possibly meeting for a chat.

She was surprisingly fast on the reply. She was on the plane, midway to Melbourne, landing around three-thirty. I texted back: "Thanks, some other time." Her next response was to suggest I contact Lachlan if it was business-related. He had stayed behind to iron out some last-minute complications with the deal done with the Chinese hoteliers.

More smoke and still no idea of where the fire lay. Was it worth reporting to Aberdare? These scraps of information failed to carry much that was truly informative so I decided to wait until something useful emerged.

Jessica's father arrived home around three, obviously too upset to stay at work, not that he could do anything at home apart from console his wife. More tea, with cake this time.

A little after four came the first real news. The local police rang to report that the car had been located in a car park behind Woolworths in a suburb way off track. The CCTV footage had proved inconclusive. The person who left the car didn't resemble Jessica, was dressed in jeans, a hoodie and wraparound sunglasses and hence unidentifiable. They said they were still working on the car and the CCTV footage in the hope of further details.

It was a relief of sorts to have some concrete facts, which, though bad, could have been worse. I texted Aberdare with the details, though he may have known if the locals were keeping him and or the AFP in the loop.

Five o'clock came and went. I decided to head back to my apartment. The situation was becoming increasingly delicate, with Jessica's parents having time to realise that their daughter was in trouble because of me. On the way out, halfway down the hallway, I stopped to open a text message: "Sheffield tonight. ASAP. No cops." No name and the number unknown.

We were all jammed up in the hallway, with Jessica's dad behind me, followed by his wife. I passed the phone to him. He read with grim acceptance. 'What do you plan to do?'

'Depends on how much we trust the police, doesn't it?' I said as he returned the phone.

Breaths were taken. Mrs Moore became agitated. I couldn't wait.

'I'll let you decide. She's your daughter, but I have to get going. I trust Detective Aberdare, but my unknown antagonists seem to be well informed of my movements. So …'

Our eyes locked briefly, both filled with grim determination and hard calculations. Jessica's dad blinked first. There was a hall table near the door with a notepad. I wrote down Aberdare's number, also Harvey's and that of my satellite phone, then explained, warning him he'd best use a payphone if talking to me or the police or do so in person. I stressed again that my communications were probably being monitored, that the satellite number was probably the best in the present circumstances and vowed to let him know what happened.

On the portico, they both stood in silent shock, faces like

death masks.

'Whatever happens, know I'll not rest until she's back safely. Wish me luck.'

Her father shook my hand with an intensity that negated further words. Turning, I made my exit and drove off without a backward glance.

Chapter Twenty Six

There was a payphone at the service station on the highway east of Deloraine, where Jessica and I had stopped before. I called Harvey.

'Yes?' His short reply reeked of annoyance and wariness.

'Julius here. Got those results we were after. Not so good, it seems, so you'll have to carry on by yourself for a while while I sort things out. Staying in Sheffield tonight, not sure after that, but the problem should resolve itself one way or the other in the next day or so. You got that?'

I hoped he'd not start asking unnecessary questions. I just wanted him alert in case I somehow got the chance to enlist his aid.

After a brief pause, he replied in his normal tone. 'Yeah. Some problems take longer to fix than others. Anyway, I'm at the farm, so will keep things going while you get things sorted. Call if you need help. Always happy to assist if you're willing to pay. Bye.'

Harvey caught on quick. He even added his usual humour in case anyone was listening. A savvy operator was my Harvey. Not that he could help much at this stage.

I picked up a burger and chips at the servo and ate while driving, wanting to be fuelled up and ready to respond to any opportunity to get Jessica to safety, but I couldn't help cringing at my food selection. It felt good going down, but what was it doing to my insides? I blocked out my answers and concentrated on driving.

They hadn't specified where in Sheffield, so I headed to the rental house.

All was in darkness. I had to use my phone torch to unlock the front door. With the lights on, everything appeared unmolested. The only change was a yellow post-it note slapped onto the middle of the dining table. It was the same screaming yellow as the pad on the kitchen bench.

"11pm. Louie Tun."

Not subtle, but I got the message. I checked the time – just after seven. What to do?

Lewington was only fifteen to twenty minutes away, so I had time to waste or prepare. But prepare for what? If they had Jessica there and I turn up, what then? Tea and scones? The only answer was they – whoever they were – would take us for a ride and bump us off. Not knowing who and why was infuriating but not as bad as not having a plan to avert the coming disaster. I decided a distraction might give the subconscious the space to come up with one. The Blue Wren seemed the best spot so I drove into town and found a table at the back, one that gave a good view of the other diners.

'How are you this evening, Mr Banks?' said Mrs Firth, the lady in charge of the front half of the café.

'In a mysterious mood, one that requires your help.' I tried to appear jovial, but I hoped my eyes said otherwise.

Mrs Firth scratched her head and studied my face, not sure what was going on.

'But I guess I'll stick with my usual, the trout and salad, and a pot of peppermint, so you can have the menu back. Hope it's all there.' I handed back the thin folder style menu, some of which had the habit of losing pages. I held my breath.

Was she curious enough to open it, read my note and then obey its instructions? It was a long shot but keeping Harvey, and via him, Aberdare, informed of my location might help. If

Harvey decided to investigate, I hoped he would be extra careful because my enemies were the murdering kind and very determined. But all these slim hopes depended upon Mrs Firth taking the effort to look inside the menu and then obey the instructions. The worrying minutes dragged by spent sipping water as I waited for her to return with the condiments. Eventually, she reappeared and bustled her way over with a tray.

'There you go, Mr Banks, the tea, and the salt and pepper. I spoke to Chef and everything's fine. Your dinner will be out shortly and after …' She paused, caught my eye to ever so briefly reveal her sober concern, then resumed her usual chirpy manner. '… I'll bring back that menu, just in case you want dessert.' With a departing smile, she turned and went back to the counter to deal with an older couple waiting to pay their bill.

Somehow I ate enough not to cause offence, after which Mrs Firth returned with the menu. 'Here's your menu back, just in case you want dessert.' She waited briefly as I pretended to scan the pages for inspiration. My post-it note was there with the addition of: "Done. If there is anything else you want me to do, order the chocolate mousse."

'Thanks, but I think I'll give dessert a miss tonight. Perhaps I'll wait until the next time I bring my girlfriend in. She can save me from over-indulging in your excellent chocolate mousse, but not tonight.'

Returning the menu, I stood and accompanied her back to the counter where I gave her the cash for my meal along with a hefty bonus, as a little something for their staff Christmas party, I explained.

I went back to the house to waste time then, at ten-forty, drove off, becoming suddenly appreciative that the car had good headlights because the moon was a fingernail clipping pasted onto a starry sky – a dark night that was about to get darker.

There had been no traffic, but a few kilometres from

Lewington, a car suddenly appeared in my rearview mirror, flashed its high beam then its hazard lights. There was a parking bay on the outskirts that I presumed was where I was to stop. I pulled over. The following car did likewise, and a weedy fellow with a long scraggly goatee got out. He was almost invisible in black pants and a dark-grey hoodie.

He knocked on my window. "Follow me," he said, then immediately returned to his car, a big Nissan four-wheel drive sprouting fearsome bull-bars covered in driving lights. He moved off. I followed.

There weren't many streetlights and not too many houselights showing either. In two turns, we ended up in the street running past the rear of the pub and the engineering works. The pub was still going though there were only two cars parked out the back. Wednesday nights were obviously quiet ones in Lewington, the others too probably. The engineering works were well lit even though the big doors to the workshop and truck wash were closed. At the last street, we turned and eventually drove through some paddock gates that led to a rambling collection of farm buildings; we went past the farmhouse, which was in darkness except for a light in an upstairs dormer window. My lights briefly revealed the building to be mid-nineteenth century from the pitch of the roof and the number of chimneys. We finally came to a halt outside what would once have been the stables, which were also in darkness, until a door opened, and light branded a rectangular patch on the gravel. Silhouetted in the doorway stood a tall, bulky man in a long coat.

The guy from the Nissan had opened my door. 'Get out. Inside. Leave the keys in the car, and don't try to be cute. Jimbo's got a sawn-off and is keen to use it … again.'

The parting remark raised a brief smirk that pleased him but not me.

The big man had stepped aside for me to enter. I moved into a long room of rough stone walls and a motion detector up high in the corner opposite the door. The room contained a scattering of tables and chairs, even a daybed, with a kitchenette along the opposite wall. A potbelly stove in the middle on the right-hand side provided welcome relief from the night's chill. The right-hand far wall was a production area with stacks of crates and cardboard boxes either side of a large stainless steel tank, on legs, connected by piping to a small bottling plant. A few bottles stood under a stainless steel contraption with a nozzle, empty but labelled with *Tarkine Mist* stickers. Was Lachlan skimming JTB product to earn a few extra dollars … flogging bootleg booze? Was he that desperate for money? But I had little time to dwell on such schemes. My mind had recognised the big man holding the shotgun: my would-be assassin in Melbourne now had a name – Jimbo.

'Tie his hands behind his back. We don't want any mistakes … this time.' Jimbo's grin did nothing for his looks. The beard was gone, but his forehead sported a big bandage while his cheeks were peppered with red marks like angry pimples. Both eyes were working, black and filled with self-assured contempt.

Once my hands were tied up with gaffer tape, I was shoved onto a plastic chair near the kitchen table. Shortly after Jimbo came over, took another chair, moved it a safe distance from me, then sat. Placing the shotgun in his lap, he eased back to gloat.

'No umbrellas to save you this time. That was a good move. Didn't expect it. Got me by surprise. Damaged my reputation you did, and we can't have that, can we?' He added a vulpine smirk to embellish his remark.

Not much I could say, so I said nothing, which didn't seem to worry the fellow. He continued to study me but now as though puzzling over the best way to eat a full plate with the maximum of enjoyment.

The weedy guy left. The silence started to pall. I decided to play the game.

'Where's Jessica?'

'Your little dressed up hussy? Ace reporter. Not far. In fact, you'll see her shortly.' Again the smarmy look.

'Who's paying you? I can triple what they're offering.'

'You'll meet them soon enough and, as for money, I'm an artist.' He stopped to impersonate a sophisticate with a wounded pride; knew he'd failed but wasn't the least perturbed. 'And you have insulted my art. And we can't have that. So you must pay. But not with money.' He scythed his hand across his throat then found it hard to suppress a chuckle.

A few more minutes crept by in dreary silence until noises came from the left, behind a solid wooden door that led to what I assumed was a very small room, probably a storeroom for saddles and such — leastways that's what I concluded from the dimensions and age of the building.

I heard muffled speech. Jimbo got up, shoved most of the sawn-off shotgun into one of the generous pockets of his waxed cotton drover's jacket, then moved cautiously towards the sink where he stood keeping an eye on all the doors and me.

'Don't try anything foolish.'

The door in the storeroom wall opened. There was a pause, as if those behind were shy of the light, then hands, also bound in gaffer tape, entered the room followed by the rest of Jessica, in white dress jeans and her red mohair jumper. She walked as though carrying an invisible gift.

That she was alive was gift enough for me. A bikie type followed. Big, all in black from his beanie to his black biker boots, he brimmed with sullen malevolence. Leading from the rear, in a grey Armani suit, was Mr Chiang.

At this point, I was supposed to reveal my Superman suit, engage in heroic fisticuffs and bring about Jessica's rescue. Sadly,

Jimbo's watchful eyes, and the shotgun, said "No".
    To which I had no reply.

Chapter Twenty Seven

'Get Miss Moore a seat, but not too close to Mr Banks. We don't want any surprises,' Chiang said with a hand waved at his leather-jacketed companion, who complied with rough but efficient movements.

The door through which they had entered remained open, revealing shelves with an ill-sorted arrangement of jars, bags and tins of various foodstuffs, with a decidedly Asian bias. It was too small a room to house three people for any length of time, which had me thinking there must be a cellar, probably a large one.

For a while, we sat, or stood, studying each other. Jimbo looked as though he was sitting in a poker game and had been dealt a good card but wanted to know more of what the others had. If it were poker, then Mr Chiang looked comfortable with his cards. The bikie muscleman seemed to be sitting out the round, a bored observer, who, like a lizard soaking up the sun, seemed content to store his energy and await developments. Jessica tried faking that she was in control, but her laboured breathing was saying otherwise. Me? I was wondering when I would get a break from the lousy deal I'd taken up, and also, what were we waiting for? Why was nobody doing anything?

Much to Chiang's and Jimbo's amusement, I was first to break the apparent impasse. 'So what happens now? What is this place and why is a Chinese diplomat slumming it with …?' I moved my head in the direction of my motorcycling "acquaintances".

'I was waiting for that question,' said Chiang as though lecturing to a particularly dull room of students. 'This is business premises from which a vital export industry is run, an enterprise of great benefit to China as a nation – as well as certain Chinese functionaries ...' He gave a slight bow. '... and a few Australians. Especially my Australian business partner who will be here shortly to ...' He paused to choose the right words. '... to remove an annoying impediment to the continued operation of that business.'

The sound of distant footsteps became increasingly distinct. Stairs were climbed, and shortly after, Lachlan appeared, wearing a business suit and a frown. He surveyed the room, barely registered Jessica and me, before turning his attention to Mr Chiang.

'The next shipment's all set to go, but I think it wise to bring it forward. These two have been sniffing around, and we don't know how much they know. But they know a lot more now.'

He didn't seem overly happy, which implied a situation not of his making. 'We still have no idea how much they've told others, more specifically, that policeman in Melbourne and the AFP.'

Chiang replied with unctuous calm. 'Don't worry. Inspector Aberdare in Melbourne and Phong in Thailand know nothing concrete. As for your Federal Police, they are a joke. Their every move is known to us. But as you say, they may become suspicious and start making inconvenient enquiries and investigations, so I agree. Bring forward the shipment to tomorrow night and then close down operations here for say ... six months. Let the police get distracted with bigger problems, which I may be able to supply if none occur in the normal course of events.' Chiang ended with a face radiating smug confidence that, in my powerless state, was particularly offensive.

I couldn't let these two snakes keep up their boasting unchallenged. 'Lachlan, you realise you won't get away with your plans. Too much suspicion is coming your way for it not to harm you.'

I had concluded by now the setup was much more than shipping sly grog and probably involving some sort of drug lab. 'This illegal drug trade you're mixed up in will land you a hefty jail term, but murder ….'

'Shut up, Julius. You've interfered too much in my life. Now, at last, you will be dealt with … permanently. And forget your police – Mr Chiang is right. They may have a few suspicions but they will never get enough to prosecute a respectable businessman, especially one with a good legal team. You know how it works. And you might like to consider that if you'd died quietly in Thailand, as you should have, your female friend here wouldn't be in the mess you created.'

He jerked his head towards Jimbo. 'If he squeaks again, persuade him to hold his tongue until spoken to.'

Jimbo nodded with a smirk, then wiggled a "come hither" finger towards his taciturn comrade. 'Eddie, go stand behind Mr Banks and keep him quiet. Use your necklace if you have to.'

Eddie, of the black leather jacket, grunted, then silently moved around the room, keeping clear of Jimbo's line of fire. He stopped a metre or so behind me. I had to crane my neck to see what he was up to, which wasn't much, but enough. He stood with bovine calm, arms hanging down, one hand gripping "his necklace"; a length of steel chain, dark and smudged from use.

Then Chiang spoke. 'Well, Lachlan, how do you plan to remove our two impediments? I think it only fair that you make the arrangements. It will engender that mutuality so important in a business partnership: the sharing of risks. It will certainly reduce your financial and karmic debts with me.'

Lachlan didn't seem too pleased at this reminder of his obligations to Chiang but was saved further discomfort when the diplomat directed his next remark to me.

'I think Mr Banks knows all about karmic debt. In a way, his death, and that of the young lady, would rebalance his karma, upset by his killing of Lachlan's assassins at the monastery.'

Lachlan was clearly unhappy that so much was being spoken of in front of witnesses. He couldn't hold back. 'Why are you telling these people all this? Why did you insist on showing the girl our underground lab and then explain the cleverness of our operation? Are you mad or …?'

'Calm yourself.' Chiang raised his hand in the languid manner of an experienced policeman directing traffic. 'I do so because I want you to know that I now have as much to lose as you do if these two aren't silenced. Admittedly, you gain more financially, but you understand my other motivations, which we have talked of in the past. So, everything I do is for both our benefits. You shall see. Which brings me back to the original question, how do you propose to dispose of these two?'

Lachlan was clearly undecided and looked ill at ease being put on the spot. All eyes were upon him, except Eddie, who continued his silent meditation focussed on the back of my head.

'First things first. I'll step outside and make the calls to get the shipment out tomorrow night. I'll be back shortly then ….'

With a dismissive wave, he headed to the door and disappeared into the night. A tongue of cold air entered unbidden, reminding me of the world outside, a world I had to find a way to re-join.

While all the discussion was going on, I had been attempting to do something towards that end. Having used my squirming to get comfortable in the plastic chair to extract my phone from my back pocket, I managed to turn it on, thanks to thumbprint recognition. And had attempted to use the redial function, which should have called Harvey. But I was almost certain that I'd failed to do so. But they didn't know it.

'You're wasting your time, Chiang. This conversation has

been broadcast so you'll ....'

I didn't get any further because Eddie had the chain around my throat and was squeezing the life out of me. My existence dissolved into incredible pain and black spots dancing before my eyes. The room started to fade.

'Release him!' Chiang's command sliced through into my fluttering consciousness. The pain receded. The room swam back into focus to the sound of my rasping breathing. I don't remember dropping the phone and so was surprised to find Jimbo at my side, bending down and picking it up off the floor, the shotgun unceremoniously jammed into my ribs.

He moved off and gave the offending item to Chiang, who chuckled again.

'Mr Banks, you really are most entertaining,' he said after eventually controlling his mirth. 'A very imaginative ploy, which may have provided cause for concern in another, less controlled environment. See the small LED display above the exit door. It lights up red for metals and yellow for transmitting devices. Both did so on your entrance, but it was of no concern. You aren't staying long, and any attempt to broadcast, well ....'

He pointed towards the tiled roof. 'Note the close intermeshing of wires below the tiles? The same arrangement is in the walls, doors and floor but hidden from view. They form a Faraday cage from which microwaves and radio waves cannot escape. So your painful efforts were for my entertainment only. I am deeply sorry.' His expression demonstrated his command of the art of diplomacy, revealing a sincere insincerity.

His attention then turned to my phone, which he held at arm's length studying it as though it was a priceless work of art. 'A marvellous device. American design and programing but, for bigger profits, made in China. But we are not without our scientists and programmers, and thus, every one of these serves two masters: the Americans and us. It is a tremendously useful arrangement.'

His odious lecturing triumphalism was thankfully cut short by Lachlan's return. Thankfulness was a bizarre response considering his return meant a fatal solution had been formulated. But, such are the workings of the emotions.

Lachlan looked upbeat. My hopes fell.

'In your report on Julius's movements – his all too numerous movements –' Lachlan glared briefly in my direction. '… you mentioned a visit to Savage River. He'd even visited the mine. Which isn't a problem as he wouldn't have found out anything. But that visit gives us a "death by natural causes" scenario. We arrange a fatal canoe trip in that thing strapped so conveniently to his car. And it's a two-seater.' His previous agitated state was far easier on my soul than the smug self-satisfaction that now oozed from him.

Chiang stood for a long moment, like a chess player considering the position of his opponent and the best counter-measures to take. Glancing briefly our way, he then returned to Lachlan and nodded. He'd apparently decided Lachlan's gambit, with Jessica and I the sacrificial pawns, was a good one. Chiang pulled a phone from an inside pocket of his jacket, briefly glanced at it then put it back. Probably checking the time.

'Three things. When? It's late, and Savage River is how far away? And how? Drowning or dashed on the rocks? And what of the bodies? You want them found, for … your further plans.' It seemed Chiang couldn't resist needling Lachlan, who responded with a sharp intake of air and narrowing eyes.

Once his calm was re-established, Lachlan offered the details. 'We'll drive there tonight – to the new mine site. There'll be no one there. Then at first light, we'll launch our pair.'

He turned to Jimbo. 'Go into the car and check out what canoeing gear he has. You know, oars, lifejackets, that sort of thing. I'll borrow your *pacifier* until you return.'

Jimbo was decidedly reluctant to give up the weapon but did so, then disappeared outside, letting in another trickle of cold air. Its freshness was strangely uplifting, giving hope that our *accidental* murder was going to be a lot easier said than done. It renewed my determination to dismiss any ideas of failure, and I vowed to focus all my energies on being ready for the slightest opportunity to escape.

In the silence that followed, I tired of Lachlan's robotic gaze and turned to check up on Jessica. Her breathing had steadied, and all her attention was on Lachlan. A chill raced up my spine. She seemed poised for an explosive lunge from the chair. My head movement must have alerted him because the shotgun moved ever so slightly her way.

It was Chiang who spoke. 'Miss Moore, I strongly advise against any ill-conceived actions. Shotguns don't have to be accurate, and there are two barrels, in case Mr Banks has a follow-through planned.'

Jessica sagged like a punctured balloon, bringing amusement to Chiang and Lachlan and relief for me. I continued to look her way until she finally glanced over.

How does one telegraph thoughts of support and unfounded optimism with only a smile and a face? I tried. She returned a weak smile, then slumped to fixate slack-eyed upon the floor in front of her. I knew how she felt, but the game wasn't over, and I was determined to win, or go down fighting, all the way to the final siren.

Chapter Twenty Eight

'Two paddles, two lifejackets, two helmets, a couple of towels and two wetsuits. There's also a basket with food for a picnic and a small backpack with a laptop, a spare phone and a change of clothes.'

Jimbo had been reluctant to enter fully into the room, giving his report a few paces from the door, presumably responding to a whiff of tension that hadn't been there when he left.

Lachlan urged him closer. 'Good. You can have your toy back but be careful: these two haven't given up dreaming of escaping.'

Having retrieved his "confidence booster", Jimbo returned to his previous position and guard duties.

'Eddie, go get Luka and get him to bring his truck around. Luka can lead the way with those driving lights and 'roo bars. I'll be in the front and Jimbo and Julius in the rear. Eddie, you'll drive the Land Cruiser, with Mr Chiang and the girl in the back.' He turned his gaze to Jessica. 'Miss Moore, I strongly advise you not to test Mr Chiang's patience. The Chinese Intelligence Service train their operatives in martial arts ... and other unpleasant things. He will be very efficient if forced to apply those hidden talents should you become uncooperative. Understand?'

It was Chiang's turn to display signs of displeasure at having unnecessary information revealed, but he said nothing. Lachlan shone with renewed confidence now that he had a plan and had apparently evened the score with his partner in crime.

While we waited, I tried hard to think of ways of freeing my hands to give me a fighting chance to do something during the ride. The odds against me would be reduced with just me and Jimbo in the backseat, if … if … My imagination failed to supply any answers.

The sound of a car encroached. Eddie had returned. Chiang circled the room to nudge Jessica to her feet. She did so reluctantly, then sent me a brief look of despair before shuffling off, sandwiched between her two escorts.

'Okay, Julius, your turn. Don't try anything heroic. It's not going to happen.' Lachlan jerked his head towards Jimbo, who cautiously moved behind me and prodded me in the back with the stubby barrels of his sawn-off shotgun. What could I do but comply? Lachlan led the way.

Once outside, the scene was ablaze with harsh blue/white light, thanks to Luka leaving the big Nissan running with all its lights glaring. My Land Cruiser, out in front, was painfully illuminated. Eddie got comfortable in the driver's seat while Chiang secured Jessica into her place in the back on the passenger's side. Jimbo prodded me again, and I obeyed, following Lachlan back to the Nissan, where Jimbo pushed me in through the open door then persuaded me to slide across to sit behind Lachlan, who was already belted up. Jimbo got in with great mindfulness, then closed the door. Neither he nor I had bothered with the jigging around required to put on our seatbelts – this had been made near impossible because the couplings were buried so deep into the rear edge of the stained seat as to be inaccessible.

'Everything okay back there?' Lachlan asked, his head slightly turned in Jimbo's direction.

'All under control. Let's go.'

Lachlan shuffled a bit, then put his right hand to his ear. I could just make out the squat aerial of the satellite phone in his hand. 'All set. Ready when you are.'

There was a muffled reply, a nod from Lachlan, followed by Luka selecting Drive. We moved off, swung into a laboured U-turn, then sedately drove past the house – still with the one light showing – and up the farm track to the gate, with the bouncing lights of the Land Cruiser occasionally splashing into our car's interior, which was a tip. The floor was strewn with crushed drink cans and burger wrappers and a spanner or two to add weight to the mix. The car was ripe with a musty, mouldy smell embellished with overtones of stale sweat and motor oil. Our driver was obviously an exponent of the grunge and grime lifestyle.

Once we cleared Lewington, now illuminated solely by the few streetlights, the swaying and bouncing tedium began. Sheffield went by in a brief series of lighted pavements and intersections with even less interruption of the dark by Gowrie Park and Moina. After that, there was no relief from the all-encompassing night until Waratah, an hour or so away.

Without seatbelts, Jimbo and I swayed at each of the innumerable bends and were constantly bounced around by the over-hard suspension. Yet Jimbo remained tireless in cradling the shotgun on his left arm, and keeping it relentlessly aimed at my abdomen. I tried to catch his eye on occasions because I wanted them diverted from my hands, which were busy fumbling with a small screwdriver I'd found buried in the crack at the back of the seat. With agonising slowness, I was working on it to stand up so the blade rested on the tape around my wrists.

With each bump and side movement, I pushed down, trying to perforate the tape without drawing Jimbo's suspicion. It was no easy task. All the while, I was afraid to try too hard in case beads of sweat would give away my actions.

There had been no traffic since Sheffield, but a car had started following after Moina, raising hopes of a miraculous rescue by

Harvey, but its lights disappeared after the Cradle Mountain turnoff. It was probably no more than a tourist returning late to the campsite in the National Park. That screwdriver was going to be my one and only chance.

Just before the right turn onto the A10, we hit a small furry animal that created a thump and little else, apart from a stupid remark from Luka at the wheel. I tried to feign tiredness when exposed to the few lights on our way through Waratah in the vain attempt to lull Jimbo into easing up. Luka again displayed surprising restraint when driving through the deserted streets because, away from town limits, he seemed to know only one speed: flat out.

Once Waratah was behind us, and after checking his rearview mirror to confirm that the Land Cruiser was still following, he went back to his usual gung-ho style of driving. I was amazed Lachlan hadn't objected but then recalled the way he'd entered his parking bay at JTB HQ and suspected he drove the same as Luka – probably considered it the norm. But it was a style one might get away with in the back streets of Melbourne, but out here, at night, in the wilderness, there were too many kangaroos and wombats to hit.

By now, I'd cut through the tape and was waiting for some of that wildlife to provide a distraction, enough for me to make a move to freedom. The kilometres ticked by uneventfully. So where were the island's fauna when I so desperately needed them? They now seemed to have taken the rest of the night off.

There was only one light showing in Luina, which, after the first bend, was soon replaced by the impenetrable black of the forest. That one light revealed Luka blinking too often. It's what I do to keep awake when I know I should pull over for a rest. He, like me, and a million other fellas, was too proud to admit to the shame of fatigue and so kept up his usual pace as we climbed the ridge that led into the next valley. A sharper than expected right-hander pushed me towards my window. A mob of roos materialised in the windscreen, silhouetted white against the green/black forest. The first one barely had time to blink before it was smashed by the unforgiving metal of the 'roo bar and disappeared under our front tyres.

The car lurched precipitously to the left, then hit two or three of the smaller ones, their mangled bodies hitting the front wheels and pushing us past the point of no return. And over we went. I had just enough time to have the thought that I'd been saved by wildlife only to be killed by them. It didn't last long. I was too busy fending off Jimbo's gun. It was way too close for comfort as we started to roll. He slid into me and, in a desperate attempt to protect myself, I kneed it away. It discharged with an almighty roar, hacking into Lachlan's right side. Jimbo tried bringing it back onto me, but I was having none of it. With my hands now free, I elbowed him violently in the kidneys with my right arm, then continued the movement to savagely jerk the barrel up with my fist. It went off with another ear-splitting roar collecting him under the chin, finishing the job of removing his face started in Melbourne.

Even with half of his face smeared across the pale grey roof lining, he continued to fight with uncoordinated grappling that rapidly lost power until he became a twitching bulk that flopped over me. The car was still falling. Snatches of luminescent guideposts fell to our onslaught. Luka's head and shoulders had rolled towards the dark mess that was Lachlan's thigh. A difficult shot, but I went for it, pulled the gun from Jimbo's weakening grip, then swung the butt at the lank-haired skull. I heard it connect microseconds before slamming up against the side window and being thrown into the back of Lachlan's seat. The car had hit the ground and simultaneously crashed into something immovable.

I must have blacked out for a second because I didn't hear

the airbags going off. Both Jimbo and I were piled like rubbish bags in the footwells, with the airbags constricting our heads, not that it bothered Jimbo. He'd passed over and had given up twitching and gargling blood. Lachlan wasn't moving much that I could see, and Luka was pinned by the airbag, looking like a babe smothered by an overlarge breast. At least they were out of the game.

A few blinks later, I began panicking about how much time I had before the Land Cruiser arrived. It had to be less than a few minutes. I had to get out and find a spot where I could ambush Chiang and Eddie. It would be two against one: lousy odds but way better than before.

First, I had to squeeze past the airbags and Jimbo. It was bloody hard work because, even in death, he was causing grief. Now his inert bulk was almost impossible to budge. It took all my strength to clamber over and around him. I had to use the shotgun to lever him off me, then with one final effort, I clambered free of him, gave the door a heave and then spilled out onto the wet grass at the side of the road.

The Nissan's lights continued to burn, so I had some illumination to get my bearings. I had to be quick because not far down the hill, I could see occasional flashes of light from the Land Cruiser rounding a bend. Would they stop before or after?

I had to keep them guessing, so I shut the door then smashed all the headlights and driving lights before rolling into the shrubbery behind the tree we'd hit. I had to remember the layout in the sudden darkness broken only by the feeble light given off by one parking light and the glow from the dashboard inside the car.

I'd barely settled when the air filled with the sound of squirming, squealing tyres protesting at being forced to turn at too high a speed. The trees lit up as the Land Cruiser swung into the corner. Eddie must have been pushing things in an attempt to catch up and had made the same mistake as Luka in misjudging the tightness of the bend. They sideswiped the back end of the Nissan, took out a swathe of guideposts, but managed to get back onto four wheels before disappearing further up the road.

The world returned to quiet and eerie darkness. What would they do? They'd have to investigate, but what would Chiang's priority be? Kill Jessica then investigate, or investigate first. I prayed for the latter. The thought of Jessica dead boiled my blood. Chiang would pay. They both would.

Scrambling back to the car, I got the rear door open and, with half my body inside, started searching through Jimbo's pockets until I found what I wanted: a fistful of shotgun cartridges. Pained breathing was coming from the front. The dash lights were still aglow, revealing the gory mess that was Lachlan's thigh. His pulsing blood had the bile rising in my throat. He wasn't going to make it. Luka wasn't moving, but I didn't think I'd hit him too hard, so he was still a cause for concern. Hopefully, the airbag would hold him.

I slid back onto the road just as the first rays of the headlights from the returning Land Cruiser fingered the trees lining the road, standing like so many silent witnesses. Then I raced across to the other side and dived into the bushes opposite the Nissan moments before they cleared the bend at a more sedate pace. They pulled over onto the narrow verge a few car lengths upslope from where I hid.

They kept the motor running. And just sat there. What were they doing inside? What of Jessica? I dared not move until the situation clarified itself. But I was ready for anything. The gun was reloaded, and I was in an ugly mood. There would be no discussions. After a painfully long time, Eddie clambered out, looked around, then started carefully angling across the road towards the wreck, his "necklace" dangling from his right hand.

I had to get to the Land Cruiser before Eddie discovered I was on the loose, but every slithering move I made towards it seemed to find a new twig to snap and crunch. It was only a matter of seconds before Eddie heard me. I made about a car length when he turned at the noise and probably glimpsed me in the shadows that I hoped would hide me. With surprising speed, and joy it seemed, he turned back and sprinted towards me. I had to get Chiang before Eddie got to me and Chiang was on the driver's side.

Slithering and stumbling on the grass and eucalypt leaves, I started up and managed to get to the car ahead of him, then kept going, getting a glimpse of Chiang, with Jessica a blur beside him. Rounding the car with Eddie's heavy breathing seemingly in my ear, I tried escaping by diving back into the shrubbery. Eddie must have launched his necklace at me because the edge of my heel shrieked from its sting. I kept moving, though now with a hobble. It was enough to allow Eddie to launch a flying rugby tackle. And he had me. Falling, I twisted, wanting to face my attacker, who landed on top of me with his head at my knees. A skull beautifully placed for a savage hit with the butt of the shotgun. I hit him two more times, each as vicious as the first, until he stopped moving, then I dragged myself from under him and lay panting for a few breaths. I dared no more.

Ripping the blood-soaked beanie off his skull, I put it on, then manhandled the body to liberate its leather jacket, which I wriggled into. In the dull red glow from the taillights, I hoped Chiang would assume it was Eddie returning, at least long enough to delay him killing Jessica. I was assuming he hadn't already done so because he seemed like a planner, the type unwilling to give up a piece while it still held value.

By now, I was slowly walking back. Chiang moved his head to check the rear mirror, and I raised my right hand in half-hearted acknowledgement, plodded closer, hunched over, keeping my face in shadow and giving the impression of exhaustion, which wasn't hard to do.

Chiang wound down his window and shouted: 'Well! What happened?'

His head was almost out of the car as I drew alongside. I had hidden the shotgun up my left sleeve, which proved a bad move because it couldn't be brought to bear quickly enough in this situation. Only one mad ploy sprang to mind. I'd never seen it done and never tried it myself, but it was all I had. Leaning forward as if about to give my report, I whipped my right hand at his face, palm up, fingers like claws and hooked two of them into his nostrils. Then I jerked his head forward and down onto the blade of the window glass that protruded a few centimetres above the sill. And ripped the door open.

Chiang sagged sideways but was stopped from falling out by the seatbelt. To finish the job, I kneed him in the head and immediately regretted it, but not half as much as he did. He flopped back, gurgling, his uncoordinated trembling hands struggling to open his crushed larynx. Unbuckling his seatbelt, I pulled him from the car, dumped him on the bitumen and slammed the door. Once in the driver's seat and strapped in, I carefully placed the shotgun in the passenger footwell.

A breath, and then over my left shoulder: 'You okay back there?' My voice sounded gravelly and strange. Jessica didn't reply. I turned further. She was awake, breathing fast and shallow, with eyes on stalks and filled with horror. Horror at me and what I'd done. But I couldn't do anything about that, for now at least.

'We're going home.'

Selecting Drive, I indicated, then slowly moved off and took my time getting up to speed. Each bend seemed to require an inordinate amount of concentration, and I had to grip the wheel tighter than normal – my hands were starting to shake.

Chapter Twenty Nine

Luina appeared quickly and just as quickly vanished into the night. By then, I had the hands and breathing under control, but the destination was less so. Where exactly were we going? Home, I'd said. But where is that?

I didn't have the energy to make it all the way back to her folks in Launceston and it was too late to stir anyone in Waratah, so Sheffield or the farm at Moina seemed the only options. But they were hardly what I would have called *home*.

Home, as an idea, became easier to chew upon as the country opened up on the approach to the farm. But the more I chewed, the clearer the conclusion was that I didn't really have one – not a place one feels really comfortable in, a place imbibed with one's spirit, one's personality – a sort of representation of oneself in bricks and mortar and a garden. I'd bought a house in Perth, rented the farm, the place in Sheffield and the apartment in Launceston, but none of them felt like a home. Even my flat in Melbourne, as comfortable as it was, lacked that missing something. Or should I say, *someone*. I glanced in the rearview mirror, trying for a glimpse of Jessica. She was a shadow created by the dull ruby glow from the dashboard display, just sitting still, her eyes slowly blinking, staring at the headrest in front of her. She was there but not there. I sighed but didn't abandon hope. We'd try for Sheffield.

The lights of Waratah were coming to an end when they reminded me that there was a world of people beyond the car I had to consider. There was a bus bay on the edge of town into which I stopped.

'Got to make a few phone calls,' I said to Jessica, who said nothing, just nodded weakly and continued her hypnotising of the headrest.

The phone was in the back, so I had to get out, open the tailgate and rummage in my daypack to locate the satellite phone, realising in the process that I was still wearing Eddie's hat and coat. Pulling the cap off, I grimaced when I touched sticky congealing blood, felt the same disgust at locating more of it on my favourite red jumper when removing the jacket. The luggage bay's cold interior lighting revealed hands smeared dark red, with an even darker red patch on my jumper that was flecked with little odd-shaped pieces of Jimbo's face. I almost puked; I didn't feel like removing the jumper, instead did a lot of frenzied wiping of my hands on the dewy grass along the roadside, then used my trousers to dry them. Feeling marginally cleaner, I was ready to start punching numbers.

Harvey first. I left a brief message to say we were both safe and heading to Sheffield. Jessica's folks were next. Unable to face a conversation, I left the briefest of messages and added her probable return being late afternoon. Aberdare didn't reply, as expected. My message to him was a little more specific: that there was a crashed car on the B23 just west of Luina, which he and the AFP urgently needed to investigate. They would also need an ambulance as well as a tow truck. I, of course, mentioned that Jessica and I were safe and heading back to Launceston, which was sort of true.

Should I have called the local emergency number? The wreck wasn't obstructing the road for anyone driving normally, and there was no one inside or out that deserved too much sympathy, so I decided to delay directly reporting the accident until Aberdare called.

I'd barely re-settled in the driver's seat when the phone

sprang to life, jabbing me with a fright I didn't need. It was Aberdare. Didn't he sleep?

'What the hell have you been up to? The Feds are hopping mad. Told me I was to report, day or night …' "Night" was said with bitterness. '… if you contacted me. Do you know what time it is? Anyway, who's in this car, and why do we care?'

After a breath to collect my thoughts, I gave as coherent a story as I could in the brief time I felt I had. He grunted as a reply, then, after a lull, said he'd fix things and then promised to catch up with me in Launceston. He ordered me to stay put in the apartment and not stray for any reason until the whole business had been resolved.

I had almost signed off before I remembered the drug shipment. 'Before you go, there's another small job for you to organise.'

He groaned.

'A big drugs delivery is to be dispatched from Lewington – tonight, probably around the seven o'clock mark and probably in a Tridee Transport truck, or trucks. The survivors of the crash may be able to help with the details. I'll give you a call later with my ideas of how the operation might work. Around noon. Need some sleep first or you'll get no sense from me. Okay?'

After another noncommittal grunt, he hung up. Not wanting any distractions on those narrow winding roads through the forests between Waratah and Sheffield, I did the sensible thing and turned the phone off.

With some of the loose ends about to be taken care of, I moved off cautiously but with a growing sense of relief. There were a couple of trucks heading north on the A10, but once I'd turned left onto the Cradle Mountain road, I had the road to myself. It was considerably narrower than the highway, with the encroaching shrubbery too close for comfort. I started praying for no further close encounters with the local wildlife.

I began to ache for the more open country passed the farm heading to Moina, where the driving would be easier. A car zoomed past in the opposite direction but braked suddenly, which had me thinking they were going to do a handbrake U-turn, like in the movies. And like the movies, it's often the bad guys doing such stunts. The hairs on my neck prickled while I strangled the wheel at the thought of another battle. Happily, they thought better of it and kept going.

It was a close call that had me wondering if it was more crooks or the Feds rushing to the crash site, who, in recognising my car, had considered chasing me before quickly giving up in favour of maintaining their course. With the kayak strapped on top, there would be no hiding from anyone, friend or foe. It was like driving around with a flashing neon arrow pointing down at us.

After that, more sweat was raised from mulling over the possibilities of what the Feds and the local police might do once they'd come to some conclusions as to what had gone down at the crash site. How soon would they come hunting me and Jessica? She was mixed up in this affair up to her neck, especially after that royal tour of the drug lab and who knew what else. And with the Chinese government involved, and ours too probably, all sorts of dirty deals were possible. Pawns like Jessica and me were decidedly expendable. I needed time to think.

And one of the things I really needed was a few aces up my sleeve, like some allies with clout. The farm was a few kilometres away. I pulled in and stopped in front of the closed gates.

'Jessica. Snap out of it!' I said, shaking her knee.

The rest must have had some effect because she took a breath, seemed to wake, blinked hard before trying to focus on my voice and my hand on her knee.

'The drama isn't over yet. I need your help. I think the Federal Police may try to arrest us and hush things up, or at the very least give us both a hard time on any number of bogus charges. You with me? You're a reporter, you must understand how …'

'Okay. Okay. I'm getting the picture.' She shook her head as if clearing the remaining fog. 'What do you want me to do?'

'We'll start simple. Be a love and open the gate and then close it after. When you get back in, dig out your phone. If you still have it. We …'

'Enough, enough!' she said, then slipped from the seatbelt and opened the door. She almost fell out of the car, her legs barely able to hold her. But she was moving a whole lot better by the time I had the car on the other side of the gate and she had strapped herself into the front passenger seat.

She glanced over and had a proper look at me for the first time since coming back to some semblance of normality. 'Jeezuz, you're a mess. Is that …?' she said with a face wrinkled with disgust and fear.

'Yeah … 'fraid so. Rescuing you has been a messy, ugly business. We now have to try and make sure things don't get any messier when the cops eventually track us down. All those dead and dying bodies ….'

'Shoosh. I'm trying to forget. Was it all so necessary? What you did to Chiang ….'

'… was the only way to get you out alive. All he had to do was a quick chop to your epiglottis and you'd have been as dead as a doornail. It was him or …'

'Okay, okay, but what about this gun?' She nudged the shotgun gingerly with a toe.

'The safety is on, but if it bothers you, stick it behind my feet. I want it close, just in case.' I didn't know in case of what, but I'd had enough desperate situations for one night and having some firepower was a confidence booster. A microsecond after that thought, I realised that I now understood how Jimbo felt — felt the seductive power a gun transfers to its master. I shook my head to free myself from the dangers of such intoxicating notions.

A minute or so later, we were at the farmhouse. Security lights came on as we passed the building to end up in the old stables. I parked the car but left the motor running, hoping Harvey had organised the bunks he had talked about – I desperately needed to catch a few hours of sleep before approaching the uncertainties awaiting us in Sheffield and later in Launceston. There was one thing I'd forgotten. Harvey had installed an alarm, and I didn't have the code.

I sat for a moment just listening to the motor and thinking. Jessica started to fidget. 'What's going on now?' she said, then added, 'You do realise that, in your company, I seem to say that a lot.'

I glanced at her, checking her face in the light from the instruments and was relieved to see a forgiving smile. What a relief!

'Sorry about that, but circumstances seem to get complicated around you.'

'Me! Don't you mean you!'

'Well – yes. You've got me there but …' I was waving my hands as further words seemed inadequate.

She relented; patted my knee; cautiously, after searching for a patch free of dubious stains. 'We'll call a truce. Is there a bed inside? I'm all in.'

I explained about the alarm. 'Call Harvey,' was her reply.

So I phoned him – four times – before he took the call. Surviving his unhappy greeting, I explained about the change of plans and my worries regarding the police. He was silent for a while, then told me the code to get in and mentioned that there were plenty of cameras around. As we spoke, he said that he had the Land Cruiser on his screen.

'I've turned the alarm off, so you can make yourselves

comfortable, though I might start the cameras rolling, they usually only turn on if an infrared beam is tripped to not waste hours looking at nothing. Anyway, you'll be happy to know you'll not be filmed while inside the house.'

'Thanks, Harvey. But we'll behave ourselves nonetheless.' We both had a chuckle.

'You reckon the cops will try Sheffield first?'

'I think they have a good idea where I'm likely to be, so it won't take them long to come sniffing around the farm. We need some sort of backup. Any ideas?' He didn't interrupt so I kept going. 'I'm going to get my lawyer in Melbourne to fly over, but that will be days away, and a lot can happen in the next few hours. I'll get Jessica to speak to her folks to get them over here, preferably with a lawyer or two. And I'll get her to talk to Higgins at *The Age* to have the press on our case. But that will all take time which I don't reckon we have. So if you can think of anything, call my satellite phone.'

Harvey ended with a: "I'll see what I can do," after which I switched off the car, grabbed the gun and my bag from the back and we headed inside. The place had been transformed with a coat of paint and a tidy up. He'd even junked the rickety dining chairs and replaced them with six metal and plastic jobs, the type used by cafés, ones you could sit comfortably in for hours. But we were interested in the bedrooms, and I needed a wash.

One room contained four new, sturdy wood-framed bunks. But no mattresses or linen. The other, bigger room, had a new Queen size bed, with a mattress and pillows but no linen. There was an ancient but solid wooden wardrobe that looked like a veteran of many house moves. Jessica investigated.

'I'll make the bed. You'd better get cleaned up,' she said from the wardrobe while assessing the linen stacked on the shelves.

Thankfully the bathroom and loo had been given a thorough clean and Harvey had reconnected the gas so I had hot water. I piled my pants, jumper and shirt neatly in a corner and, after a splash, returned dressed in my spare clothes; blue jeans, T-shirt with a lumberjack shirt on top, feeling foolish to be fully dressed in preparation for bed, but I didn't know what arrangements Jessica had in mind.

She was on the phone, now plugged into a socket near the left side of the bed, talking, probably to Higgins from the sound of the conversation. I was amazed she'd managed to raise him, then stood for a while looking surplus to requirements until she became annoyed and pulled the sheet open on the right side and distractedly patted the sheets for me to get in.

So I stripped back to my T-shirt and undies and slipped in. I was starting to relax, and though desperate for a few hours of shuteye, I couldn't while Jessica was on the phone. She ended the call.

'That was Higgins. I used his emergency number. He'll have a film crew over at dawn in a helicopter. I'll ring my dad. Get him organised, then join you.'

'Good. If I nod off, which is unlikely, set the timer for two and a half hours. I hope it will wake us, as I reckon we don't have much more time than that before they figure out where we are.' I gave her a smile then settled down to study the ceiling and listen to her attempts to call her folks.

She got through surprisingly quickly, considering the hour, which was getting close to four. She gave them enough information to explain some of the whys of our situation, sufficient to have her dad see the serious possibilities we still faced. There was a brief pause, then Jessica nodded as if in agreement and hung up.

She sat for a moment, breathing heavily, then seemed to calm as if becoming comfortable with newly arranged thoughts. She spent a few seconds setting the alarm on the phone, then left the phone on charge on the floor beside the bed. She rose and, turning, saw the silly expectant look on my face.

'Forget what you're thinking. Nothing but sleep is going to happen. And there's no need to be so happy.' But she was smiling when she said it.

Despite her warnings, I still watched as she stripped down to bra and panties then neatly put her clothes into the wardrobe before turning off the light switch on the doorframe. In the sudden dark, she collided with the bed end, turning the darkness blue with very colourful remarks, after which she collapsed onto her side.

Allowing a few moments for her to settle, I rolled over and sent an exploratory hand towards her hip, found it warm, soft and oh so inviting – for a nanosecond. She shoved it aside with tremendous vigour.

'It's okay. I just wanted … You to know how happy I am to know you're safe.'

She didn't turn, just released a long slow breath and spoke into the darkness. 'I'm happy too. And truly thankful for all you've done, but I'm tired and still a little frightened about what happens next. So …'

I rolled back and let things subside, for a while listened to the silence of the house and then quietly said to the darkness: 'Good night, Jessica.'

'Good night, Julius,' she mumbled, her breathing already at that slow steadiness that precedes slumber.

My last thought was that maybe some progress had been made in my wooing of her. At least I could truthfully say to myself that I had got to the stage of sleeping with her. Laughing at myself was the last memory before the blessed blanket of sleep closed over me.

Chapter Thirty

Thirty seconds later, or so it seemed, Jessica was kicking me awake: none too gently.

'The alarm!' she spoke into her pillow. All I could do was grunt and try to get my eyes working. She kicked again. I got the message: I was getting up, and she was sleeping.

I managed to get the phone unplugged and silent again, then grabbed my clothes and dressed in the kitchen/lounge room; put on the central light and instantly regretted it, but persevered. It was a little before six. The sun would be up shortly, then the fun would begin. I pulled back a few curtains, thick, aqua blue and very new, and saw signs of the yet to rise sun trying to make an impression on an overcast sky – overcast and iffy, just like my prospects of a good day ahead.

I sent Harvey a text just to let him know we were awake, went back to the car to rescue my picnic basket then made a start on breakfast. Harvey replied with a text: "Be there, 7:30, with some of the boys. Make sure Jessica is dressed, don't want to excite them too much."

Not sure what "some of the boys" meant but having some witnesses around would make the police, of any persuasion, a little more amenable to reason, or so I hoped. I reset the alarm for seven-fifteen, then brewed tea and dished up the food I'd organised for the day before. I went to fetch Jessica, but she was sound asleep, so I ate and cogitated alone.

At seven-fourteen, I was shaking her awake and having a hard time fending off her punches. Finally, with a scream of exasperation, she flipped over to glare at me, then threw the covers off and pushed me roughly aside before thumping over to the wardrobe. I watched her dress, enjoying that male pleasure unleashed when studying a beautiful woman in motion.

She glared again on the way to the bathroom. I yelled, 'Tea and breakfast is on the table.'

The sawn-off shotgun was in my bag with the laptop and a few other bits and pieces. It would be useful to have it handy should things go pear-shaped, so I took the bag and placed it on a spare chair at the table, next to my spot.

I didn't have to wait long for things to happen. A roar of approaching cars desecrated the silence, resulting in me racing to the window in a panic that it was the police, not Harvey and friends. The pulse soon came back under control when I recognised Stanko's big Nissan Patrol in the lead. Eight more Nissans followed, all serious off-roaders with mud plugger tyres, suspension kits, aerials, bars and lights. Harvey's truck was bringing up the rear. They lined up either side of the house, in a shallow V, like a guard of honour, and kept their motors going for a while, probably enjoying the raucous symphony generated by overlarge exhaust pipes. In an irregular wave, they grew silent and Harvey stepped out, sauntered towards the house, on the way giving some of the cars a slap on their bullbars or their drivers a smiling thumbs up.

We met on the verandah.

'You and your boys certainly know how to make an impressive entrance.'

'Yeah, pretty awesome when you get a bunch of serious four-wheel drivers together. You can thank Stanko and his buddies from the Patrol Club. Had to spin a bit of a story about you being falsely accused of using the farm as a drug lab. Said that if you got banged up, Stanko and the rest of the crew would be out of a job unless something wasn't done to get those dickheads to see reason. Stanko is the Patrol Club's captain. It's almost Friday, so a bit of fun wasn't hard to sell to the rest of the members. I've told them to stay close to their cars just in case. I wasn't specific.'

I waved to the guys, received a chorus of air horn blasts in reply, and then ushered Harvey inside.

'Left a few cars at the gate, on the inside, blocking the way. Don't want to make things too easy for the coppers. You certain the cops will show?'

'Yeah. Sort of involved in the death of …' I had to do a quick tally. '… three, and maybe two more. And left plenty of evidence behind, like fingerprints and my phone. So it wouldn't be too hard to stitch me up for murder if they decided not to listen to my side of the story, which is likely. There are national and international considerations involved and, when that happens, you really are up the creek.'

'As in Shit Creek in a barbed wire canoe.'

'That's the one. The news people will be arriving at some stage by helicopter, so I'm promised. And Jessica's parents and possibly a lawyer will hopefully turn up. The more witnesses, the harder for them to cover things up and pin the blame on me, and Jessica.'

Harvey grunted in reply.

By this time, we'd made it inside, leaving the door open. Jessica was just getting started on her breakfast and patted the seat beside her. I made a start towards it, but Harvey beat me to it.

'Good to see you, Harvey. Have you come to rescue a damsel in distress?'

'Yes, ma'am. Me and the boys are here to serve.'

They were both laying it on thick just to put me in my place. I joined them in their fun then suggested more tea. Jessica said no, but Harvey was game, though insisted on the fortified version, so I had to hunt for the bottle of *Tarkine Mist* and hope there was still some left and that it was bottled in Australia and not the "supercharged" export product. I checked the label: it was the homebrew.

Harvey had scoffed down a piece of toast and was making a start on his tea when he received a call. He put it over the speaker. A very excited voice started narrating the unfolding drama being recorded on the screen. A swarm of marked and unmarked cop cars, flashing like Christmas trees had arrived, choking the entrance, with officers banked up behind the gates demanding that the fellows working on the first car open up and let them in. But the car was jammed up against the gate, with both rear wheels off and the back resting in the mud. A couple of wheels lay close by, and a balloon jack lay under the rear diff but was uninflated.

Over the excited yells of the cops, you could just hear the driver, a bulky guy in jeans and a checked flannelette shirt, trying to explain the difficulties they were having getting the car fixed.

'Who's doing the filming?' I asked.

'I think it's a bloke called Steve – he owns the second car. Told them to take the rear wheels off and promised that we'd pay for any damages.'

'Steve, don't put up any resistance to these guys; just do what they say. You're doing a great job. See you soon, down at the farmhouse. Just follow the track … assuming they let you. Got lawyers and a helicopter of journalists arriving shortly. Take it easy but keep filming as long as possible. Bye.'

'No probs, Harvey.'

A bunch of guys in black with high-powered rifles then jumped the gate and started marching down the track. 'Better go,' said Steve, and the filming ended.

I didn't like the way things were developing. 'Jessica, maybe it's wisest if you grab your phone, a few towels and then lie down in the bathtub. If those idiots with the guns get stupid, hopefully that cast iron tub will protect you. You could try calling your folks. Tell them the police have arrived but explain we have plenty of supporters. Try to …'

'What about you?'

'I'm their target so … Look … one last time. Please just do what I say.'

After a moment of intense scrutiny, she stood, came over and, with hands on my shoulders, planted an intense, open-eyed kiss on my lips. Then, without a word, she dashed off to the bathroom.

Harvey and I exchanged looks and then had a think. The sound of a 'chopper approaching decided the issue. 'Grab a chair and your cup. We're going to meet them on the verandah, for all to see. Hope they've got the cameras going up there. Get your phone out and start filming and get your boys out of their cars and on their phones and filming too. We don't want any of the action missed.'

'Smart thinking. Let's go.'

The line of men in black crested the ridge, jogging in a skirmish line, rifles to their shoulders and swinging them from side to side, again like in the movies. And, just like the movies, they encountered an army of cameramen taking in their every move. They slowed, then about a hundred metres out, stopped, dropped to their knees but continued to swing their guns around, though with less enthusiasm, perhaps confused by having too many targets. The helicopter had landed briefly, it seemed, somewhere behind the house, then, by the sound of things, had taken off again. I caught a glimpse of it as it made a wide and high circuit over the scene.

One of the riflemen had a hand to his ear and seemed to be in conversation. Then he gave orders to his troops to relax, or whatever the military term is because they all stopped waving their guns, choosing instead to lie prone on the cold, wet grass with guns cradled in their arms. Perhaps some sanity was starting to emerge.

The man with his finger in his ear was still talking. The helicopter continued to circle. The next development was a bunch of regular police and three guys in dark suits hoofing it down the track. The regular police stopped in an irregular line behind the ranks of prostrate shooters while one of the plainclothes men, a big fellow in a dark blue suit, consulted the Tactical Response Squad's commander.

Noises from behind the house became a "Hello" from the contingent off the helicopter. Jessica appeared cautiously at the front door.

'It's Higgins, with a cameraman. I told him to go slowly around the front and meet me here.'

I shook my head. 'Wow! He got here quick. There's no stopping him if a big story is in the wind. Wow.'

Higgins and assistant must have become visible to the watchers because all eyes turned, and a ripple of tension ran through them. The head detective shook his head, spoke to the commander of the gunmen then started to stroll down towards the house. The guys in black looked decidedly disappointed.

Higgins left the cameraman to do his thing and, armed with a microphone, joined us on the verandah.

'Jessica, be a darling and bring out two chairs. One for you and one for your boss.'

She frowned but disappeared and soon enough returned banging and clattering the chairs, then with little grace thumped them down either side of us. She was not amused but kept silent as Higgins reached the steps. He nodded to her then took up the seat next to me. She sat next to Harvey, who smiled as though he'd won a prize.

'Morning, Higgins; this is Harvey. As you can see, your star reporter is alive and definitely kicking.'

We exchanged smiles, mine mischievous. Hers was harder to define. At least her frown had softened.

'And this fellow must be from the Federal Police. Am I correct?'

Harvey was still filming, making the fellow, who was undoubtedly Mr Confidence in most situations but with us more like a rookie dealing with his first domestic dispute, and with his sergeant watching on and keeping score. His discomfort was encouraging.

'Harvey, we have an important visitor, so perhaps we'll leave the filming to the professionals.' The cameraman had followed the guy in and stood a few paces behind him.

I stood up as the fellow came in range for a handshake. He was an Aussie, clean-shaven, with a chunky build going soft, probably from too much desk work.

'Julius Tiberius Banks. I guess you are with the Federal Police?'

He shook my proffered hand – for the cameras – then was unhappily silent for a second as he scanned my support crew, who returned his gaze with a confidence that seemed to sap his. Eventually, he spoke in an educated Aussie accent, 'Alonso Picarri.'

'Well, Alonso, are you here to sort things out? Here to find out the truth or to stitch us up?' There was no point beating around the bushes.

'And I hope you guys haven't given up on tonight's big drugs shipment. It needs to be dealt with. We suffered too much to get that information and hence don't want our near-death exploits wasted for political reasons.'

He didn't like the way things were going. 'Just take it easy, Mr Banks. Perhaps there is a more private space to discuss matters.'

We were less than a metre apart, so to soften him up further,

I fixed my gaze directly at him, eyeball to eyeball. Us fellows find such situations most distressing. I hoped he was no different from the rest. He resisted at first, tried to divert his eyes, but I stayed with him. The tussle ended with him blinking first. He was no longer in command. It was just like those bouts we had at the temple when learning to use the staff, learning to capture the Chi energy of your opponent before you made your first strike. Do that, and a win was almost guaranteed.

'Okay. We'll do as you wish: go inside for ten minutes or so, for a nice cup of tea and a chat. But first, tell your buddies to move back to the crest of the rise to give us all a bit of breathing space, calm the situation, and to signal the genuineness of your intentions.'

He was none too happy but did so with his colleagues equally reluctant to comply. Once inside, I sat him at the table but on the opposite side of my bag, in which the shotgun lay. He had his back to the door, which I had left open. It was an uncomfortable position for him, designed to further sap his remaining Chi. I was going to set the agenda and would do so from a position of physical and psychological superiority.

'It's herb tea, so probably not your usual drink, but it is hot and it's still pretty cool in here.' I slid the mug across to him and then took up my seat opposite.

'I think it best if you tell me what you know, or think you know. I presume you have been tracking my movements and have been up to the crash site.'

He was reluctant to talk, but I reminded him that unless he did, I would blab everything to Higgins and it would be on the internet and national television within minutes. My version of events, not his.

We covered the basics but there was too much to clarify in one ten-minute conversation, so we decided on a location for the next one. It wasn't an easy task as he wanted it behind closed doors in some government office. But I didn't have that much faith in him, and even less in the government. A compromise was reached. A date, time and place was agreed on, as well as contact numbers and email addresses.

We rose together, but I stopped him before we moved off. 'You never showed me your ID. I'd appreciate it if you did now just so we keep things on the straight and narrow.'

He hesitated, presumably not used to being put upon, more practised at applying the pressure. But he did as asked, pulling a badge from an inside pocket of his jacket, in the process revealing a pistol strapped in a shoulder holster. He saw my knowing grin, then suddenly lightened up as he passed me the badge. Perhaps we were beginning to understand each other.

'Nice photo,' I said as I returned it. 'Didn't think you were AFP. I hope your masters in Canberra don't try anything stupid. I'm a wealthy man with expensive lawyers to call on, and this episode won't disappear from the news if your lot, shall we say, try to ration the truth. I think the best way out is to concentrate on the drug shipment going out tonight and gloss over the international implications of Mr Chiang's involvement.'

He nodded, and we reached the door. I let him go first then stopped him before he got to the steps. 'Just for our comfort, it would be beneficial if you could call your friends on the hill and explain the arrangements. We'll wait here until they comply.'

He was circumspect but pulled out his phone and told the person in charge to move the troops back and send them back to barracks as the situation had been clarified. It had been a false alarm.

'If you could wait a minute or two to let your men get clear, I can drive you to the gate. It's quite a walk and all uphill.'

I think Higgins was disappointed at the change in the situation. The drama was leaking away.

An interminable time elapsed before the Tactical Response

Squad and police left, and the helicopter returned to retrieve a disappointed Higgins. The one good note was Jessica's parents arriving.

Once the family reunion was over, Jessica and her mother kept themselves busy scouring the cupboards for supplies, after which they cooked a big stodge of bacon and beans and whatever else they found as breakfast for the lads from the Nissan Patrol Club. While the situation was dispersing, I handed Alonso the sawn-off shotgun wrapped in a towel then had a long chat with him near Stanko's car, though both of us were careful not to get too close to its grimy exterior. It was a more casual sizing each other up exercise, which resulted in us having greater hopes of a sensible resolution to the situation. I even suggested a chemical theory as to how the drugs were being smuggled out undetected.

Once he received the call to say they'd all gone, save his partner with their car, I drove him to the gate, shook hands and watched them disappear down the road. I waited a long while to make sure they weren't trying a sneaky return, but mostly just to relax. Leaning on the closed gate, the metal still damp and cold, the simple act of breathing in the freshness of the country air proved wonderfully therapeutic as was the quiet, disturbed only by the occasional sound of birds or a cow complaining in a far off paddock. I was invigorated by a sense of freedom last tasted a lifetime ago.

Eventually, I went back to the car, did a U-turn then cruised down to the farmhouse filled with confidence that the tide was finally turning in our favour. 'Our' favour? As in Jessica and me? That concept was still harder to untangle than all the subterfuge surrounding Lachlan's behaviour, the drug lab setup and its workings, not to mention all the international political game playing that lay behind it.

No, I wasn't home yet. Whatever I meant by the term.

Chapter Thirty One

We had a conference standing around the dining table, Jessica, her mum and dad at the sink tidying up the dishes. I thanked Harvey and the boys for their efforts, then made a big point of saying the drilling program was continuing and that I'd sorted out the misunderstanding over drug labs. I advised them not to share their footage with too many others because delicate negotiations were ongoing. Soon after, joking and laughing, they jostled out through the door and moved off like a trumpeting herd of elephants going flat-out up the farm track towards the gate.

The shock of the ensuing silence left those of us remaining too stunned to put words in our mouths. The moment passed. I escorted Harvey out to the steps to see him off. Jessica's dad came out to join us on the verandah, where together we watched silently as Harvey's big four-wheel drive vanished over the rise.

'Jessica's told me some of the ordeal she and you had to overcome. Seeing all those police certainly caused me a turn, I can tell you.' He paused, probably felt as awkward as me, but undoubtedly for different reasons. 'I think it best if she comes home for a while, assuming you feel the police will keep up their end of the bargain you seemed to have struck with them.'

The thought of Jessica once again slipping from my fingers left me feeling less than enthusiastic, but I had to say something. 'You're probably right. She's been through the meat grinder in the last few weeks, and all because of me, I'm sorry to say. But none of it was of my doing. As much as I can figure, it appears my business manager, Lachlan Lucas, started it all. Seems he was cursed with too much ambition and too little sense. Got himself suckered into debts he couldn't manage. He tried killing me to have his wife-to-be – my soon to be ex-wife – inherit all my fortune, not just a third as per our prenuptial agreement. I reckon if it came down to it and Lucinda didn't give him full access to her inheritance, he'd have found a way to become a widower.'

'So how does this drug business come into it? Jessica tried to explain but …'

'There's a global financial war going on between China and America. You must have heard about it on the news, the effects at least, if not the rationale behind it. The Chinese saw Lachlan as a way to contribute to one aspect of that war by using his money problems as leverage to get him involved in an illicit drug smuggling scheme, which involves a mine, possibly, and definitely a distillery here in Tasmania. The distillery belongs to my company, JTB Holdings Limited. I think some fancy biochemistry, provided by elements in the Chinese government, was being used to add undetected into our whisky some chemical components that are either extracted at the destination and sold as some novel but devastating recreational drug, or perhaps left in, with its effects being more subtle but probably as insidious.'

He looked incredulous.

'Yeah. It's all too bizarre to believe and I sometimes doubt it myself, but Jessica had a tour of their underground drug lab … and the numerous attempts to kill, first me, and then the both of us, are proof enough. And it's not over yet. I still have to negotiate our official release from being associated with this mess, of which I am hopeful but not certain. She can help by sending a detailed email of everything she learnt during her tour of the lab. I'll give it to Alonso when I see him tomorrow. That's her first job. Hopefully, it will suffice, and she can be spared a grilling.'

He nodded and seemed thankful that Jessica was going to be kept from further involvement.

'But everything is still in flux, so keep an eye on her. You saw how easy it was for her to be abducted. I think you are old and wise enough to understand how keen authorities are to find suitable scapegoats to take the wrap for situations they find embarrassing or too hot to handle. My task over the next few days is to ensure Jessica and I regain some normality in our lives.'

He nodded again. Shortly after, we were joined by Jessica and her mother. I knew what was coming.

'Time to go?' I said to make our parting a little easier.

'Yes,' said Jessica in a weary, almost melancholic voice.

'I'll be in touch. Your dad has a little job for you when you get home, which should keep you from further drama. This affair is still touch-and-go as far as I'm concerned, so don't get separated and stay vigilant.'

I was lecturing again but couldn't help myself. They seemed to understand. Jessica gave me a hug. I shook hands with both her parents, and they walked over to where they'd parked the car. With departing waves, they soon joined the cavalcade of those who'd disappeared over the hill.

I went back inside. It was just me now, and all I had to do was a last-minute tidy up, lock the doors and drive off, once I'd texted Harvey to set the alarms.

The cloud cover had eased by the time I got back to Launceston. I'd left the kayak and the roof rack back at the farm and felt marginally less conspicuous as I parked the Land Cruiser. I took the lift up to my apartment, had a long shower, had a meal sent up and spent the rest of the afternoon stretched out on the sofa, my time split between dozing and bouts of worrisome thought experiments.

Somehow night arrived, then turned into day. Around nine, Jessica's concise and detailed email came through that, after reading it, I forwarded it to Alonso. It gave him a few hours to study it. A minute or so before noon, I strolled into the city library seconds ahead of Alonso, who followed me as I scanned the room for a suitable location. We eventually settled at a small nest of tables with no one in earshot. Spotting a few suspicious characters trolling the shelves, I assumed they were Alonso's flunkies there for backup.

Earlier, Ravi had messaged to say he couldn't make it, so we decided he'd stay in Melbourne and attend via the phone. Alonso wasn't happy sharing our chat with the phone but acquiesced, though with Ravi listening in, he was most careful with his language and tried not to give away too many compromising details.

His news was all good. Luka was recovering from my tap with the gun butt and was being held on charges relating to the drugs operation. But the most important outcome was that Alonso felt confident Jessica and I would survive the ongoing enquiries unscathed, thanks to Chiang's involvement. Though damaged, he'd survived but wouldn't be making too many long speeches from now on. Apparently, he was already on his way back to China, thanks to diplomatic immunity. But his prospects upon return weren't promising. I wasn't shedding tears.

We were almost done when I felt compelled to ask for more on the drug bust in Lewington. I'd spent much of my time the day before and in the morning scanning for news relating to our troubles. There had been a report about the blockage to the B23 with a few blurry aerial shots of the crash. It was theorised that it was caused by a deadly internal dispute amongst drug dealers. They then tied it in with a siege at a remote farmhouse, which included more aerial shots showing the farm, the sheds and the cars lined up with the besieging tactical response squad doing their thing. But no mention of me, Jessica or Chiang. I guess Higgins had to be happy with the crumbs he'd been allowed to air. Apart from that, there had been nothing.

'So, what happened last night in Lewington?'

'Two trucks and their drivers were taken in. We raided the farmhouse and found the drug lab. It was a neat set-up with a tunnel connecting it to the fake underground fuel tanks at the engineering works – all the staff there and at the farm were rounded up and are … assisting us with our enquires.' He smiled, which was a rare event.

'It will take a while to figure things out, especially the sneaky way they were shipping the drugs, but preliminary lab test seems to confirm your suspicions. The export whisky was doped up in Lewington. That bottling operation in the shed was just a blind to keep the publican sweet, thinking he was getting bootleg booze for nothing. It got rid of the siphoned off whisky that allowed room for their magic additives whilst putting the publican in their pocket.'

'So the local version of *Tarkine Mist* was kosher, only the exported stuff was doped up?'

'Yeah. I talked to one of the drug squad guys involved, who said his chemists were very excited at the novel way they'd done it. Too complicated for me but apparently involved two ingredients, not overly exotic or harmful in themselves, but when combined with ethanol and digestive enzymes, it did some weird and powerful stuff. All too technical for me but apparently with big implications. And when I say big, I mean international. So it's another reason I reckon they'll let you guys off in return for your silence. They'll get you to sign an official secrets act declaration. A small price, I'd say.'

We shook hands. He looked around as if to get his bearings then walked off. A few minutes later, the loiterers in the aisles left, singly, in an attempt to be unnoticed by the general public.

I waited for twenty minutes or so to feel sure they'd all gone before I made my exit. Walking back to the apartment, I was extra vigilant, just to be on the safe side.

Over the next few days, Alonso called a few times to clarify details and I had a call from Aberdare to explain he was now totally off the case. I told him I knew all about it and thanked him for his forthright assistance and apologised for causing him unnecessary grief. At some stage, a text from Lucinda arrived. Brutally short, it announced that Lachlan had died in a car accident and gave me the funeral dates. After much thought, I texted back that I wouldn't make it to the funeral and left it at that. I talked to Jessica and her parents over the phone a few times just to keep them informed. Harvey phoned a couple of times to check on progress and was relieved normality was looking possible. He resumed drilling on the Monday.

That Monday morning, I sought distraction from a gnawing uncertainty by cleaning out my wallet, which had grown decidedly obese. The floor near the bed was soon littered with redundant business cards and EFTPOS receipts. A simple act, but the thinner wallet lightened my mood.

The only other thing that happened on Monday was a text from Amir saying he was keen to buy my kayak. It was the last thing I wanted. Dodgy goings-on at the Savage River mine was off my agenda for the foreseeable future, so I texted back to say thanks for the offer but the kayak was no longer for sale and intimated that other parties were interested in it. After that, I spoke briefly to Alonso to inform him of my inconclusive visit to the mine and the tip-off I'd received, anonymously, warning me of some dodgy operational procedures there. I suggested it could have some connection, now or in the future, with more Chinese machinations and hence worthy of further investigations. He was non-committal but said he'd look into it, eventually. We left it at that.

Tuesday morning arrived. But I hadn't. Instead, I lay skulking in bed, propped up with pillows, just thinking. As the days had piled up and the tensions had gone down, I was finding getting out of bed harder and harder. I knew why. I had been replaying my life and not happy with where I was but unsure how to move on.

Ever since that bullying incident at school, I'd chosen money as the way forward, the way to gain respect, status and the freedom to call the shots. But in succeeding, in becoming rich, what had happened? I'd been taken in by a gold-digging society girl who flattered my ego enough to keep me on the money-making treadmill until everything hit the fan with my burst appendix.

I'd always known, in some measure, that accumulating money wasn't the end goal, that I wanted to do something with it other than collect the stuff but once involved, one doesn't know when to stop. It had become my life despite it no longer giving me pleasure. I'd ended up like a junkie who shoots up not for the buzz but because shooting up and scoring hits had become the only meaningful things he did. Though not entirely. There had been attempts to break the mould, to do something more meaningful.

That something better had instigated the ill-fated Mount Gambier project. It was the drive behind the current drilling program and my architectural dreams of building factories and homes that worked efficiently, ecologically, and would be inspiring to look upon.

Geothermal energy I considered not just the way of the future but a beautiful idea because of its simplicity, no moving parts, and inexhaustible. But I'd come to realise that beauty was a far trickier concept than first thought because of its subjective nature. All beauty is in the eye of the beholder and no more so than when judging a person. Jessica was physically a beautiful woman, but it was her inner, intangible beauty that intrigued me most. But it was also proving the hardest to see and understand. I knew I was in love with it, as much as the body it dwelt in, and hoped she saw similar goodness in me. Though again, my hopes in that department were fading.

Suddenly life had become all too complicated. I couldn't move, and so I lay in the gloom, forced to consider the prospect of more days of indecision, stymied by the when, how and in what role Jessica would be incorporated into my life. Until that was resolved, I couldn't think of other things worth doing. We hadn't spoken much recently, yet there was so much that needed to be said with seemingly less and less inclination to do so.

Business emails had filled in some of my time, as did the drilling project. The architects had emailed for further instructions on Monday afternoon. But I had delayed answering. The architectural dreams they were working on had lost their lustre.

Eight o'clock came and went. Then eight-thirty and I was still moping in bed. At eight-thirty-six (I checked the time), there was a knock at the door. Too early for room service. The police or new enemies? The knock returned, more rapid and louder. I'd gone to bed naked, so jumped out, floundered around in the wardrobe for the complimentary fluffy white bathrobe then cautiously approached the door.

'Who is it?'

'Room service! And if you don't open up, I'll ….'

She didn't get to finish. I opened the door so fast she almost fell into the room.

'What are you doing slacking in bed? The forecast is for the cloud clearing, sun around lunchtime but rain in the evening so we haven't got all day.'

She was in the room, the door closed. She was looking fabulous in the outfit she'd worn when I'd met her folks.

No discussion was permitted: she simply shooed me towards the shower and told me not to waste too much water. On my return, she watched intently as I dressed but gave me the hurry up when I stopped to show off my naked magnificence. Once fully clothed, I was herded towards the door but had to dash back to the bed to retrieve wallet, car keys and the satellite phone, the other having been permanently lost to the police evidence store. I bundled all into a leather waist bag that I always travelled with but rarely used.

'Where are we going?' I said on the way to the lifts.

She smiled teasingly before replying, 'You'll see.'

She drove my car. We ended up back at Cataract Gorge for another amicable stroll followed by a leisurely lunch, at the same café as last time. I made a point of mentioning my building projects. Jessica's questioning revealed both an interest in the concept I was hoping to enact and her ability to make interrogation a pleasurable experience. I realised then how she had been able to so easily win over Harvey.

We arrived back at the apartment around four. The sun, which had made a brief appearance around eleven, had been smothered by rapidly developing thunder clouds that had been preceded by warmth and humidity, conditions apparently caused by tropical air being funnelled south as a result of a slow-moving high-pressure system being squeezed by an intense low coming up from the southwest – knowledge gained from checking the weather map while waiting for our lunch.

We were standing at the railing of the balcony splitting our time between sipping tea, occasionally checking the comings and goings in the alley below, but mostly trying to catch the flashes of lightning that now played across the increasingly dark clouds building up in the southwest.

After a particularly violent outburst of lightning, Jessica moved quietly back from the railing, placed her mug on the tiny steel and glass table in the corner, then slowly turned to me and murmured, 'Thunderstorms are very exciting, don't you think?'

Her expression was one no weather girl would be allowed to display on air without first requiring the report's rating to be changed from General to Restricted.

Suddenly, the sense of expectancy brewing in the air coalesced around her and then me. My mug joined hers on the table, touching it with a *clink*, mirroring our embrace as we temporarily moulded ourselves to the other. A kiss followed. It was the kiss that I'd long dreamed of, filled with passion and an intermixing of souls. I turned towards the bedroom, started to move, but she yanked me back.

She must have seen the confusion on my face and created more when she responded with a smile before placing a finger to my lips.

'Give me your left hand.'

I was going to say something about wanting to give her a lot more than just my hand: I wanted to do a Frank Sinatra and sing: *Why Not Take All of Me?* but she kept her finger to my lips for one more second before shifting both hands in an attempt to jiggle my wedding band from my finger. It proved to be no easy task. But she was determined to remove it. The ring was equally determined to stay. It almost descended into an all-in wrestling match, but eventually, with zero grace, the deed was done.

Panting, we stood for a moment leaning against the railing. Then Jessica turned me to face her and handed back the ring.

'You know what to do with this?' she said with a resolve usually reserved for hardnosed business negotiations, which was probably appropriate considering we were on the cusp of committing to a *joint venture*. Her intensity had my throat suddenly dry.

I hesitated, tripped by uncalled for images of Lucinda from my hospital bed, followed by recollections of the terror felt in junior high when I'd been dared to jump from the highest platform at the pool, all extinguished by the glimpse of a similar fear leaking from behind Jessica's outwardly determined expression. So, she too understood there were no guarantees in life yet had found the courage to risk her future with me. It was then I fully realised that moving forward without Jessica at my side was incomprehensible. It was another high diving moment.

Moving back to face the laneway, I scanned the angry sky wanting it to bear witness to my decision. A distant flash of lightning seemed to acknowledge my intentions. Taking the cue, I tossed the ring with all my might up and out for the gods of fate to accept. I tried to track its golden flight but soon lost sight of it. It, and the vows it represented, were dissolved to nothingness. Would those gods bless the new vows bubbling up within me? Would Jessica?

Turning, I searched her upturned face for clues; saw a mix of intense happiness and perhaps a little anxious expectation. A trickle of tears trailed down her cheeks, upstaging the rains to come. I read her answer as a silent shouted yes.

Words no longer seemed necessary. It was now up to our bodies to finalise our unspoken pact. Grabbing hold of my hand, she led the way to the bedroom, our progress faltering every few metres as we shed clothing, all thoughts of the future displaced by a shared desire to live intensely in the glorious here and now.

About the Author

D. Alan Petersen spent his formative years in New South Wales.

In the late 1980s he moved to Western Australia. There he found a wife and soulmate, and came to realise the veracity of Voltaire's assertion that: "Paradise is where I am."

His paradise is located at their home in Rockingham, Western Australia.

He can be contacted by email at: petersenalan59@gmail.com

9 781922 343925